CH00825735

THE SHADOW ON THE BRIDGE

CLARE MARCHANT

Boldwood

First published in Great Britain in 2025 by Boldwood Books Ltd.

Copyright © Clare Marchant, 2025

Cover Design by JD Smith Design Ltd

Cover Images: Shutterstock

The moral right of Clare Marchant to be identified as the author of this work has been asserted in accordance with the Copyright, Designs and Patents Act 1988.

All rights reserved. No part of this book may be reproduced in any form or by any electronic or mechanical means, including information storage and retrieval systems, without written permission from the author, except for the use of brief quotations in a book review. This book is a work of fiction and, except in the case of historical fact, any resemblance to actual persons, living or dead, is purely coincidental.

Every effort has been made to obtain the necessary permissions with reference to copyright material, both illustrative and quoted. We apologise for any omissions in this respect and will be pleased to make the appropriate acknowledgements in any future edition.

A CIP catalogue record for this book is available from the British Library.

Paperback ISBN 978-1-83603-047-8

Large Print ISBN 978-1-83603-048-5

Hardback ISBN 978-1-83603-046-1

Ebook ISBN 978-1-83603-049-2

Kindle ISBN 978-1-83603-050-8

Audio CD ISBN 978-1-83603-041-6

MP3 CD ISBN 978-1-83603-042-3

Digital audio download ISBN 978-1-83603-043-0

This book is printed on certified sustainable paper. Boldwood Books is dedicated to putting sustainability at the heart of our business. For more information please visit https://www.boldwoodbooks.com/about-us/sustainability/

Boldwood Books Ltd, 23 Bowerdean Street, London, SW6 3TN

www.boldwoodbooks.com

To the best virtual office colleague and writing buddy, Jenni Keer

1

1569

Dinner was almost over and I was attempting to conceal my boredom, putting my hand over my mouth as I yawned. Further down the table my grandmother frowned at me and shook her head slightly. She was more conscious of the civil rules I should be abiding by, although I cared little if I appeared rude.

Our stepfather, the Duke of Norfolk, was visiting and this required us all, myself and my three younger siblings, to attend dinner with him, during which he ignored us anyway. After our father Lord Greystoke died, his fortune and estates were entailed to my younger brother George, who was then just five years old. Fiscally compromised, our mother had married the duke in haste, but less than two years later she died in childbirth, the babe with her.

Subsequently we had been dispatched, together with our maternal grandmother, to live here at Barnhamcross Hall; an old, converted convent in Norfolk where we had been for these past two years. It had few of the opulent comforts of Arundel Castle where we'd lived previously, or even Greystoke Castle in Cumberland where we'd all been born; the ancestral home of our father and now awaiting George to come of age and inherit. He too was now bored and restless, and I couldn't help smiling at him, his jerkin askew as he fidgeted and squirmed on his seat. With no mother and our poor grandmother too old to keep his manners much constrained, it fell to me to look after him and teach him as best I knew what would be required of him, given he was now the fifth Baron Greystoke.

It seemed our grandmother could contain him no longer because with a flash of his dark green breeches George slipped away from the table and out of the door. I slid my eyes towards the duke but he didn't seem to have noticed and I breathed a sigh of relief. If he thought my brother ill-behaved he may well decide to send him away to live with another family as was customary, so he could be taught the ways of a nobleman. It would surely happen at some point, but I was not ready to see him go yet.

I had barely taken two mouthfuls of the cinnamon custard in my dish when there was a hideous scream followed by a crash from the gallery above us. It was where George's most prized possession, his huge, life-sized rocking horse, Hal, lived. Jumping to my feet I ran to the stairs as the rest of the household followed. The duke took the stairs two at a time, but I was fleet of foot and arrived at the terrible scene first. As he caught up with me the merest wash of a grim smile flushed across the duke's face, and then it was gone.

George lay on the floor, a pool of blood spreading around his head in every direction flooding the floor. His eyes were open and staring, but his head was at an impossible angle, and I knew immediately that he was looking at nothing, for there was no life left within him. His thin legs in their green were still tangled up with Hal where the horse also lay on the floor, and I could see that one of its front legs was no longer attached to the torso. I had to step over it to reach George, where I dropped to my knees. The space was filled with a horrendous noise, a roaring screaming sound and I wished it would just stop. Then I realised it was coming from me, carrying on and on as though it may never end. Someone was trying to pull me away but I resisted, lifting George's head onto my knees so I might cradle it there.

The light through the tall gallery tracery windows, still in place from the convent days, fell in a shaft of brilliance to illuminate a halo around his head. A halo for a fallen soldier, just as my brother used to pretend to be as he rode his horse. The metallic smell of the blood rose in my face and I could taste sweet cinnamon in my mouth as the food I'd just eaten threatened to rise up my throat. Hands beneath my armpits pulled me away, and from my prone position I watched as our steward, Richard, scooped George up and bore him away, drops of blood leaving a trail behind him. His sightless eyes did not leave mine as though imploring me to do something, to save him. It was too late now.

I clambered to my feet, not easy in my heavy, now bloodstained, gown. I could see my stepfather, the duke, standing to one side and as I watched, he wordlessly held his hand out and a person I did not recognise dropped two wooden pegs into it. He slipped them into his pocket and strode away towards his private rooms. I looked at the horse again and with a sudden flare of lucidity I understood what had just happened. Hal's leg was no longer attached to the rest of the horse because the pins had been removed, now I knew I could see they were missing. It had been deliberately sabotaged so that George would fall. My spirited, mischievous eight-year-old brother had just been murdered, killed at the behest of our stepfather. Why on earth he ordered such a heinous thing?

* * *

The Hall remained in mourning for the following month. My mood alternated between heartsore, abject sorrow because our brother was gone, and a white-hot fury because I knew the truth: it was no accident. My grandmother kept to her rooms, only appearing for the funeral. A quiet and small affair, it was held in the chapel which was once a part of the convent and afterwards he was buried in the cemetery alongside the nuns. My sisters didn't attend, and they'd been kept in the nursery since. I was expected to remain with them but I ignored my orders, instead stalking the corridors, hiding in shadows to listen to conversations I was not supposed to be privy to, searching for answers.

I found them six weeks after my brother's death, when I was resting on a window seat in the gallery, gazing down at the kitchen garden below. A young lad was digging up onions and I almost raised a smile when he picked one up and, swinging it around his head by the leafy top, hurled it at a maid who was picking flowers and laying them carefully in a basket she carried. With his perfect shot the onion hit her on the bottom. She placed the basket on the floor and turned to see who had thrown it. Although I could not hear her remonstrate, I could tell from the way her hands were folded in front of her that she was most displeased. And then to my delight she swung the onion round and threw it back at him, making him dodge out of the way to avoid being hit. Life went on, even though for me it couldn't.

The gallery was where I felt closest to George. The floor where Hal once stood now had dimples in the floorboards where the heavy horse's rockers had damaged it. That day I was obscured by the thick embroidered drapes hanging at the window so wasn't spotted by the duke and one of his men as they entered, talking in low voices.

'Are you sure this is truly so?' the duke asked. 'Everything must go to his sisters – the Cumberland estate and the fortune too? They will be very rich when they inherit. And I absolutely must have those lands; so close to Scotland they are of huge strategic value, and not just to me. To others who would also wish them. The boy is dead and yet I still do not have what I want. Unfortunately then, there is more work to be done.'

He walked from the gallery towards the stairs and I waited until I was certain they were gone before I climbed from my hiding space. My suspicions were correct, our stepfather had ordered that Hal was tampered with to create an accident which would kill my brother, and I'd just overheard his motive for doing so. He wanted the Greystoke estate for its position so close to Scotland and all the money that came with it, which had now reverted to myself and my sisters. A sour acid burned in my chest as I stood where George's blood still stained the floor when it had pooled in the dips Hal's rockers once rested in.

* * *

A week later carts were being loaded with the duke's belongings as he readied to move on elsewhere. It was what he did: spend his time either at court with his cousin the queen, or travel around his many homes. He rarely came to Barnhamcross Hall and I hoped fervently he never had reason to do so again. But I would make him pay for what he did, however long it took.

Just as the final carriages rolled away, I was summoned to his rooms. He was wearing a travelling cloak and sitting beside the fire, his long legs stretched out before him in tall shining leather riding boots. I walked in and stopped in front of him, my legs shaking but my knees locked straight as I refused to curtsey. There was a long pause as he expected this sign of reverence, but he would be waiting a long time for I held no respect for him. The silence lengthened until eventually he cleared his throat and got to his feet.

'Anne, I have been giving some thought to your marriage,' he said.

Now I could not keep my counsel. 'My Lord, you seem to have forgotten that I am but twelve years old, too young to be wed. Perhaps if you had visited us more often, you might have known that?'

'I am aware of your age,' he snapped. 'You shall be betrothed to my eldest son, Philip. The heir to all I possess, my riches and lands will one day be his and you will be Lady Howard. A much-exalted place to be, I am sure even you can appreciate that. Your sisters will also be betrothed later to my other two sons, William and Thomas. And I will manage your fortunes until you all come of age.'

'I shall not have it,' I hissed through my teeth, and I watched his face as a red stain rose up from his neck until his face was a deep scarlet with suppressed anger. 'I shall choose my own husband when I am ready, just as my own parents would have wished. And I do not bestow on you permission to touch our inheritance.' Even as the words left my lips I knew I had no means to stop him.

'I am your guardian.' The duke got to his feet so he could look down on me, a threatening position as I was forced to tip my head back and look up at him. I was painfully aware of how exposed my throat was to someone who only weeks before had so blithely arranged the murder of my sibling. 'No man may marry you without coming to ask my permission and it will never be given. As your protector it is for me to choose who you will wed, and I have done so. There will be a small betrothal ceremony as soon as it can be arranged and then a marriage ceremony when you are fourteen.' Without another word he strode from the room, almost knocking me off my feet as he swept past and knocked my shoulder, and I staggered to the chair he'd just vacated and sank into it. I had thought my life could not get any worse, and yet now it had. I would be tied to him forever, until he was dead. I looked across at the doorway he'd just walked through.

'You must forever watch your back.' I spoke the words clearly as though he might be standing outside the door listening, although I knew he wasn't. I could hear shouts in the courtyard where he was mounting his horse, preparing to leave. 'Come what may, I shall avenge my brother's death.'

2

2025

Sarah pulled in to allow the car approaching her to cross the narrow bridges. She could sense the house away to her left, its gloomy façade seeming to block out the sunlight, watching and waiting. For her. It had taken twenty-one years but now, finally, it had drawn her back.

She'd spent several weeks trying to think of a reason to not accept the request to visit, but in the end, she couldn't find the words for the reply she really wanted to send. Cordelia's letter had hinted at dire circumstances and Sarah felt the heavy weight of obligation. Nobody else would go, she knew that. And that her godmother – her father's second cousin – wouldn't have asked her unless nobody else would suffice. Nevertheless, the effort it had taken to pack a suitcase – a small one; she didn't intend staying a moment longer than necessary – and let her neighbour know she was going away, had been exhausting.

But here she was, having just driven through Thetford, and in a moment she'd go over those three bridges spanning the place where the two rivers, the Thet and Ouse, converged. The

Nuns' Bridges. She gripped the steering wheel, her knuckles white as she slowly moved forwards.

Now she'd arrived she just wanted to carry on driving, to be anywhere other than here. But she was expected, and however hard this would be, she knew she'd turn left after the third bridge and follow the track to the large imposing iron gates hung on old brick pillars at the entrance to her godmother's home. A building which had started life in the fourteenth century as a convent and following the reformation had been gifted to the fourth Duke of Norfolk who'd subsequently converted it into a house. It had been added to later by the Georgians and despite its size and faded grandeur, for many years it had been a place of sanctuary. Now though, for Sarah, it was just the place where her sunny childhood memories ended.

The gates were open, one of them leaning slightly askew and, judging by the amount of grass and weeds crawling up and weaving their way through, they hadn't been closed for some time. Sarah frowned, that wasn't going to help with security, the least she could do while she was there would be to arrange for someone to clear the ground and repair and repaint the rusty iron. The drive was in a similar state, the centre a small mountain range of ridges and tall goosefoot grass which caught on the chassis of her car and made her wince, hoping she wouldn't leave her exhaust on the drive behind her. Pulling up outside the house she parked next to a blue Mini, whilst to one side sat a gleaming orange motorbike.

As she got out of the car and stretched her back, tight after hours of driving, there was nowhere else to look but up at the stern façade of the house. It was no longer inviting, nor did it exude the warmth it once did. Her heart beat hard in her chest and she bit her lower lip as tears formed in the corners of her eyes. It looked exactly the same as it did when it came to her in the dark hours of night, the awful violent dreams which still interrupted her sleep all these years later. The ivy across the front had definitely grown, now almost obscuring some of the upper windows, but the huge wooden front door, studded with iron bolts and held to the frame with thick, black, two-foot-long hinges, was exactly the same. The dense, weathered wood had kept out those who were not permitted to enter for eight hundred years. She wished it would refuse her now.

Someone must have been watching out for her, even though when she'd telephoned, she'd only confirmed the day she was arriving, not the time. It had been a long drive from Cornwall and yet in front of her the door, groaning at having to move when it clearly rarely did, swung open revealing a small woman wearing faded jeans and a T-shirt bearing the slogan 'I Incite This Meeting to Rebellion'.

'Sarah?' she asked, opening the door wider. 'I'm Amanda, Cordelia's housekeeper. Come on in, she's been on tenterhooks waiting for you. She seemed dubious that you'd turn up, although I did tell her she was being ridiculous.'

Cordelia knew her only too well, Sarah thought as she stepped through the porch and from there into the hall. It was all exactly as she remembered it. The umbrella stand in the corner was still there, although it no longer contained the two umbrellas which used to reside in it. Beneath her feet the old flagstones looked as though they'd recently been given a sweep. Inside, the temperature had dropped ten degrees and she gave a shiver and swallowed hard.

The musty smell of dust, damp and ancient stone, mixed with old leather furnishings and heavy, silk, floor-length curtains washed over her in an unexpected wave of melancholy. The sound of her feet as she walked echoed around them before scattering into the distance down corridors snaking away from where she was standing. All achingly familiar, despite her wish to forget it all.

This wasn't designed as a home, and nor did it feel like one. The hall in which she now stood had originally been part of the chapel, stripped of all its religious artefacts after the reformation, but still with the magnificent, vaulted ceiling, coloured bosses marking each of the intersections of the carved wooden beams. Thankfully it seemed they'd been too high up for the sixteenth century vandals to desecrate. The windows along the front wall still retained a few of the original stained-glass panes through which the light outside now filtered in around the ivy, leaving flickering movements of dancing colour on the flagstone flooring. She was sure, despite the intervening centuries, that she could still smell remnants of incense.

This part of the house felt every bit as foreboding as it ever had. It was always cold here; the air hung with the prayers of centuries and the unseen nuns who once knelt here and offered their souls to God. Beneath her feet some of the slabs, uneven and worn down by centuries of people passing over them bore inscriptions dedicated to the ancient custodians of the building. Out of habit she stepped over them.

Sarah followed Amanda towards the back of the house. There was still no mention of why she'd been summoned, but she assumed at some point everything would be explained. And it would need to be a good reason. Through another heavy wooden door in the far corner, they walked into the bright and sunny Georgian extension to the rear of the Hall. Even as a child, she'd always preferred this part of the house, but now as an adult Sarah realised how incongruous it was. No planning official these days would allow something so out of place to be added haphazardly on the back of such an ancient building.

From this still lofty, albeit brighter, inner space lay the

drawing and dining rooms, and also a corridor leading back to the kitchens which, with the other formal rooms, were all in the old part of the building. Amanda waved her hand towards the drawing room.

'She's in there, you go in and say hello and I'll make a pot of tea, I expect you're parched.'

'Thank you, I am,' Sarah replied. She opened the door slowly, feeling it catch on the thick Aubusson carpet and walked in. Her legs were shaking as though they may give way at any moment but she'd come this far, she couldn't back out now.

The room looked different, but that was hardly a surprise after so long. The pale faded pink walls and green moiré silk curtains with their dusty swags were the same, the fabric no longer shining as it once had, and the wide marble fireplace was exactly as it was. But most of the elegant furniture had been replaced by a modern corner sofa unit, a wing back chair and sitting on top of what appeared to be a mahogany bow-fronted Victorian chest of drawers, a widescreen television showing a quiz show.

'Is that you, Sarah?' A voice, instantly so familiar, came from the chair and she hurried across, putting her misgivings at being there out of her mind, just for a moment.

'Yes, it's me, hello.' She tried to keep her voice steady as she bent down to kiss the old lady on the cheek. The scent of Chanel no.5 wafted up to meet her, instantly so familiar, but that was the only thing she recognised in her godmother. The tall, robust woman who'd always looked as though she'd just arrived from an army parade ground and who spoke as if she was commanding troops, was now a small, wizened old lady with sunken cheeks. Her skin was thin and pale yellow and her hair, once thick and dark was now sparce and white. Sarah tried not to gasp or show her shock, although she was sure her face was displaying her emotions.

'Hello.' Her voice came out in a whisper as she tried to gather herself together. 'Long time no see,' she added, immediately regretting saying something so thoughtless. She was as guilty of their infrequent communication over the past decade as Cordelia was.

'Hello yourself, my darling,' came the reply. 'Sit yourself down,' she said, waving towards the big sofa. 'That thing is a monstrosity but the springs and horse hair were coming out of the old chesterfield, and as Amanda sits in here with me in the evenings, I insisted we got her something more comfortable. She chose it. I hate it, but I don't have to sit on it so I'm thankful for that.'

Sarah perched on the front of the nearest seat. She agreed it didn't fit with the aesthetic of the room, but that old sofa had indeed been extremely uncomfortable even back when she used to visit, so goodness knows what it was like in more recent years.

'She seems nice, she's just making us some tea.' Sarah could hear her voice babbling on like the rivers outside, unable to stop.

'I couldn't do without her, she's such a help. Cook, cleaner, nurse, general dogsbody although don't tell her I said that.' Cordelia smiled to herself.

Before either of them could say any more they were interrupted by a quiet knock on the door and, as promised, Amanda arrived with a tray bearing a teapot, two mugs and a plate of Rich Tea biscuits. Some things never changed, Sarah noted; the same importance of using a teapot, although thankfully the bone china cups and saucers were no longer there, possibly long since broken.

'I'll leave you to pour,' Amanda told Sarah. 'Dinner's at six thirty. Bring your suitcases in when you're ready and come and find me in the kitchen, I'll show you which room you're in.'

'Thank you.' Sarah's voice caught in her throat. Please God don't let it be the same one. She turned and poured two cups of Earl Grey and offered the biscuits to Cordelia who took one and broke it in half before putting both bits back on the tray.

'I'm glad you came,' she said. 'To be honest, I didn't think you would and I wouldn't have blamed you, not one bit. I appreciate how hard it must be, coming back here after all this time.'

'I can't lie, I wanted to turn the car around a hundred times,' Sarah admitted, 'especially when I had to drive over the bridges.' Her voice faltered for a moment, and she took a deep breath to try and stop the wobble she could hear, as well as feel. She mustn't let her guard down or there'd be no stopping her emotions, bound so tightly inside.

'The first time is always the hardest. I hope when you've heard what I have to tell you, you'll feel less anxious that you came.' She took a mouthful of tea, an audible clunk as she swallowed it echoing around the room, before taking a deep breath.

'I don't have long to live, perhaps six months, maybe less. That's why I now have Amanda here, to help me. Anyway, I'm not going to beat about the bush, I've left you this place in my will.' She held her hand up anticipating an interruption. 'Wait till I've finished before you say anything.' Sarah, who had indeed opened her mouth, shut it again. 'What happened all those years ago wasn't your fault, and I feel huge remorse at what happened, how the fallout has echoed down the years. It seems you've spent your life in hiding, and I'm guessing that's why you don't now have a husband or a family of your own. The few times we've corresponded, you've always told me how much you enjoy your illustrating work but how are you going to meet people when you work on your own? You can't keep blaming yourself for that summer, you were just a child. When I've gone, lay those ghosts to rest and come back to live here. Take your finger off the pause button to your life, you of all people know how precious it is, how quickly it can be snatched away. There, I've said my bit. I actually asked you here now because the house is full of my personal belongings and I don't want anyone rummaging through my memories when I'm gone. I'd like you to help me sort everything out before I head off into the afterlife. Will you do that for me please?'

Finally Sarah was allowed to speak, but when she opened her mouth nothing came out. Nobody spoke of what had happened, and now in one fell swoop Cordelia had taken the lid off Pandora's box. And also told her she was to inherit the one place in the entire world she didn't want nor would ever live in.

'Will you?'

Sarah realised Cordelia was waiting for an answer. There was only one she could give, despite the fact that with her whole being she wanted to refuse.

'Yes, yes, I'll stay and help. And thank you, but I don't want this place. Leave it to the cats' home or wherever.'

Cordelia laughed. 'We can discuss that part of the deal later, I hope by the end of the summer, you'll have changed your mind. This place gets under your skin, surely you can remember that.'

Sarah nodded. It did. It had once been the fairy tale palace of her dreams, but not now.

3

1571

I stood perfectly still as I had been instructed, my arms out to each side. Just for once I was quiet, my teeth biting my lower lip, stopping the words from escaping, but my foot was tapping as I sought release for the anxiety coursing through my body. Already my head was hurting from the number of pins used to hold my hair in place. Strings of pearls and round cabochon emeralds, gifts from my stepfather, Thomas Howard, the fourth Duke of Norfolk, were woven through the intricate arrangement. In less than an hour, that man would also be my father-in-law.

'Nearly finished, my dear Anne,' my maid, Kate, said. She was more than a maid but my companion too; ever since I'd seen her remonstrate with a garden boy about a thrown onion I knew she had a spirit to match my own and she could be a friend in a world where few could be trusted.

She tied the white silk sleeves, gathered into little pleats and stitched with yet more pearls, to the pale yellow stomacher I was wearing, the ribbons flicking in and out of the eyelets as she worked. My insides were hurting and I didn't know if it was nerves, or the tight garments which barely left room for me to breathe. On the bed lay a dark green velvet gown embroidered with tiny lilac flowers. Already I felt weighed down, not only by the heavy clothes, but also with the burden and emotion this day brought.

My stepbrother Philip and I had already wed two years previously, but that ceremony was a formality due to my age. Now at fourteen I was considered old enough to properly take my vows. Two years my senior, Philip would shortly leave for Cambridge to study there, and I would join my father-in-law at his London home.

It meant leaving my younger sisters, Elizabeth and Mary, with our grandmother at Barnhamcross Hall where it stood beside the convergence of the rivers Thet and Ouse, as they met in bubbling, foaming fury over which the three bridges of Icknield Way spanned the water. Whenever there was heavy rain, the waters rose and flooded the area. Despite its raw bleakness it had become my home, a place with memories made with my siblings, the last remaining years of my childhood before I would be thrust into my new life – that of court and, I had no doubt, subtleties and behaviours I'd struggle to understand.

'There, you look beautiful.' Kate interrupted my thoughts as she stood back to admire her handiwork, before holding out the gown for me to slip my arms into. Despite needing last minute alterations, it still swamped my diminutive figure. I would have to walk slowly to prevent myself standing on the hem and falling flat on my face, I could only imagine the duke's displeasure should that happen. Kate threw her arms around me and squeezed tight. 'It's your wedding day,' she whispered, 'and you are marrying a fine, handsome lad. Put aside your misgivings for today and enjoy everything.' I hugged her back, thankful again for her friendship and insight. During the years she'd worked for me she'd grown to know me almost as well as I knew myself, and

I couldn't deny that her description of my husband to be, was correct.

'Thank you, my friend.' I spoke into her ear as I returned her hug.

Outside the room I could hear the bickering voices of my sisters, who were overexcited that we were all at the magnificent castle of Arundel for the nuptials. They couldn't remember living there with Mama, they'd been barely more than babes in arms.

'Are you ready?' My grandmother, also resplendent in a new gown, walked in. The duke had ensured we were all dressed appropriate to our station for this auspicious occasion, even though he cared not how we lived at Barnhamcross Hall. 'Your sisters are fighting over who carries which end of the bower, so it may be prudent for us to make our way to the chapel now, before someone's new dress is ruined.'

'Yes, I suppose so.' I didn't need to disguise my desolation at the situation. In front of my grandmother, there was no require-ment to sound happy or excited, for she understood how much this day pained me. Leaving my family was breaking my heart, but we both knew I had no choice. Since the death of our mother four years ago, my siblings and I had been under the guardian-ship of the duke and what he wanted, he got. That had been made palpably, horribly, clear when George had been made a pawn in the chessboard of our lives. The man was a tyrant, and for the rest of my days I would labour to see him pay for his terrible deed.

4

2004

'Mummy. MUMMY. Sarah won't help me with my bag, and it's
toooo heavy!' Emily's whining voice was already beginning to get
on Sarah's nerves. She'd managed to make the word 'too' last for
about thirty seconds. Rolling her eyes, Sarah lifted the case from
the back of the car, earning her a ruffle of her hair and a conspir-
atorial wink from her father. Emily's headstrong nature was
silently acknowledged, as was her own tendency to comply with
her demands in exchange for a quiet life. At ten, Emily was
younger by just eighteen months, and yet Sarah felt a decade
older in her attitude.

'Let me help you, darling.' A large freckly hand took the case
from her and Sarah looked up into the smiling face of her
godmother, Cordelia. The sun was still high and it shone behind
her making her dark hair, now shot through with glimmering
silver-grey glow like a halo. Cordelia, a distant cousin, was hers
and hers alone. Not Emily's godmother, someone she didn't have
to share with her sister like she did with everything else. And she
knew she was the apple of childless Cordelia's eye.

Eavesdropping one day, Sarah heard Mummy tell her friend

that Cordelia had once had an important job and travelled the world. Then she'd inherited this huge old house, part medieval nunnery and part Georgian mansion and it was where she now lived, in isolated splendour. The grounds of the house led down to three narrow bridges and the place where the two rivers met. Daddy had explained it was why the town was named Thetford, but she'd tuned out when he'd started a history lesson. He could save those for his students at the university where he taught.

All she and Emily cared about was that every year they spent the month of August at the hall with their parents, while Daddy was on holidays. Here they had access to the extensive gardens and beyond those, the wilderness which ran down to the river. And this year Daddy had brought an old tyre in the car, saying that he'd fix up a swing, so they could fly out over the river. Mummy had already decreed that Emily wouldn't be allowed to play on it unless one of the adults was present, but as she was eleven, almost twelve, Sarah would be allowed to play on it whenever she wanted. Not that she'd ever be alone to do so, her sister followed her everywhere.

'I'm glad the good weather has kept until we could get here and enjoy it.' Mummy pushed her oversized sunglasses onto her face and kissed Cordelia somewhere in the air close to her cheek. Leaving Daddy to carry the rest of the luggage, they trooped inside, the cool interior of the house a contrast to the brightness outside.

Sarah and Emily immediately began to skip around the spacious entrance hall which was originally the nave of the nuns' chapel – another history lesson from Daddy – with its austere walls, pale sandstone blocks soaring up to beamed rafters high above. The floor still had stones dedicated to two abbesses sunk into it and, despite her joyous dancing, Sarah was careful to hop over them, believing it would somehow be unlucky to step on them. Emily had no such concern, paying little attention to where her feet landed.

The adults disappeared towards the back of the house where the tall-ceilinged Georgian rooms were. Mummy was carrying a bag which clinked with the sound of bottles; their holiday was starting as it always did. Their parents would spend all day and evening drinking wine, whilst Cordelia made sure she and Emily were fed at regular intervals. That was where any adult supervision ended.

With Emily following, Sarah carried their suitcases up the narrow staircase at the back of the hall and then along the endless corridors to their room, the one they always stayed in. It was in the former convent part of the building but the sunlight from two tall, gothic-arched stone mullioned windows with leaded lights stopped it feeling gloomy. The sunshine now pouring in shone on the dust motes which their exuberant entry had disturbed.

The familiar twin cast iron beds were covered in new matching yellow duvets which looked more grown up than the Disney ones they'd had previously. And they brightened the oak-panelled wall behind the beds.

Emily was pouting in disappointment to discover that Mickey and Minnie hadn't greeted them and she immediately ran back downstairs to request the old covers were reinstated. Sarah began to unpack her clothes into the tall chest of drawers she always used, shoving items in haphazardly. Along the top was her collection of items found in the garden still left from the year before.

Going to the window, she gazed down at the glorious sight of the manicured lawns stretching into the distance, all tended by Cordelia's gardener, Pete, who was permanently at her beck and call. The roses, set out in six big flower beds, were a mass of colour, all shades of white and cream and yellow. Sarah knew how wonderful they smelled, filling the air in the garden with their delicate scent. From where she stood, she could also see the hammock shaded by the boughs of a pair of rowan trees from which it hung, and her mind went to the library books she'd brought with her. The summer stretched out in a miasma of blissful, sun-warmed fun, and a smile widened across her face.

Later, just as she'd expected, the evening descended into her parents drinking copious amounts until they were almost asleep, and by the time the sun set and long shadows stretched out across the lawn, Cordelia was the one who hurried the two girls to bed. As she lay awake listening to an owl softly calling from somewhere in the woods and the regular sigh of Emily breathing gently in her sleep, it was as perfect to Sarah as it could possibly be. She had, she considered, arrived home.

5

1571

Philip and I remained at Arundel for five days after our wedding, before riding to Howard House, which lay just outside London's city walls. It was many miles and the journey from Sussex was long and arduous. In deference to mine and Kate's lack of riding expertise we travelled at a leisurely pace, but I felt no gratitude. The day after the wedding, I'd had to wave goodbye to my sisters and grandmother, as they began their return journey back to Norfolk. With every ounce of my being, I wished I was going with them, to a familiar place which, although held painful memories, was also filled with love. I doubted there'd be any of that at my new destination and most of our travels, broken up by overnight stops at various houses belonging to friends of my father-in-law, where Kate and I stayed in a room of our own, was made through a veil of tears. Even Philip, who during the time we spent together had shown himself to be a funny and entertaining companion, kindly rode alongside me, instead of riding on ahead with his father, trying to distract me by pointing out the deer and hawks inhabiting the rolling Surrey hills. But his best efforts couldn't cajole me from my misery.

Finally, we arrived in London. Despite my gloom, I sat up straighter and looked around as we approached the bustle of this great city. I'd read plenty of descriptions of it in news pamphlets and despite my woes I felt a spark of excitement to see it for myself.

As we rode across London Bridge, the tall buildings along it crowding out the light I looked down at the brown swirling water of the Thames and was immediately struck by the difference from the clear rivers beside my home, where you could sit in silence and hear the rush of water dancing over the stones below, catching the grasses as it raced by. Where the quiet was punctuated by the angry squawks of ducks and geese who nested beside the shallows, and where the stillness of the heron watching and waiting for the flash of a fish was a familiar sight.

Here, the crowds of people going about their daily business were overwhelming as they darted in front of my horse, causing it to dance sideways as I fought to control it. This was completely different to anything I had imagined. Philip shouted to his father, who was attempting to push his way through the people ahead to allow the entourage to pass and a young yeoman guard, Luke, was sent back to take hold of my horse's bridle and lead it.

The noise of hawkers shouting and the smell of hot food mixed with excrement and the dirty water from below as all manner of things were thrown into the fast-flowing river, was so overwhelming I thought I would pass out. For a moment I closed my eyes and when I opened them again, we were almost at the other end of the bridge and my eyes spied something attached to the walls. Tall pikes which swayed slightly in the wind, topped by round black balls of tar. It was only as we drew level and I could see teeth gleaming in rictus grins that I realised they were the heads of those executed as traitors. My stomach churned and immediately I looked down at my fingers twisted in my horse's mane, keeping my eyes averted until we'd passed beneath the gate and were within the city walls.

Passing along Gracechurch Street with its cluster of churches, several bells rang in a musical discord to chime the hour. Already it was mid-afternoon and as the duke had decided we wouldn't stop for dinner, my stomach growled. It was many hours since we'd broken our fast. A wide street, which Luke informed me was called Cheapside, was lined with stalls selling all kinds of food and I breathed in the scent of warm bread and pies and roasting meat. Just for once, I was thankful the duke's position would ensure food was produced the moment we arrived at our destination. I sincerely hoped it wouldn't be much further.

After thirty more minutes riding, where the city gave way to green fields reminding me of Norfolk, we finally arrived. Howard House had previously been known as Charterhouse, another religious establishment dissolved and the building subsequently given to the duke. He seemed to make a habit of acquiring properties due to the misfortune of others.

The impressive entrance porch led into a great hall with a huge sandstone fireplace and wood panelling around the walls. My father-in-law was quick to show off the large screen decorated with fashionable motifs that we walked beneath, which he'd recently had installed. His initials were engraved on it as though someone may visit and not know which illustrious person lived there. Philip was eager to give me a tour of my new home, but after our journey, I apologised and informed him it would have to wait for another day before asking to be shown to my rooms.

Philip took me to one side. 'I instructed my father you must have your own apartment here,' he told me. 'You are still too young to be in the marriage bed and I would not have you forced to undertake that yet. We have many years ahead and I will be away in Cambridge soon, we can grow to know each other slowly when I visit.'

I leant my head against the soft velvet of his doublet for a moment. He was so different from the monster that his father was and I felt a spasm of guilt about the vow of retribution I had made for George. I may inadvertently bring Philip down too, although I would try my very best not to do so.

'Thank you,' I whispered. He smiled and nodded.

'I cannot promise your rooms will be spacious,' he said. 'I sent word to Gilbert to prepare them but he will have chosen where you are to be. Perhaps you will be squashed with your maid in one of the cramped monk's cells which remain here?'

I felt his chest rumble with laughter, and stepping back I swatted his chest with my palm.

'If that happens, I will be arranging an exchange for your rooms the moment you are on the road to Cambridge,' I replied, not able to stop the smile which played at the corner of my mouth.

'Send word if you are displeased,' he told me. 'Or speak with my grandmother, Lady Frances. She appears imperious for she holds an important position as the dowager duchess, but she is truthful and kind and she will ensure you are equipped for your new life here.' He gently kissed my cheek before disappearing into the bowels of the building until he was swallowed up by the shadowy corridor. I felt a pang of disappointment that I was unlikely to have much time with him before he left.

* * *

As I'd been warned, my rooms were indeed small. My bedchamber overlooked the courtyard and entrance at the front of the building, whilst the parlour window had an outlook to the old cloisters. It was a pleasant view but not the one I was used to and once again a wash of homesickness flooded over me, taking my breath away. Curling my hands into tight fists, my nails dug into the soft flesh of my palms. I would not keep thinking that way, I told myself; I would embrace everything this new life could offer. It was time to harness that which stirred deep within me. I was known – indeed complained about – at Barnhamcross for my stubborn attitude and my ability to achieve what I desired whatever the cost, and now I would apply that strength to what I must do.

'Well, this is all very different,' I said to Kate, catching her hands and whirling round on the spot with her. 'What new life shall we have here? All of London, this great city at our disposal.'

'It seems so big and unfriendly.' Kate's mouth was starting to turn down at the corners, but I wouldn't let her nerves spoil my excitement.

'You have me, I am your friend,' I admonished. Although I agreed silently that whilst it didn't feel homely yet, I was sure it soon would. Once I'd stamped my own position within our new surroundings.

Within minutes of our arrival, with the duke's steward, Gilbert, still at the front of the building, shouting at the servants who were carrying the luggage and furniture that had travelled with us inside, a knock at the door revealed a young maid. Her eyes were cast down and she was carrying a bowl of warm water scented with sprigs of dried rosemary. She placed it with a piece of linen for drying onto the top of a press in front of one of the windows.

'Mistress, I am to ask if you require any sustenance?' Her voice came out as barely more than a whisper. I was keen that the staff would know that I was not as grand as my father-in-law, nor as discourteous, as I suspected he often was.

'Thank you,' I replied. 'Both myself and Kate have not eaten since this morning so we would indeed like some food, together with a jug of ale please.' The young girl nodded and disappeared out of the room.

I splashed my face and hands with the fresh smelling water and then bade Kate to do the same whilst it was still warm. We were both dirty from travelling and our gowns would need to be cleansed of the dust they'd collected. Before we left Arundel, I'd insisted Kate was properly attired. She might be a servant, but it would not show the duke in a good light if a member of his household staff wasn't appropriately dressed. Thankfully, as appearances were everything to him, he'd readily agreed, and Kate had been provided with new shifts, kirtles and a riding gown.

I too had many new clothes, as nothing I'd ever possessed before. I'd previously owned just four gowns, one of which was my black damask worn for mourning, but now – including my wedding attire – I had a further six which had been sewn by the duke's tailors, together with several pairs of new sleeves, silk hose and soft lawn shifts. Even my old boots had been replaced with ones of the softest leather, together with velvet slippers for inside the house, and lambskin gloves for if I wished to go riding. I honestly couldn't imagine ever wanting to do that again. What a shame the duke hadn't thought to furnish my sisters and me over the years with better, warmer clothes to combat the chill of our Norfolk home.

The maid reappeared with two others all bearing platters of food and jugs of ale which they laid on the table before curt-seying and leaving once again. It had all been undertaken in silence.

'Thank goodness,' Kate said, placing the garments she was holding onto the bed. 'Let me help you with some food.' She moved towards the platters and poured some beer, holding it out to me.

'When it is the two of us in here, please Kate, just be as you were in Norfolk,' I told her. 'You do not have to wait on me as the other servants expect to do. Yes, you are my maid, but foremost you are my friend. Come now, let us help ourselves to food and sit together and eat.' Using a spoon, I placed some roast goose and veal on a trencher and added a piece of the white manchet bread which was so much finer than the rough brown alternative we'd been used to. There were dishes of purple carrots and artichokes in a shiny pungent sauce, and a small two handled cup containing a saffron infused caudle sweetened with honey. My anxiety was quietened for a few minutes as we both tucked in, but I knew this was just a momentary pause. I had a mission to undertake here in London. It would be dangerous and probably life threatening, but I would not fail. I had made a promise to myself, and I never reneged on a promise. My father-in-law had no idea of my plans, and nor would he until it was too late and his hours were numbered. Then he would know why retribution was mine.

6

2025

Carrying her suitcase and backpack into the house, Sarah found Amanda waiting in the hall for her.

'Cordelia asked me to air a room for you the moment she'd sealed her letter,' she explained as she led the way to the stairs. 'So convinced was she that you'd come.'

'She had more foresight than me then, I wasn't certain until this morning that I would,' Sarah admitted.

At the rear of the hall were the stairs. They had at one point led to the convent dormitories and solar, once the private chamber of the abbess and now Cordelia's bedroom, and nobody had ever thought to move them to a more prominent place, so here they remained.

Having climbed the stairs – she'd forgotten how steep they were, or perhaps it was just because she was now older that they felt so – Sarah followed Amanda across half landings and up more stairs along the familiar corridors, still lined with dark portraits of austere people who'd lived centuries before. Her heart began to thump. Please God, don't let her have put me in the same room. She could see the closed door ahead, the past lurking behind it waiting to drag her back to that summer. To engulf her in the horror lodged permanently within her, waiting for any chance to creep back out.

'Cordelia insisted you have her old room.' Amanda opened a door to her left and stepped inside. Sarah let her breath out slowly, as she walked into a room she'd barely ever been in, somewhere that was out of bounds to small children.

'Her room?' she questioned. 'Where does she sleep now?'

'The stairs are too much for her now, we've set up a bedroom in the dining room, and the old cloakroom beside the kitchen has been converted into a wet room. It's much more convenient and I'm happy not to have to keep walking up and down those steps every day.' She chuckled. 'You've got young legs though, you'll be okay. Dinner will be in the drawing room; you may have noticed there's now a small dining table in there. We tend to eat together, it's easier. If there's anything you need, just let me know.'

'Thank you,' Sarah smiled at her, 'you've been very kind getting all this ready for me, you really shouldn't have gone to so much bother, I'm very grateful though.'

'Nonsense, Cordelia says you're staying several weeks, so you'll need somewhere pleasant to escape to when you want to be on your own. It can't be easy coming back here, Cordelia told me briefly of what happened when you were a child. Living in the village of course I knew of rumours but nothing more.'

'No,' she agreed, 'I'm still not sure I've done the right thing, but I want to help her so here I am. She was very kind to me when I was a child, when I needed her, and now she needs me. I don't know how long for, but I must do it and put my own thoughts aside.' Sarah didn't add that there had been a time when Cordelia was the only person to show her any love, and she realised that she shouldn't have let the relationship drift as it had.

When Amanda left the room Sarah walked over to the window that was partially shrouded by the ivy she'd spotted when she first arrived and looked down at the gardens below. From her vantage point she could see they were now mostly overgrown other than a small patch of lawn. The grounds were extensive, she did remember that.

Turning around she surveyed the room. It was dark, a combination of both the ivy and the low ceiling, the windows decorated along the borders with stained-glass panels similar to those in the hall below. She hoped they still opened so she could attack the foliage.

The walls were covered with old lime plaster, once painted yellow but now faded to an ochre colour. Sarah ran her fingertips across one and looked at the fine film of powder which coated them. The house, as well as the garden, needed a lot of fixing, and if Cordelia had her way, it would soon be Sarah's responsibility.

So many idyllic summers spent here. She leant her head to one side, for a moment thinking she could hear the shouts of happy children running through the hall grounds. The dens they'd built, the games of hide and seek, long hot summers when they'd tanned to a crisp – her parents rarely thought about sunblock, she thought ruefully – only returning inside when the lowering sun indicated it was time for dinner.

And the swing over the river. That summer, their father had spent an afternoon constructing the rope and tyre contraption, deliberately choosing a place where they could drop into a pool, the water deep enough to prevent injury but still shallow enough to stand up in. They'd spent almost every afternoon there; it had been one of the hottest summers on record with no let-up in the continuous high temperatures. The air then had held a stillness as though it was holding its breath, waiting for what was to come.

Despite her vow to never return, here Sarah was. She had absolutely no desire to own the hall, the idea was abhorrent. If she couldn't dissuade Cordelia, it would be sold as soon as it was possible to do so. She'd paid a heavy price every day since that final summer and needed no reminders.

* * *

Dinner, salad *Niçoise* followed by tarte Tatin, was a quiet affair. Cordelia simply pushed her food around her plate, eating little. The temperature was still in the twenties despite the time of day, the humidity making Sarah sweat. She wondered if, as well as Cordelia's wet room, a shower had been installed anywhere else during her twenty-one-year absence.

Thankfully Amanda chatted during the meal keeping the silence at bay as she explained how her son, Jed, was currently home from working on oil rigs in Asia and helping out with some necessary and urgent tasks around the hall and grounds. There would be plenty to keep him busy, Sarah thought to herself. He was staying at Amanda's cottage in the village, whilst she now lived at the hall to be close to Cordelia if she was needed during the night. Jed was often present at lunchtime, but he didn't eat dinner with them unless he was in the middle of a job which required him to stay on until evening.

Once dessert was finished, Sarah helped Amanda carry the dishes back to the kitchen, intending to do the washing up. She suspected that the house didn't have a dishwasher, and she was right.

'Oh, there's no point with just the two of us,' Amanda said, turning on the big brass tap over the Belfast sink. 'And Cordelia explained she never bothered with one. It won't take me long to get these washed. We usually have a cup of tea before your godmother turns in; she likes to go to bed early. I think she'd probably enjoy a chat whilst I'm in here, she's talked of nothing else but your arrival for weeks. I'll bring the tea through in a little while.'

Sarah walked back to the drawing room. Cordelia was still sitting at the table and, offering her arm, Sarah helped the old woman who also leaned heavily on her walking stick, over to the chair she'd been sitting in earlier. The message about the forthcoming tea was relayed.

'Good, then we have time for a talk whilst we're alone,' Cordelia said. 'I need to explain what I'd like you to do whilst you're here. This house is big, you know that, and I've spread my belongings throughout it during my time here. The joy of all those years working for the Foreign Office meant frequent postings abroad, but I'm sure you can tell that from my many souvenirs around the place.' She looked around the room and smiled at the various ornaments, many of them oriental in style. 'And there's also the library, a lot of books have been added to it over the years, I've no idea what is even in there these days. I've occasionally bought some first editions of childhood favourites; I can't resist a Noel Streatfeild if I spot one in an auction. I'd like you to go and have a look and sort it all out in there. It doesn't even get dusted any more, there's too much other work for Amanda.'

'I've never been in the library. It was always out of bounds when...' Sarah took a deep breath, 'when I visited as a child.' Even as she said the words she knew she was lying.

'No indeed, I didn't want small people charging around in there, perish the thought. I think I can trust you to act with more decorum now. And the loft space, that's also full of items shoved in there over the years, not just by me either, my predecessor – the great-uncle from whom I inherited the hall – left all sorts of rubbish. And those who lived here before him too, I have no doubt. I barely gave it a second glance.'

'I'll start tomorrow,' Sarah said. The sooner she began, the sooner she could be away again. As much as she loved her godmother, she couldn't stay and surely Cordelia knew that. The other woman nodded slowly as though she could read Sarah's thoughts.

'There's something else,' she said. 'An old family maxim I suppose you could call it. A riddle, a message handed down through the owners of this house. And given that will soon be yours, now is the time for it to be passed on to you too. *"Search for that which you desire, for here it awaits you, and it shall be yours. Courage alone is invincible."'*

'I don't understand it.' Sarah pulled her eyebrows together. 'What does it mean?'

'If I knew that, I expect I would have solved it,' came the reply, although Cordelia was staring out of the window into the distance instead of making eye contact and Sarah wasn't sure she was telling the truth. 'I can only repeat what I was told.'

'It's probably like Chinese whispers and over the years the original message has been distorted by people repeating what they've heard,' Sarah said, mentally rolling her eyes. 'Like the priest hole you once told me about, I spent hours fruitlessly exploring for that too.' She wasn't going to be dragged into some sort of ancient search for treasure, looking for something which had been lost for centuries and all with a timescale of potentially a few weeks.

'Is there anything else you want to talk about while it's just the two of us?' Cordelia asked.

Sarah could guess what she was hoping to get into the open, but she wasn't going to oblige. 'I've just one question, although I feel uncomfortable asking. Can you tell me what is making you so ill?' she said.

Cordelia pulled a face and placed her hand on the front of her body. 'My liver has packed in. Or at least is very close to doing so and my kidneys can't cope. There's nothing that can be done now. I caught hepatitis whilst working overseas years ago, before there were vaccinations.'

'But that's awful,' Sarah exclaimed. 'If the Foreign Office sent you out there, they should be paying you compensation now you're ill.'

'What's the point?' Cordelia shrugged. 'All the money in the world won't make me well again and I don't have any dependants to leave it to. I certainly don't have enough time for a court case. I've saved quite a bit over the years, although as you have prob-ably guessed, not enough for everything that needs doing here. Sorry I'm going to dump it on you.' Sarah opened her mouth to say that was the least of her problems but she was interrupted by Amanda who with a cheery 'tea's up,' arrived bearing a tray, and after placing it on a coffee table she set about pouring and adding milk.

After they'd drunk their tea, Cordelia watched an episode of *University Challenge,* answering most of the questions before the students had even opened their mouths. It was almost eight thirty and after her long drive, Sarah was exhausted. Bidding goodnight to the other two women, she climbed the flights of stairs to the first floor. As she paused at the top, her head turned towards her right where she knew beyond the landing, lay the gallery. Where she'd witnessed something which had terrified her all those years ago. For a moment she thought she heard the faraway shout of a child's laughter. Pushing it from her mind, she hurried to her bedroom. But all the while she knew any ghosts which remained here at Barnhamcross Hall would wait for her, biding their time.

7

1571

Within a week, Philip left for Cambridge. He came to say goodbye, holding my hand and looking deep into my eyes.

'Stay safe, and do not cause ripples in the house,' he said, his face serious. 'Speak not of anything you are unsure about, if you need to ask questions find my grandmother. She will be a friend to you if you approach her, for she understands your position in the world now. One day you will be duchess too. In fact, I believe if my father has his way, one day you will be queen.' I kept my face straight as with a dawning recognition I realised what he was telling me. What his father's wishes were.

We'd spent little time together during those seven days; he was either studying with the tutor who'd travelled with him, or out hunting with his father, and I found I was disappointed we had not seen much of each other. To my surprise, I was already very fond of him. I ruminated over the fact that he and his brothers were all given the finest education and yet we girls, although considered good enough as wives for the brothers, had not been furnished with any sort of teaching. As our family covertly followed the old faith, we were however – from time to time – secretly instructed by a Jesuit priest who travelled to our home from Norwich. It had resulted in all three of us being far more knowledgeable than the duke doubtless realised. Not only was I able to read and write, being especially fond of poetry, but I also knew of the duke's sojourn in the Tower of London.

Perhaps he believed that being so far from London our family hadn't heard of his misdemeanours, but printed news pamphlets were brought daily from London to Norwich, which – with its busy port – was second only in importance to London. From there, the peddlers who walked the Icknield Way to Cambridge passed by our door and brought us news. It might have taken a little while, but the happenings in London eventually came to be known throughout the country.

Whilst I had waited for the time when I would be officially wed to Philip, I was able to follow the traitorous actions of my stepfather. I already knew him for what he was, so I wasn't surprised to learn about his part in the Northern Rebellion, as he led the lords of the north in their attempts to overthrow our queen and place Mary, the Queen of the Scots, on the throne instead. Wherever there was instability, misconduct, he was there in the midst of it.

I had, however, been shocked to discover that he had also been wooing the Scottish queen, just months after my own mother had died in childbirth. It seemed he'd once had aspirations to overthrow Queen Elizabeth, and wasted no time after he was widowed attempting to orchestrate them. Did he still secretly hold these wishes, to see a Catholic queen upon the throne?

Being of the old faith was an act of treason, and by practising it at Barnhamcross we too had put ourselves at risk. There was a tiny, concealed space called a conveyance, where a priest could fold himself away if the inquisitors came calling. My grandmother had told me that when the building was still a convent, the space was used to store the religious order's money and valuable sacrament gold. Now very little was used for mass, for the less we had, the less we needed to hide.

Thankfully though, we'd never been searched and Father Benedict was only of slight build; we already knew he could fit into the space if needed.

It would be a different set of circumstances though, if the duke chose to flout the law. Outwardly he presented himself as a protestant, and yet if he had thought to marry the Catholic Queen of Scotland, he would have to at some point reveal that he still secretly followed the church of Rome. For a man who spent a great deal of time at court, he knew the danger he put his household in. Either that or he was convinced he was infallible, and I was certain the latter was true.

* * *

We were just settling into our new home when something untoward happened. At first, I wondered if I was reading too much into what I had witnessed, so desperate was I to discover anything that might bring about my father-in-law's downfall.

Poor Kate had developed a crippling headache and lay for two days with the shutters closed and a cool cloth laid on her brow. I had spent the first of those days writing a new poem about my wedding and once completed, I was disappointed I couldn't read it to her.

> *A gathering of guests assembled,*
> *A peacock breast of coloured gowns,*
> *I follow the bower of wood and flowers,*
> *Whilst the scent of rosemary sharp and pure,*

Dances amongst those who gather,
Awaiting me at the church door,
Is the man to whom I am betrothed,
His fine doublet of red and gold threads,
And wise face, open and kind,
My wedded life awaits me now,
As I go to him.

Eventually, I was so bored of my own company I decided to let her be and further investigate Howard House.

I walked downstairs to the main hall where guests were received. It was also where the servants ate at the long refectory tables, however it was currently empty, still being two hours before dinner would be served. Only the enormous wolfhound, Blade, was present, stretched across in front of the fire. I had little experience of dogs, and he was huge. Until that point, I'd managed to avoid him but as I stepped off the bottom step into the hall he lifted his shaggy head and looked across before lumbering to his feet – his enormous feet – and trotting towards me.

I stood rooted to the floor in fear as he began a thorough examination, sniffing every part of my gown. His head was almost level with my chest and I knew that if he chose he could easily knock me down. After a moment I began to relax as I realised he meant me no harm, and eventually he gave an enormous sigh before laying down with his head resting on my feet. Carefully, I slid them from beneath his warm body intending to traverse the hall, deciding to explore one of the corridors which led from it, one which I'd seen the duke frequently use. There was a sense of similarity with Barnhamcross Hall; another residence where dark, shadowy monastic passages led further and further into the distance. To a warren of rooms and buildings joined haphazardly to each other until they seemed to disappear into places where no one trod. His office and rooms must be here somewhere, and although I currently had no plans as to how to achieve my end objective, it may be useful later to have this information.

As soon as I stepped forward though, Blade was once again on his feet and walking beside me, keeping his steps level with my own.

'Go and lie down, you annoying animal,' I admonished, giving him a shove with both hands. He didn't falter and just continued walking; it appeared I'd gained an ally. I approached the corridor I was interested in, but almost immediately encountered the steward Gilbert and behind him, my father-in-law in conversation with a tall, well-built gentlemen with dark hair.

'Mistress, I see you have become acquainted with the duke's dog, Blade,' Gilbert said. I stepped to one side to allow the men to walk past, Blade keeping close to my side.

'Were you coming to find me?' the duke stopped and asked, frowning. His companion however didn't appear so disconcerted, and smiling broadly he bowed low and introduced himself as Señor de Espes del Valle. I hadn't heard of him, but I responded in kind before explaining to the duke I was merely acquainting myself with the arrangement of the building.

'This corridor leads to my private apartment,' he snapped. The Spaniard turned to look at him, his eyebrows raised. Whilst I was used to this exacting and barely polite version of my father-in-law, clearly those he wished to impress saw a different, more congenial, side to him. Because he had two – at least two – faces. Like Janus, looking to his murderous past, whilst also turning towards his plans for the future. And what that future might hold was what I was intent on discovering.

'My apologies,' I also raised my eyebrows and met his eyes,

staring for a moment before lowering mine demurely and dipping my knee to him. 'I did not realise that areas of my new home were prohibited to me.' I pretended to appear subservient, but I hoped he could tell from the tone of my voice there was more than a trace of challenge to it. Why was he so keen that I stayed away from his rooms? Instantly my intuition was pricked.

And keeping company in his own home with a Spaniard, an enemy of our queen and our country immediately heightened my suspicions. Did he not consider I knew the state of affairs between our two nations? Perhaps he believed that, as a young girl I was not interested nor understood the politics. How wrong he was, I was not the docile, malleable child he believed me to be.

Without a word I curtsied again before returning to the hall with Blade. Now I had just the smallest suspicion all was not as it appeared, and the thought of it made me smile to myself. This critical moment was quite possibly the commencement of my plan to gain revenge, for gain it I would. I would move slowly like the snake and watch like the owl, and retribution would be mine.

* * *

Thankfully, the following morning, Kate was feeling a lot livelier, and I told her about my attempted investigation the previous day.

'If only I could find a way to delve further,' I said. 'It is very irregular is it not, a Spaniard here talking with the duke, the man who is closest in both importance and nobility to our queen. And now I have been given instructions not to venture down that corridor, I am sorely curtailed in my explorations. I must discover a way to go there unobserved.'

'You would be best advised to leave the duke well alone,' Kate said. 'No good will come of it. Why do you wish to know who he associates with? It does not concern you and you will only antagonise him further if you are found prying.'

'I will not leave him be.' I gripped her arm tightly. Seeing her wince, I let go again but kept my hand resting there. 'I told you when you first came to be my maid what he did to George, and that I intend to find a way, by whatever means, to avenge my brother's death. That resolve has not changed just because we are now in London. Indeed, I am perfectly placed here to seek out any wrongdoings, any crimes he may be involved in. Even though he has already endured a spell in the Tower, I believe it is possible he may become involved again in something treasonable. And if he does, I shall expose it or die trying.'

'Do not speak of death,' Kate admonished. 'I know there is not a way for me to dissuade you, I have been your maid for long enough to be fully aware of your obstinate nature. I can only ask you to take the greatest of care.' She paused for a moment holding her chin up and by the light of the fire, I could see a sparkle of mischief in her face. 'I do, however, believe I know of a way for you to continue your work. I was unsure whether to tell you, but I have heard tell of secret passages which thread their way through this building, a remnant from its monastic origins. They are supposedly haunted, Luke told me.'

Immediately I knew I'd been right in not preventing the tiny buds of friendship I had suspected was growing between the two servants. They'd become friendly on the journey from Arundel, twice he'd arrived at my rooms to deliver messages and both times I'd noticed their eyes meeting when they thought I wasn't watching. I was sure I'd heard them whispering outside my parlour one day when Kate had gone to the kitchens to ask for ale. Naturally, someone who'd spent all of his working life in the building would know its secrets. I'd heard of similar passages at Barnhamcross, where supposedly there were spaces between walls, wide enough to allow a man to walk through, yet still narrow enough that nobody would notice that the walls were especially deep. My sisters and I had searched for an entrance in vain but finally gave up, deciding they were a myth.

'Then he must tell me also,' I replied, my chin jutting out. 'If this is to be my home now, I wish to know everything about it. When he next pays us a visit I shall question him.'

Annoyingly it was three days before Luke put in an appearance. I was almost at the point where I was going to send Kate to find him with a thinly veiled excuse in case she was questioned, when there was a knock at the door and he entered, carrying a letter on a silver tray. A long wavering sigh from beside the window, where Kate was perched to use the light to assist in her fine embroidery, rather gave away the girl's attraction to him. Luke's eyes slid towards her as presented the tray and I removed the letter, holding my hand up as he turned to go.

'Wait for one moment, if you please,' I commanded him, and he turned back to me. Having to speak with authority did not yet sit comfortably with me, although it was something I would have to become accustomed to. I felt my face flush with awkwardness. I pointed to the chair opposite to me and asked him to sit down. He looked across at Kate and then back to me, a frown burrowing its way between his eyebrows. 'You do not need to worry,' I added, keen to put him at his ease, 'I just have some questions which I believe you may have answers to, and they are ones I do not wish others in this household to be privy to.'

'I am happy to assist, mistress,' Luke said, sitting on the edge of the chair he'd been directed to, his fingers twisting together.

'Kate, will you join us please?' I asked. I hoped he'd feel less anxious if she were also party to our discussion, that I held no secrets from my companion. Indeed, she was akin to a sister to me.

'I have heard there are rumours of a number of concealed passageways from the era when this was occupied by monks, is that true?' I hoped he wouldn't question why I was asking him, that he knew it was not his place to do so.

'Yes, mistress there are *rumours*, they are spoken of in the servants' hall,' he replied. 'It is said that because monasteries were sometimes used as strongholds and sanctuaries by soldiers, the monks may have needed to escape. But nobody in living memory knows of their whereabouts, they are just a myth, nothing more. There is a tale of a monk who went in, got lost and subsequently perished in there. He is supposed to haunt them and some of the kitchen maids claim they have heard noises and moaning.'

'Surely somebody knows?' I questioned. I couldn't believe nobody had ever gone looking for them.

'Not any more,' he repeated more slowly, as if explaining to a child.

'Well, thank you anyway, and also for bringing me this letter,' I held up the folded vellum I was holding. 'That is all.' He stood up and bowed and without a word, Kate also rose and followed him out of the room. I let her go because I was too busy wondering how I was going to discover if the passages actually existed.

It was five minutes before she reappeared, a broad smile on her face. In the meantime, I'd read the letter which had been delivered and suddenly, any thoughts of secret paths had fallen from my mind. The missive was from one of the queen's ladies, requesting my presence at court to be introduced to Her Majesty. Apparently, now being wed to the duke's heir came with responsibilities. The thought of having to undertake something so monumental caused a lump to form in my throat, preventing me from swallowing. Wordlessly I passed the letter to Kate who, although she read slowly, was able to make her way through it, reading out loud and following each word with her finger as she went. I stood staring out of the window, hoping my heart wouldn't burst it was beating so fast.

'To meet Her Majesty,' she breathed. 'My Lady, this is such an honour. Think how proud your mama would have been.'

I turned from the window. 'I am too scared,' I blurted out. 'I am not used to court ways, I cannot attend.'

'Nobody argues with the queen,' she pointed out, ever the voice of reason. 'And it does not say when you are to go, the duke will probably accompany you. Put it from your mind until then.'

I doubted I'd be able to do that, but I knew she was right. I may be wilful at times, but even I could not refuse the queen. I would seek out Lady Frances and ask her advice. I had only seen her once at a dinner before Philip left and she was as frightening and haughty as he'd warned. But I knew he'd have advised truthfully if she was someone I could trust.

'I shall distract myself by searching the house for these secret corridors then,' I announced. 'Rumours rarely start without some truth.'

Kate narrowed her eyes as she looked up at me. I deliberately kept my face blank and stared back. She knew me well enough to believe I would not listen to any words of warning.

'If I make my way around the building in a methodical way, I will not miss anywhere,' I continued. 'When I searched at Barnhamcross I was too haphazard, I realise that now. I cannot believe nobody here knows of them, but if anyone does, they are obviously keeping the information to themselves. As will I if I discover them. Thankfully I have already laid a seed in my father-in-law's mind of my intention to familiarise myself with my new home, and Gilbert was present to hear me say so. Thus, if I am again found wandering the corridors I have the perfect excuse. Pass me a piece of parchment and my quill, I must start drawing a map of the rooms I already know with due haste.'

Beginning in the middle with the cloisters and great hall I added the newer great chamber recently added by the duke and from there the stairs and corridors leading to my own rooms. The establishment was vast and there was a lot I had no idea about, but I intended to rectify that.

8

2025

As Sarah climbed into bed, dusk was closing in, the night ready to claim its time. Somewhere a pigeon called, and in the distance a car horn sounded. It was easy to forget they were only half a mile from Thetford.

She opened her kindle, but the words remained unread, her head churning with all that had happened during the day. If she closed her eyes, she could see the bridges she'd driven over earlier. It had been a dry spring and already a hot summer, and the levels of the rivers were low, yet all she could hear was a torrent of wild, frantic water washing away all in its path. Carrying all before it towards the sea.

And now she was sleeping in a room just yards from the one she'd used for all those summers. She wondered if it still looked as it had back then, two simple wooden beds with faded Disney duvet covers and a large oak chest of drawers with the collected treasures displayed on top, as if in a museum. Which is exactly what the room would be now, a museum to her childhood, the one she lost that night.

Closing her eyes, she lay down on her side and let the tears she tried so hard to keep locked away slide across her face and into the pillow. She didn't even know what she was crying for, that part of her life which had altered her so completely, leaving her permanently mourning what might have been, or the shadow of a life not lived.

* * *

Awake the following morning at seven o'clock, she lay on her back in the silence, wondering whether her godmother was a late riser. She'd forgotten to ask if there was a specified breakfast hour, but she was sure nobody would mind if she made herself some tea and toast and then she could start work on the house. Despite her distress, she'd agreed to undertake the task, and she was keen to get on. The sooner it was started the sooner it would be finished, then she'd leave and never return.

Already, the sun was warming the room despite the thick stone walls, and when she drew back the curtains she could see the sky, a pale azure with soft, scattered brush strokes of wispy clouds. The herald of yet another warm day. She pulled on some cargo trousers and a T-shirt and went to find the kettle and toaster.

Downstairs, both the dining room and drawing room doors were closed and she headed to the kitchen, where she found Amanda ironing and a man sitting at the table eating a large bowl of muesli. He looked up and smiled at her.

'Morning, love,' Amanda greeted her, placing the iron on its stand. 'This is my son Jed, the one who's very kindly doing all the jobs I can't manage. If you find anything about the house or grounds that needs fixing just let him know. Now, do you want some breakfast? Tea or coffee?'

Jed looked nothing like Amanda, who was short and round-faced with curly hair. He was rangy, Sarah could tell that from what she could see, his black T-shirt hanging from his shoulders displaying tanned muscular arms. His auburn hair was cropped close to his head and his green eyes, the colour of new acorns, were already showing lines at the edges which disappeared into creases when he smiled.

'Hi.' She held her hand up in acknowledgement before turning to Amanda and adding, 'I'll just have a slice of toast and some tea if that's okay, but I can get it, you're busy. Then I'll get started in the library.'

'Like Mum said,' Jed put his spoon down, 'anything you need doing round the house, just ask. I'm off to tackle the old kitchen garden today, it's completely overgrown but I'll probably see you at lunchtime.' Now he was on his feet she could see he was tall, well over six foot. At the sink he started to wash his bowl and Amanda told him to leave it.

'You need a dishwasher,' he remarked. At least Sarah could agree with that.

After breakfast, during which Amanda explained Cordelia rose later in the morning these days, Sarah made her way to the library. To reach it she had to enter from the main staircase, where one of several half landings led to a short flight of five steps up to the door. The house was a maze of small passages and secretive tiny rooms, spaces which must have had their uses centuries before, when the house was converted from a convent into a home for the fourth Duke of Norfolk.

The door was just as she remembered it: polished wood decorated with inlaid carved panels down each side, Tudor roses at each corner. Thick and heavy, built to keep out unwanted visitors. Once inside she began by opening all the shutters, soon realising that they hadn't been moved for a very long time. Festoons of cobwebs swung down from them like the elegant gowns worn by the ladies who'd probably once used this space for reading years, centuries, before. Returning to the kitchen, she found an old feather duster, now missing half of its plumage, and used it to sweep away the worst of the mess.

The room smelled musty, and Sarah wondered if there were already small insects burrowing their way into the pages and eating their way through the knowledge and beliefs housed there. She'd arrived just in time, and however upset she was at being back at the Hall, someone needed to save the contents of this room before it was too late. It looked like it was going to be her.

Now bathed in a brighter light, she could see how it had been altered over the centuries, made larger where original walls had been removed, leaving stone pillars and thick heavy beams traversing the ceiling. The sections of wall between the windows were roughly painted, more flaking lime plaster lying in little piles of dust on the floor. At one point a piece of plaster had fallen away and Sarah could see the original stonework laid bare. This repair would need specialist intervention, possibly by English Heritage or a similar organisation.

Pulling her phone out of her back pocket, she took some photos and added a note to ask Cordelia if there was any restoration planned, although she'd already inferred there weren't the funds to do so. It was desperately needed before the house fell down. Looking at the blank screen she realised that since arriving at the Hall she hadn't received a single message, not a text nor an email. She had few friends, preferring to keep her life private, nobody knew where she was, and nobody cared. Which suited her just fine.

In the middle of the room stood a large refectory table which Sarah decided to utilise. She'd stack the books on it before assessing what there was and then each evening she'd discuss with Cordelia which ones may be potentially valuable. She began to lift the heavy tomes from the shelves and carry them over.

An hour of carrying books back and forth made her arms feel as though they were on fire, the muscles burning. Her idea that she thought she could sort the house in a week was, she now realised, ridiculous. The realisation she'd possibly be there for the whole of the summer made her stomach clench. This was not what she'd signed up for, not mentally at least.

Going to an old chair in the corner of the room and hoping it wasn't riddled with woodworm, she dragged it over to the table and flopped down, rubbing her hands down her trousers. Pulling the first book towards her she examined the leatherbound cover, once dark green but now faded along the spine, the corners scuffed. Opening it to assess the state it was in, she coughed at the sharp mildew smell which rose up. The entire book between the covers slumped forward, the glue no longer able to hold the heavy pages tight and a dead silverfish fell out. The pages were a mottled grey around the edges, the ink now faded and difficult to read and large sections were stuck together as though they'd become damp at some point. Sarah worried that this would be the case for the majority of the contents of the room, left to decompose like the rest of the house, and she considered what a waste it would be if her assumption turned out to be correct.

Looking round at the books on the shelves surrounding her, she felt her heart drop even further. She had no idea where to start. Perhaps Cordelia was awake now and could give her some guidance.

Running back downstairs she was pleased to find her godmother now sitting in her chair, an open book on her lap.

'Have you finished already?' she asked, smiling.

'Honestly,' Sarah flopped into the chair opposite, 'I admit I have no idea where to start, let alone finish. Do you have any records of what's in there? Even if they predate your occupancy, it would be a good start.'

Cordelia pursed her lips, the thin skin on her face falling into deep grooves. 'There were some papers in a file somewhere, done by one of my ancestors. Goodness knows where they are now though.' She frowned as she gazed out onto the lawn. With the day now hot, the terrace doors were open, and the sun lay across the carpet, bleached into pale rectangles where it had fallen year on year. Sarah could remember lying in that warm space reading books.

'What about the butler's pantry? It was previously used as an office, there's an old desk in there. Do you remember it? You used to hide...' She stopped talking abruptly. Sarah knew what she was about to say.

'Yes, good idea, let me go and have a look.' She jumped to her feet and hurried out. Neither of them knew what to say any more, unable to speak the unspeakable, skirting around the subject to avoid touching upon it. So many silences. That summer was now a locked box, not to be opened.

The butler's pantry was off the corridor leading to the kitchen in the older part of the hall, and it was as dark and fore-boding as the Georgian drawing room was light and welcoming. The two halves of the house seemed to bear no relation to the other, pushed together like members of a dysfunctional family at a Christmas party. Here, just like the rooms above, it was gloomy, despite the beautiful weather outside.

It reminded her of the gallery, which she intended to avoid as much as possible. There were some memories of that summer she couldn't help recalling; they arrived unbidden in her mind. A murky shadow which suddenly moved, appearing to sweep across one end of the gallery, a strange darkening that was there one minute and gone the next. At the time, she'd been too frightened to tell anyone, believing that by doing so, she'd make whatever she'd seen real. Perhaps if Cordelia hadn't told her the ghost story, it wouldn't have put the idea in her young head. Maybe now was the right time to mention it, because if she didn't, then it would be too late.

She sat down at the desk in the captain's chair and, just as though she were eleven years old again, made it swivel around three hundred and sixty degrees. Despite the passage of time, it still moved as smoothly as it ever did. Through the door at the back of the room which led into the kitchen, she could hear Amanda singing along with the radio and the sound of crockery being stacked up against each other. This small room was now just an unused passageway which nobody had any reason to enter; the kitchen having a more well-used door. A familiar layer of dust coated everything. They should probably put some covers over the furniture, she'd suggest it later.

The desk drawers produced household expenses ledgers going back generations, a booklet on hanging game birds and a big file of what appeared to be legal documents. Beneath those was a scant inventory of the contents of the house dated in the 1980s which may have been when Cordelia inherited it. Apparently, her predecessor had also travelled extensively throughout his life so didn't settle down and have a family, hence why eventually Cordelia had inherited, despite her only being a distant relation. And then she hadn't married, and now it was 2025 and here Sarah found herself. Yet another descendant, with no chance of having a family, she of all of them didn't deserve one.

Taking the papers she'd just found back upstairs, she walked up the steps from the main staircase to the library, realising as she did that she must now be above the butler's pantry. She could still hear Amanda singing, now a fairly out of tune Abba rendition, somewhere below her.

* * *

After another two hours of taking books from shelves and listing them on a spreadsheet before dusting everything and returning them, Sarah decided that she deserved a cup of coffee. She'd take one to Cordelia and have a chat about buying some dust sheets.

As she walked back down the steps to the main staircase, she paused for a moment. Turning, she stepped back up to the library and then down again, more slowly. Her hard-soled sandals hit each step, but she could hear that the bottom two sounded different to the others. At first she thought she'd imagined it, but after several trips walking up and down, she knew she was right. The last two sounded lighter as if they were hollow, compared to the top ones which had a much flatter resonance. Something else to mention to Cordelia.

Finding Amanda vacuuming the hall floor, she suggested coffee and ten minutes later the three women were sitting in the drawing room with their drinks and the biscuit tin. Sarah noticed that although she and Amanda were helping themselves, Cordelia ate nothing and only took the occasional sip of her coffee, which Amanda had made with warm milk.

'Anything to get some calories in,' she'd explained to Sarah as she'd poured the frothy drink into a mug.

'How's it going?' Cordelia asked. Sarah described her lack of progress and made the suggestion that as she moved around the house they covered everything with dust sheets to preserve it. Thankfully everyone was in agreement and Amanda said she'd investigate where they could be bought from.

'I have just noticed something rather strange though,' Sarah said. She went on to explain that the steps leading up to the library were above the butler's pantry, and how as she'd descended them, the bottom two sounded different beneath the clumping of her feet. 'Is there a loft space in the ceiling above the kitchen?' she asked. 'I wonder if there's a trap door anywhere. I looked while we were in there making coffee, but I didn't notice anything.'

Cordelia shook her head. 'I've lived here on and off for almost forty years,' she said, 'and I've never noticed anything different about those steps. It must just be the way they were constructed when the place was converted from a convent. Over the years I've become used to the odd flights of steps and strange little spaces between corridors and rooms.'

Sarah nodded and took a sip of her drink. Cordelia had just accepted the house how it was, but for herself it would always be a place of hollows and shadows. To find something odd wasn't a shock, it was almost as though it had been waiting for her. This house held secrets and dark memories that were never spoken of; what were a few more?

9

1571

I was keen to get started on my search and, as soon as we'd broken our fast the following day, I announced we would begin. Kate rolled her eyes and said nothing, she knew too well I wouldn't be dissuaded.

'Let us start on this floor of the building.' I continued ignoring her truculence as I tucked my partly drawn map inside the sleeve of my gown and led the way.

We walked along the corridor from my apartment until we reached an adjacent wing of the house on the north side of the cloisters. Lady Frances had rooms next to mine and beyond that was Philip's apartment.

Despite the candle flames flickering in the sconces on the walls, it was an especially dismal part of the building, another reminder of home. I wondered why anyone even bothered to light them – I was quite sure we were the only people who'd walked these corridors for many days other than the fire boys, charged with trimming the wicks and snuffing out the flames at the end of the day. Eventually we walked almost a full square as we arrived in a corridor leading to the one where my rooms were situated. This one was even darker and bleak, with no candles lit.

'According to Luke, this was part of the infirmary when the building was a monastery,' Kate whispered. 'He said those who died of the Black Death still haunt it. Let us return by the way we have already trodden. Please,' she added, tugging at my sleeve. I ignored her and continued walking as the gloom enveloped us. I wished I'd thought to bring a lamp, I was already wondering why this part of the hall wasn't lit. It still bore an incipient aura of illness, and death.

There was a musty damp feel to the air and the few windows let in little light. It was also very cold, this corridor not having the wooden wainscotting of the others, although an occasional tapestry was hung, a poor attempt to prevent the outside weather from penetrating.

Perhaps it was my previous experience at Barnhamcross – of draughts cutting into the skin as they found their way inside a building – that made me more aware, but as we crept past an old hanging, I felt an all too familiar slice of cool air nip my ankles where my gown did not quite reach the floor. I stopped walking.

'Mistress?' Kate said. I held my hand up to stay her questions and stood in front of the hanging, bending down with my hand around the edges. Sure enough, as I reached the bottom I felt the same icy breeze.

'Do you not feel it?' I asked, pulling her hand down to where mine was.

'I do now,' she said. 'Where is that coming from?'

'I hope we are about to find out,' I said. 'I felt it against my ankles as we walked past. I was just thinking about how cold Barnhamcross can get with its old ill-fitting doors and windows and then there it was, the same sensation as if I were home.' My disturbing of it produced a cloud of dust and Kate started coughing, and I definitely heard a 'tut' from her.

'You may return to my rooms if you wish,' I said, continuing with my investigation.

'I shall remain with you,' she stuttered before starting another paroxysm of coughing. I was too intrigued with what I had discovered to be concerned about her as I pushed my hands behind the tapestry and my fingers snagged on something cold and metal. Despite its weight, I lifted the hanging away from the wall a little to try and see what it was.

I'd found a door handle. A narrow, plain wooden door made from simple rough planks set deep into the wall hidden behind the strategically placed wall hanging. I could hardly believe my luck, emitting a little squeak of excitement.

'I think I may have found something.' I spoke quietly, despite wanting to shout in delight.

'Good, may we go now?' Kate asked. 'You absolutely must not enter the passages if that is what you have discovered, you heard what Luke said, there are the ghosts of lost monks wandering them.' There was a tremor in her voice and she was shifting from foot to foot as though anxious for the moment of agreement so she could flee.

'All houses are reputed to have ghosts, and he only said one monk. One ghost,' I replied, my voice sharp. I suspected she'd be too frightened to follow me into the passage, and my hand twitched with the urge to give her a slap. She was being ridiculous and at that moment I had little time for it. 'There were at least two at Barnhamcross, I saw a ghost that looked like an old abbess at the churchyard once.' I paused for a moment as I thought of George, I'd left him there, the place where he should have been safe. Perhaps one day I would get the chance to go back and lay his spirit to rest. 'I need to know what is here, you go back to my parlour and I will be with you shortly.'

'Then I must accompany you.' Kate put her hands on her hips. 'Although, as we did not bring a candle with us, I cannot imagine you will be able to see very much.'

I nodded in agreement, wishing I'd thought to bring a lamp and cursing myself for my own stupidity. 'Run and get one, quickly,' I told her. She looked at me in silence, her eyes narrowed, before turning on her heel and walking away, her back upright, reappearing a short while later with a brass pricket candlestick with a lit candle.

'Please hold this tapestry,' I instructed her as I took the light. 'And I will see if I can prise the door open.' I waited whilst Kate grasped the heavy embroidered cloth in both hands and pulled it to one side before I lifted the simple metal latch on the door and gave it a hard push. Flakes of rust fell away but with my shoulder pushed against it, the door swung open with a loud creak making us both jump. Kate gave a nervous giggle. I was starting to feel a little less confident, but I wasn't going to show it. If there was ever a point when I might need to use these secret corridors – and who knew what the future might bring – I had to quash my fear.

I carefully stepped in through the doorway, but found myself in a small, empty room, barely larger than a cupboard, similar to ones I remembered at Barnhamcross. Kate stood outside, peering around the doorframe.

'There's nothing here,' she said with a note of satisfaction in her voice, and I let my breath out slowly, nodding. But as I turned to step back out the draught which had originally alerted me bit into my ankles again.

'I still feel something disturbing the hem of my skirts,' I said, stepping further into the space, holding my hands towards the floor. 'Come inside and lift the candle.'

With more light I could now see two of the walls were rough stone, but opposite the door it was clad in rough panelling, dull and unpolished. It was incongruous to find it in a cupboard and I knocked against it with my knuckles. The responding noise was deep and echoey and I turned back to Kate, my eyebrows raised.

Slowly I began to feel around the edges of the panelling until my fingers ran over the smallest of clasps and pushing it down with both thumbs I was rewarded with a grating sound as it moved and the panel swung open. It was dark as night and I could see nothing beyond our limited candlelight other than an uneven stone floor and damp walls.

'Come,' I beckoned and with a scowl on her face, Kate did as she was bid, letting the door close gently behind her.

In front of us, a dark, narrow passageway with a low ceiling stretched into the distance. I could only see a few yards in front, beyond the pool of light the flickering flame threw, all was darkness. The leaping shadows up the walls resembled a congregation of shifting, dancing, ghostly monks and I hoped Kate wouldn't notice. Something scuttled past my skirt, its claws scratching on the stone cobbles beneath my feet. We were both used to vermin occupying our living space after rural Norfolk and neither of us made comment.

As though we too were mice, we hurried along the passage, our eyes searching our way forward in the dim light. As we approached the far end I stopped abruptly as I realised we'd reached a steep flight of stairs curving downwards away from us. I held up the candle so Kate, who had almost walked into the back of me, could see.

'We must go steadily,' I whispered. Now I had no idea where we were in relation to the rest of the hall, and who may be able to hear us. I had lost all bearings. Holding the light as high as I was able, I walked slowly down with one hand holding my skirts whilst leaning my elbow on the wall to guide me.

Eventually we reached the bottom where there was a junction and turning right, we continued. Just at the point where I wondered if we'd actually find anything, my feet tripped on a slight step as the floor level changed a little and I could see a thin strip of light ahead. I crept forward until I realised it was beneath what appeared to be another door and I pressed my ear against it, listening. I wondered if this too was hidden behind a wall hanging and how nobody had noticed it.

It took my ears a minute to work out who I could hear, the voices muffled and sounding distant, but eventually there was a voice I recognised. William Barker, one of the duke's secretaries who'd travelled with us from Arundel to London. Was I close to my father-in-law's offices here? I fervently hoped so, because it was the perfect place to eavesdrop. Turning to Kate, silently I ushered her back the way we'd come. I'd discovered all I needed to for one day, my pursuit of justice for my brother had stepped forward, just a little.

10

2025

After lunch, and with the weather still warm, Sarah decided to take a few hours off to sit outside whilst Cordelia was in her room having a rest. Settling herself on a lounger on the terrace, she closed her eyes, enjoying the hot sun against her skin. It had taken courage to come and sit here, a place which held so many memories, but if she was staying for a while she needed to conquer some of her fears. Although she hadn't originally planned to stay longer than a week at the most, now she'd somehow agreed to undertake Cordelia's wishes, however long it took, and there was a lot to do. She could afford a few weeks away from her illustrating work having recently finished a book, but she needed everything to be finished by the end of the summer.

She could feel her limbs growing heavy as she began to slide into sleep, when she was interrupted by a call from across the lawn. 'You look relaxed!' Sitting up and shading her eyes she spotted Jed. Beside him stood a wheelbarrow piled high with chunks of rock.

'Well, I was until you turned up,' she muttered under her

breath before chastising herself for her uncharitable thought. 'I couldn't resist the sunshine,' she called back. She hoped he'd disappear to wherever he was going and leave her to her sunbathing, but instead he strode across the lawn towards her. His jeans were tucked into sand-coloured boots and she couldn't help noticing how tight his T-shirt was against his chest.

'I need to repair the back boundary wall.' He indicated the barrow. 'Do you want to come and lend a hand?'

Sarah opened her mouth then shut it again. No, she didn't want to go, it was a place which held memories of that summer. Nothing bad had happened there, she reminded herself, it was simply where the old medieval graveyard was situated, a place to be left in solitude and peace without noisy children disturbing it. She used to sneak there despite being told not to, but that wasn't Jed's problem, it was hers; she needed to come to terms with her emotions and the demons she was battling.

'Of course,' she shouted before getting to her feet and following him into the woods, where the heavy verdant leaf canopy helped keep the temperature cooler. Beneath her feet layers of dry leaves and brown chestnut cases left to build up over the years crackled. All around small saplings strived to grow, despite the scant sunlight which now filtered through.

'You might want to suggest to Cordelia that she gets someone in to clear this a bit,' Jed said as he steered the wheelbarrow around a fallen branch. Sarah nodded. Over the past decades it had definitely become far more overgrown. In fact, other than the lawn, everything outside appeared to have just been abandoned, left to grow wild.

As they reached the other side of the woods the sun filtered through the sparser canopy, the warm air full of flies and butterflies. Here the grass was waist high, just as it always was. A jungle, she could remember calling it that. *'Don't go to the jungle, Em.'*

The area where the wall had collapsed was thankfully not close to the graveyard and she was able to help remove the old stones, attacking them with a harsh bristle brush before Jed replaced them, mixing in the new ones. Neither of them were stonemasons – that was indisputable – but by the time they'd finished they agreed it hopefully shouldn't fall down again for a long while.

'I reckon we deserve a drink to congratulate ourselves on a job well done,' Jed said as he wiped his hands down his jeans. 'Mum's house in the village is two doors down from the Duke of Norfolk Arms, how about meeting me there later?'

Surprised by his offer Sarah opened her mouth to apologise and make an excuse when suddenly she decided to live recklessly. She'd already come down to a part of the garden she thought she'd never visit again, so why not do something else which would take her out of her comfort zone? And spending a couple of hours with Jed had been far more enjoyable than she'd envisaged.

'That sounds great, thanks,' she said. 'Dinner is usually early here as you no doubt know, so once I've spent some time with Cordelia, I'll come and find you. I reckon I'm owed a glass of wine.'

'Then I'll make sure there's one waiting for you.' Jed grinned and spinning his barrow round he headed back through the woods, leaving Sarah standing on her own. She went to follow him but then stopped. If she walked further along, she'd arrive at the back corner where the graveyard was, in fact looking now she could just make out the railings through the trees. Despite everything her head was telling her, her feet turned and started to walk towards it. Perhaps she could lay some ghosts? She certainly had enough to put to rest.

When she was within thirty yards, she stopped for a moment. She was all alone, she knew that and yet she could smell her father's cigarettes hanging in the hot summer air and hear his voice in his mobile phone. Soft, whispering and sometimes a gruff bark of laughter. It was only now, years later she guessed why he was constantly sneaking away to talk to someone else. As a child she hadn't understood he was having an affair, and yet now it was obvious. After all he'd told them about not going in amongst the graves, he'd ignored his own rules. Which was why all those years ago she'd decided they didn't apply to her either. And now he was no longer here to stop her. One of the hardest things she had to accept about that summer was that she lost the one person she could depend on, he was her ally, always there for her. She could go to him with any problem, but then suddenly she *was* the problem. Slowly she continued walking, her hand catching the tops of the grasses, gathering the seeds and sprinkling them from her outstretched fingers.

The original gate to the burial ground was now gone, just visible leaning against the railings further along. Sarah knew when Cordelia had been more active, she used to keep the foliage down, in particular around the small stone situated just outside the railings. Her much loved dog Nero's gravestone. But now the tall grasses and wildflowers had reclaimed the area for themselves, slowly obliterating any sign that they'd once been disturbed. Sarah made a note to find the shears and cut back the vegetation again.

As she stood silently, her mind somewhere in the past, she realised abruptly that she was no longer alone. The same aching cold atmosphere as she'd encountered in the house as a child all those years ago, encompassed her. She recognised it instantly, the presence of someone with her. The light brush of an arm against her own, so soft she could almost believe she'd imagined it. The sadness she carried always in her heart tugged a little and she felt her eyes well up, but this grief came from the air, the stillness around her, not within.

'Hang on, wait for me,' she called to Jed even though she could no longer hear the trundle of the barrow wheel as she began to run towards the trees.

* * *

After their post dinner coffee that evening, Sarah excused herself, explaining she was going to the village pub. Earlier she'd suggested cutting back the vegetation in the graveyard and she was pleased when Cordelia enthusiastically agreed.

'I feel bad I've been unable to,' she said.

'I'll do it after I've tackled some of the inside,' Sarah promised.

After a quick bath she pulled on some clean jeans and a white short-sleeved blouse. Thankfully her blonde, pixie cut hair required nothing more than a ruffle through with her fingers and she applied a quick swipe of mascara and some lip salve. Already her face was beginning to turn brown, a constellation of freckles decorating her cheeks and nose.

It took five minutes to drive to the village; she could have walked but with no pavement it was safer to take her car. It transpired the motorbike she'd seen when she first arrived belonged to Jed and he used it to travel back and forth to the hall.

Inside the pub she paused for a moment letting her eyes get accustomed to the gloom after the sunlight outside. It was still only seven thirty and she wasn't expecting Jed to have arrived yet, however, as she stood in the doorway she heard her name being called. He was sitting at a table close to the bar as if placed where he could see anyone arriving. Immediately he jumped to his feet asking her what she'd like to drink.

'A white wine spritzer please,' she replied, 'with tonnes of ice.' She collapsed into the chair beside the one where he'd been sitting, admiring his back view as he leant over the bar.

Once they had their drinks, Sarah asked him about where he'd lived and worked abroad, and how it felt to be back home. Anything to stop him from asking her questions, after many years she'd learned how to deflect them.

'I'm only staying with Mum temporarily,' he explained. 'I've separated from my wife, and she and our two daughters live in Cambridge. So, I need to find another job and somewhere to live locally so the girls can stay with me at weekends.'

'I'm sorry,' Sarah said, 'I didn't mean to pry.'

'It's no secret, I'm surprised Mum hasn't already told you. With me working abroad, my ex, Laurie, and I drifted apart, too far to get back to where we needed to be. We're still good friends and I often go over at weekends to see the girls.'

'How old are they?' Sarah asked.

'Poppy is eight, and Skye is four. Here, look.' Jed scrolled through his phone before showing her a photo of his daughters. With their red hair and green eyes, they both looked exactly like him.

'So, you'll be moving away soon then?' she said. 'I expect your mum will miss you.'

'I won't go far, not halfway across the world like I was before. I need to find a local job first, engineering jobs like I do aren't as plentiful around here, that's why I ended up working away. I might have to rethink my career.' He took a large mouthful of his pint. 'But the most important thing is seeing the girls more often.

Hopefully I'll have found something by the end of the summer, and at least this work for Cordelia is keeping me busy while I apply for jobs. So, let me get this straight,' he asked, changing the subject, 'she's what, your aunt? You're her only living relative, is that why she's leaving you the house?'

It seemed that Cordelia's will was common knowledge. Sarah raised her eyebrows and he went on to explain he'd been asked to witness it.

'She's my godmother, but also a cousin of my father, once or twice removed,' she explained. 'And I'm not happy about the will. Apart from anything, the house is going to need a lot of money spending on it.' Even to her ears the words sounded sharp and immediately she regretted them.

'So why isn't she leaving it to your dad?' Jed asked. 'Surely he's the next in line to inherit it?'

Now he was asking questions she definitely didn't want to answer, to even think about. The fact was that there was no reason on earth that would bring her parents back to Barnham-cross Hall. Not now. And she couldn't blame them either, if there had been a way of her avoiding being here, then she'd have taken it.

'I assume she asked him and he said he doesn't want it.' The explanation sounded lame and untrue, even to her. 'Old houses like Barnhamcross Hall can be a millstone around the neck if they're unwanted.' Just as it would be to her, if she couldn't make Cordelia change her mind. They'd all lived that summer, watched it play out, so why would she of all people want a life-long connection to the place? She had more to regret than any of them. What had happened had been her fault, and hers alone. And now she was back and, she suspected, the ghosts were too. They'd been waiting for her.

11

1571

I was reading my latest poem describing our journey to London to Kate, who was congratulating me on my clever words when a sharp knock at my parlour door was immediately followed by the arrival of Lady Frances de Vere, the duke's mother, my new husband's grandmother. Kate and I quickly got to our feet and curtsied. She was followed by a maid who laid a sumptuous gown in deep red taffeta, decorated with hundreds of tiny pearls, on my bed. Both Kate and I gasped as we saw it.

'My son is visiting court today whilst it sits at Greenwich and you are bade to accompany him. He leaves in two hours. You must be suitably attired, my maid shall attend you, and dress your hair.' As she said the final words her eyes flicked towards Kate, whose eyes widened a little although she said nothing. We both knew it was a slight to choose someone else; Kate had been trained by my own grandmother's maid and was proficient in the skills needed for someone in the employ of the highest classes.

'I cannot.' I shook my head violently. 'I know nothing of courtly ways and my father-in-law will be angry if I disgrace myself. Lady Frances you must decline on my behalf.'

'Shush child.' She sat on the chair Kate had just vacated. 'All will be well. But remember there are many currents which shift and eddy beneath the waters at court, you must be wary to whom you speak. You will soon learn who is a true friend and who is not to be trusted.' She looked me in the eye and as Philip had promised, I knew she was someone I could depend on.

Having been given only two hours in which to get ready, I soon wound myself up into a frenzied panic as to what I was required to do when presented to the queen.

'Assuming I shall be introduced,' I pointed out to Kate. 'This is my first visit to court and to be honest I would rather just observe from a distance. Perhaps there will be a second time when I am more confident.' I stepped into the gown chosen by Lady Frances. There was a starched ruff, far stiffer than I was used to, forcing me to keep my head upright so it didn't scratch the soft skin of my face. To my consternation it started chaffing against my throat within a minute of being attached to my shift. I wore a new pair of soft leather shoes held on with a silver buckle. They had a low, blocked heel and were unlike anything I'd worn before. Although they gave me some much-needed height, walking in them was a skill I wished I'd had the opportunity to master before I had to wear them for such an occasion.

'I hope I do not fall,' I said, pulling the corners of my mouth down as I slowly traversed the room, my arms held out to my side to balance.

We were interrupted by the maid who, as promised, had arrived to dress my hair. It took thirty minutes of curling and pulling and pinning, by which time, my eyes were watering as I tried to keep still whilst I was tugged sharply from side to side. The additional weight of the headdress now adorning my head felt as though it might tilt over at any moment.

No sooner had she left the room but to Kate's visible pleasure, Luke appeared to inform me the carriage to take me to the duke's barge was waiting in the front courtyard. Picking up a small red silk purse tied at the top with ribbons and with a nervous smile to Kate, I followed him downstairs, each step precarious as I walked in the already despised new footwear.

At the front entrance I heaved a sigh of relief when I saw the duke had chosen to ride, so I'd be on my own in the carriage. I fervently wished Kate were with me for support, but I knew it was deemed unnecessary, I did not require a chaperone when accompanied by my father-in-law.

The journey to the river was interesting, albeit rough over the rutted street, making me bounce up and down on my seat. I was almost thrown to the floor when we stopped suddenly as a flock of sheep ran across in front of us. As I'd hoped, there was a myriad of things to look at as we travelled alongside the city wall and passed by the Old Bailey and the Fleet Prison. The smell from the Fleet River was disgusting and I held my pomander to my nose. I was fascinated by the narrow streets we passed with their tall buildings squashed tightly together, their upper floors built out further and further until they all but touched at the top. Everywhere was tinged with the soot from the fires and the air I breathed in felt thick with smoke. Everyone was wearing dark or dun-coloured clothing as though the gloominess of it all had adhered to them.

Eventually we arrived at the Thames, alongside the old Blackfriars monastery and close to the huge, glowering Baynard's Castle, which rose up out of the black murky waters as though grown from them; a dark swirling mass. As I alighted from the carriage, the duke explained it was the home of the Earl of Pembroke, a close personal friend of Her Majesty's and I wondered if he was as daunting as his home was.

The barge was waiting at the stairs, decked out in the Norfolk livery and with his guards already on board. It was much larger than any other craft on the water and carefully I navigated the steps down to the jetty, each one feeling perilous in my uncomfortable shoes. In front of me, one of the duke's yeomen walked backwards holding one of my hands to steady me. Despite his own precarious position his face didn't reveal any fear he might fall backwards into the water which swirled dangerously below us. When I was finally on board I breathed in shakily, gratefully sinking down onto one of several elaborately carved wooden chairs fitted with thick, sumptuous velvet cushions.

With a shout from someone below we moved away from the mooring and out into the busy river, surrounded by many small wherries sculling across the river with single, or occasionally two, passengers. Out here in the middle of the river I could feel the brisk wind buffeting the barge as the rowers struggled to keep the vessel moving forwards and, feeling shaky, I gripped the sides of my chair. It was not a sensation I was enjoying.

Despite the fact that we rarely conversed at home, the duke was in a talkative mood.

'These houses along the river change hands frequently,' he explained as he waved his arm towards the big oak-framed buildings perched on heavy stone foundations. Many of them had tiled roofs to protect them from flying sparks which could rage through thatch in a matter of moments. Majestic windows with tiny panes glinted as though hiding pairs of eyes watching them. 'People come and go in the queen's favour, and when they are gone, they have no need of a comfortable home.' He kept up a running commentary as we passed, often with an unkind snipe about the occupants.

'Do you not wish for a home on the river?' I asked.

'Ah,' he smiled showing his teeth, 'I am so oft at court Her Majesty has pleaded with me to find a home from where I could travel more swiftly, but I cannot acquiesce to her requests. I prefer to keep myself away from the tumult that occurs here in the city.'

Or away from where clandestine visitors may be spotted, I thought.

As we approached London Bridge I kept my eyes averted, now knowing what was displayed above us. The waters beneath the bridge were eddying and chaotic and the duke explained that in a lesser boat we would have to disembark and walk across the bridge to get back in the other side. Thankfully though, with his robust barge, we could stay where we were, although the ride would be rocky whilst we negotiated the rise and fall of the water. I clung onto the arms of my chair more tightly, my eyes shut as I said a Hail Mary in my head and prayed I would not be thrown out.

Finally, with one last swirl of water as it spat the boat out from beneath the bridge, we continued our journey. The magnificent yet terrible Tower of London glowered down throwing a despondent cloak over all who passed beneath its dark shadow, and I couldn't help glancing across to look at the duke's face. He had, after all, spent several months imprisoned within it. His hands, resting in his lap were pulled into tight fists and his knee was bouncing up and down. Perhaps he was still haunted by the time he'd spent there. One day, God willing, I would see him returned when I took my revenge for what he did.

* * *

The landing stage at Greenwich was magnificent, especially compared to that at Blackfriars and after we alighted, I followed the duke towards the gatehouse, where his yeomen stood to one side and we continued without them. A gentleman to whom I was not introduced appeared to be waiting for us and immediately he fell into step with the duke, their heads close together as they talked in low voices. I walked behind, still a little unsteady in my shoes which were now pinching my toes, whilst attempting to eavesdrop.

The duke's acquaintance disappeared once we were inside the building and we walked together, him with long strides and me almost trotting to keep up. He pointed out things of interest, portraits of former members of the royal household and favoured statesmen.

After traversing a long, sunlit gallery, a wall of windows topped with thin panels of stained glass throwing coloured shapes onto the rich blue carpet beneath our feet, we entered into a small chamber where a dozen people were sitting talking. I held my breath, my lower lip caught with my teeth as I quickly scanned the women for one with red hair and a commanding presence. We'd walked past several portraits of her, and I was fairly confident I'd recognise our sovereign, but as my eyes roved around the room, I realised she wasn't present. Slowly I let my breath out again. My palms were sticky with sweat from the apprehension and I slipped them into my pockets, searching for the piece of linen put there just in case.

At the duke's behest I followed him around the room as he introduced me to the others present, although I soon forgot the names. The women were an unidentifiable mass of sumptuous, colourfully embroidered gowns with huge skirts, lace and extravagant jewels. I wished that my own gown, so highly thought of when it had been presented to me that morning, was more fashionable. I felt dowdy, and also noticeably younger. For the first time I was thankful Lady Frances had sent her own maid to do my hair, at least I knew that part of my apparel was in keeping with the other ladies present.

Suddenly everyone in the room sank down on one knee, the huge gowns causing a draught as they all lowered at the same time. Immediately I followed suit, keeping my eyes trained on the floor – another thick luxurious carpet – until the duke took my elbow and brought me to my feet. I wobbled slightly.

Still gripping my arm tightly, he drew me forwards, waiting for a moment while the queen's ladies helped her sit down and arranged her skirts before positioning themselves on cushions at her feet. A young man sitting in an oriel window began to play the lute and the talking in the room resumed, albeit at a more hushed level.

As we approached the throne, a large wooden seat intricately carved and decorated with cushions embroidered in golds and reds and placed on a dais, I kept my eyes lowered. Beside me the duke bowed again and having no idea what was expected of me, I curtsied once more.

'Norfolk, who do we have here?' I heard the queen, a deeper voice than I had been expecting, and feeling, rather than seeing the movement of the duke standing up straight again, I followed suit.

Despite my nerves, I was eager to examine the monarch at such close quarters. My sisters, and for that matter Kate, would all want a very detailed account of my visit and to be so close to the queen was something I could have never imagined happening when I was confined to Norfolk.

As I was expecting, her skin was painted with white Venetian Ceruse to cover the smallpox scars that littered her face, giving her a slightly ghostly appearance. She exuded a confidence, a supremacy so visceral I could feel it emanating from her in waves. This was not a woman to cross, ever. I thought about my family's clandestine religious tendencies and a flush of fear warmed my face.

'This, your majesty, is Anne, the new wife of my eldest son, Philip. She is also my stepdaughter from my marriage to the late Lady Elizabeth Dacre.' The duke swept his arm towards me as he made the introduction, and still having no idea what the correct etiquette was, I curtsied once more. I just hoped that by behaving in a demure and subservient manner I wouldn't offend anyone.

'Come here, child.' The queen spoke more gently and on shaking legs I approached the throne. 'Sit at my feet and talk with me.' Turning to a young page who looked no older than seven or eight, the same age as my sister Mary now was, she snapped, 'Bring a stool.' Mary was still playing in the nursery at home and yet I knew this boy would have arrived at court from his family home fairly recently to learn how a gentleman behaved. First as a page and then later as a courtier. It would have been considered a huge honour to the family in question for their son to be raised in the royal household and from there to make a judicious marriage. Perhaps George would have also been here, if he'd lived beyond eight years old. I looked at the young boy again and bit my lip to stop it quivering. I realised that there had never been talk from the duke of where my brother may have been sent, because there was no expectation that George would ever achieve adulthood. The plans for him had been laid the moment our mother died. George's riches, his estates, had been very firmly in the duke's sights.

A low velvet footstool appeared and, smiling my thanks, I perched on it arranging my skirts in a similar way to the queen's ladies.

'Have you come recently to London?' the queen asked.

'Yes, Your Majesty.' My voice was trembling, and I cleared my throat before continuing. 'Previously, I lived at Barnhamcross Hall near Thetford in the county of Norfolk with my grandmother and sisters. But since my marriage some weeks hence, I have come to live at Howard House.'

'With your grandmother?' the queen questioned. 'Both your parents are dead?'

'They are. My father died in 1566. Subsequently, my mother married the duke,' I inclined my head towards him, 'but she was then sadly taken from us. She died in childbirth, the babe too.'

'And how are you finding our fair city, have you visited many people yet?' The queen seemed to have grown bored of my potted history, and although I'd hoped to mention George's untimely death, I didn't get the chance.

'Unfortunately not,' I replied. Now I had seen the activities at court, I realised exactly how isolated I was at Howard House.

'Do you sing, or play an instrument? I am always looking for more ladies who may entertain me,' the queen said.

'Not very adequately,' I said. 'I do write poetry though,' I added. I didn't want her to think I was a naive young girl from the countryside with no skills who spent her days bored and unable to entertain herself.

'How charming,' the queen smiled. 'You must write some poetry for the court, and return to read it to me, I should like that very much. I will arrange for parchment and quills to be sent to you.'

I felt my heart sink. I enjoyed writing, but my poems were for my own enjoyment, or occasionally that of my sisters or Kate, who were never critical. The thought of reciting them in a setting such as this was too dreadful to contemplate. I opened my mouth to explain they weren't of a quality for court, but already the queen had turned to speak with a gentleman who'd just arrived. He was dressed in a heavy, voluminous, black velvet cloak, trimmed with ermine and was wearing a close-fitting black cap on his head.

'Lord Burghley,' the duke whispered in my ear as he helped me from the stool and back to my feet. I curtsied for the final time before walking backwards for three paces as the duke had previously instructed me to do. The room was more crowded now the queen had arrived, courtiers hoping for a private audience or simply to be noticed by her. Despite my own nervousness I couldn't help but be impressed by the aura of rule which came from the woman: small compared to the men who circled her, but mighty in her sovereignty.

I followed the duke back to the gallery where people were congregated, talking to each other, whilst still keeping one eye on the doorway to the private rooms. As if there may be a subtle opening, through which they could slip and be drawn into the queen's inner circle. The two guards on the door, complete with polished pewter breastplates and helmets, their pikes crossed to bar entry were a sign that there was little likelihood of admittance for anyone other than those for whom the doors of power were always open. Such as my father-in-law.

He had now approached a small, slim man who was talking with another, standing in one corner.

'Gentlemen,' he acknowledged them and paused as they bowed to him. Being the only duke in England and second only to the queen in status, he commanded a level of respect I was just beginning to realise. If only all these people knew he was a common murderer, that these people cared what had happened to my brother. But all would come right, George had me to right the wrongs.

The gentlemen were introduced to me as Sir Francis Walsingham and John Dee. 'Walsingham is the queen's spymaster,' he explained. 'It is upon him to know of any plots that could put her in danger, and Master Dee is her astronomer.'

'I am pleased to meet you both.' I was surprised Walsingham

looked so unassuming for someone who held such a powerful position, one of extreme importance to the queen.

After we left the chamber, the duke suddenly halted and told me to wait, before he hastened along the gallery towards two men who were standing some way away in the shadows, talking. I immediately recognised one as the visitor at Howard House, Señor de Espes. Their heads were bent close together as though they were worried their words may be overheard.

'I see your father-in-law is having a private word with our friend, the Spanish ambassador.' A voice in my ear made me jump and I turned to see Sir Francis Walsingham standing behind me.

'I have seen him before,' I said, before realising that perhaps I should have kept this information to myself. It was too late now.

'When you have been at court?' he asked.

I shook my head and told him about encountering him at Howard House. 'I came upon them by accident shortly after I moved in, I was wandering the house trying to find my bearings. I rarely get the chance to leave, and it soon becomes tiresome being within the same four walls.'

'Then I must instruct my wife, Lady Ursula, who is one of the queen's ladies, to request you visit her. It is not healthy to spend all of one's time confined to home.' He tapped the tips of his fingers against his mouth as if he was considering what to say next. 'As you are recently to London, you will not know that previously there has been treason afoot in the Duke of Norfolk's home. And yet it appears once again he entertains those who are an enemy of our country,' he said. I didn't admit I already knew of this. 'Perhaps, my dear Anne, you might keep your eyes and ears open to anything unusual whilst you are at home, hmm? Anything which could be considered treasonous? If a plot were to be discovered the ramifications would spread like spilt ale and I would not wish for you to become inadvertently implicated. Your father-in-law, he was your stepfather before? That is a most unusual state of affairs.'

My heart was in my throat. His words, the feeling that he was looking into my soul made me hesitate and without me speaking a word he nodded as though he understood everything I hadn't said. Bowing briefly, he slipped away out of the gallery before my father-in-law had probably even realised he was there.

After a further few minutes, the duke returned to me, making no mention of my talking with Sir Francis. Instead, he was smiling broadly and without a word we left the palace.

The journey back along the Thames was less pleasant than the outward one. The gentle breeze which had helped us travel downstream had whipped up into a sharp, squally wind and the oarsmen were now rowing against it, making our passage slow going. Canvas sides were attached to the canopy within which I sat, the material cracking like a whip as they flapped. Like a giant water monster breathing in and out. Despite the shelter, the wind still found its way inside, making my eyes run and pulling coils of my hair from the pins which secured them.

This time the duke did not sit with me, preferring to stand outside and watch the other river users and the people going about their business on the banks. I suspected he liked to know as much as he could about anything – everything – so he was as fully informed as he could be. Lining up the pieces on his chessboard and considering his next move.

12

1571

Eventually we reached Howard House again. The carriage had moved swiftly through the streets, rocking me from side to side until I felt nauseous and by the time I was finally in my rooms once again, I wanted nothing more than to take off my outer garments, especially the uncomfortable tight stomacher, and lie on the bed in my shift, with the drapes pulled. I knew Kate was desperate for a description of my day, but I couldn't relay it until I was feeling better. Within minutes I fell into a deep sleep, punctuated by dreams of shadowed faces and jewel-encrusted garments.

Darkness was starting to fall outside when I awoke. Sitting up, I moved the curtains to find Kate beside the fire sewing, waiting patiently.

'Have I missed supper?' I asked, suddenly realising how ravenous I now was, having not eaten since early morning.

'It was an hour ago, but I requested that a platter was sent up for when you awoke,' Kate said. 'Come into your parlour and eat now, my dear Anne. Then you can tell me every detail of your day. I wish to hear it all.'

I wrapped a silk robe around myself and followed her into the parlour, where the candles were already lit against the falling light, their dancing flames throwing shadows across the walls. Immediately I drank two beakers of ale and followed them with several slices of cold goose and beef, a piece of manchet bread and finally a bowl of stewed figs flavoured with ginger. Kate kept quiet whilst I ate, even though out of the corner of my eye I could see her fidgeting.

'Now, pray tell me all of what you saw. Was the queen present, did you see her?' Kate put aside the sewing she'd brought through from the bedchamber, all thoughts of doing any now abandoned.

'She was.' I went on to tell Kate everything. The clothes, the fashions, the furnishings, every little detail had to be recalled. When I explained how I was presented to the queen, she squealed in excitement.

'Is she beautiful?' she asked. I shook my head.

'Not really,' I said. I described her, including everything she was wearing. 'But her looks did not matter. She is so strong, so commanding that it shines forth from her. She is the Queen of England and it almost blinds you, her magnificence.' I reflected that I must garner strength such as hers to help me fulfil my undertaking.

'And did she speak with you?' Kate clasped her hands together, her face alight.

'She did,' I replied, before pulling a morose face as I explained how the queen had requested that I write some poetry to recite for the court. 'I fear I have now made myself more visible, when my hope was to do just the opposite. Going to the palace was enjoyable until I had to converse with the queen, I was happy to simply observe everyone, and everything.'

'Perhaps she will forget she has asked you,' Kate suggested. 'You are unlikely to be attending her again.'

I nodded my agreement. 'Something else happened whilst we were there,' I said. I hadn't been sure how much to tell Kate, but I may have needed a collaborator if I was going to find a way to drag the duke down and see him as dead as my brother now was. I went on to explain about who the duke had spoken with, and what Sir Francis had subsequently said to me.

* * *

Unfortunately, my wish that the poetry for the queen would soon be forgotten, were not to be granted. Two days after my audience, a package wrapped in a piece of green silk, beautifully embroidered with tiny bees and flowers, was brought to my rooms. With it was a letter, the wax on the back imprinted with the royal seal. I laid it on my lap for several minutes staring at it; there was nothing to indicate it was anything to worry about, and yet it burned my hands with fear.

Using a sharp silver knife provided when I arrived for this very reason, I slit it open, the brittle wax falling to the floor. Quickly I scanned the contents before opening the package. The note explained this gift had come from the queen, a beautifully bound book just about the size of my hand, its leather binding etched in gold. Inside each parchment page was blank. She commanded me to fill it with poems for her, for the court, to enjoy.

I swallowed hard trying to dispel the apprehension rising in my gullet. More than ever, I wished I were back in Norfolk. London had taken a frightening turn, possibly a dangerous one and I didn't know what the perils were in order to avoid them.

Like the flat lands beside the rivers at home with their concealed marshes I could slip into something life threatening with a single step because I didn't know where the threats lay.

13

2025

'Morning.' Jed grinned from his usual place at the kitchen table where he was drinking a large mug of tea and eating toast. He was wearing an olive-green T-shirt which made the green of his eyes sparkle and the deep auburn of his hair glow. 'I've just been telling Mum about our evening at the Duke of Norfolk.'

'You didn't mention at dinner that you two had a date,' Amanda said as she laid a plate in front of Sarah and pointed to the toast rack, which was full of crispy golden slices.

'Mum, I told you that it wasn't a date.' Jed spoke sharply and Sarah guessed this was a conversation they'd already had.

'Nope, not a date,' she agreed. They needed Amanda to understand, or they'd endure a summer of being watched, teased and potentially pushed together, however well-meaning the sentiment was. 'Just two people who'd mended a wall and decided they deserved a well-earned drink.'

Jed drained his cup and pulled a 'told you so' face at Amanda before disappearing out of the back door. She didn't look convinced, but Sarah just helped herself to marmalade and said nothing else. The fact was, Jed was a good-looking man, but romance was off the cards, and he probably didn't fancy her anyway. There hadn't been any flirting, and if he'd wanted to then he'd had the chance.

Returning to the library, Sarah wondered again about the steps. There was something odd about them that had been nagging at her. Once again, she walked up and down several times stamping her feet, her head cocked sideways as she listened for the different tone. Eventually she sat down beside the lowest one. There was a tiny landing, no more than six foot long and kneeling on there she knocked each wide floorboard in turn with her knuckles. She wasn't imagining it, there was something different about some of the stairs.

Running downstairs, she stood in the butler's pantry again, examining the ceiling. It was low in here; if she could find a step she'd be able to reach up and touch it. It was lower than either the kitchen where the ceiling soared up high enough for herbs and meat to be hung, and the dining room which had a beamed vaulted ceiling as befitted a chamber of the Duke of Norfolk. This was a strange space between two worlds, a pausing place.

Slowly she walked back upstairs and sat on the steps. Leaning forwards, she pushed her fingertips against the wood, making her way along from the wall at one end to the other, but there was no difference. She started again on the step below: tap, tap, tap. Then, as she was about to give up on the whole idea, she realised the wooden riser at one end had a sliver of wood along the top as if it had been inserted to infill a plank which didn't fit flush. Many of the wooden panels in the house had such additions, very little was in a straight line in a building as old as this one. She pushed her forefinger against it not expecting anything to happen but to her amazement and delight it slid out slightly and a barely audible click beneath her released the step she was sitting on. Jumping up she ran her fingers along the edge. There, they snagged on the shallowest of grooves which was just enough to fit her fingertips in and lift the wood up.

The flap was fixed to the second step with a pair of small iron hinges which creaked and rasped loudly as they allowed both steps to be raised, revealing a space beneath that was barely more than five feet by three. Sarah exhaled slowly.

'Ohhhh,' she said as she let her breath out. The space was empty and remembering her conversation with Cordelia only days previously, she ran down to the drawing room.

'You won't believe what I've found,' Sarah announced, before going on to explain. 'It must be the priest hole, surely? All those times I searched for it but it's far better concealed that I'd have guessed. In fact, I don't suppose I'd have discovered it if I hadn't realised the ceiling in the butler's pantry was too low. Sadly, there aren't any gold chalices or jewel-encrusted crosses in there though, no treasures.' And nothing to indicate she'd found the answer to the family motto.

Leaving Cordelia again, Sarah returned to where she'd left the hole open. Walking back up the main staircase and turning to the steps gave her a different eyeline. As the sun poured down the stairs from the landing above, through the stained glass, it speckled the polished wood with a myriad of colours. Sarah paused for a moment stretching her hand out to watch the colours dart across her skin as she moved it up and down, causing a shadow to pass across the priest hole. As she did so, she spotted a tiny outline in the corner, a knot in the wood which was more prominent that the rest. Crawling in on her belly Sarah ran her fingers over the bump which wobbled slightly and giving it a sharp push she almost fell onto her face as the back wall of the space swung open. It was another, smaller cavity.

This was in complete darkness and Sarah pulled her phone out to use the torch, shining it to the back. It would have been a

very tight fit for a man to hide in, only about four feet square.
But if indeed this was the actual priest hole, how ingenious to
hide it behind a dummy one in front. As before, there was no
treasure, but in the back corner lay a small package. Gingerly
she pulled it forward. As she did so, she felt an exhale of breath
brush against her face.

14

1571

Two days after the queen's book was delivered, Kate and I arrived for dinner in the great chamber. The duke had proudly informed me he'd had this space refurbished and it now contained two enormous fireplaces along one wall, the high ceiling decorated with gilded plaster mouldings of his insignia and Latin motto, *Sola Virtus Invicta*. Courage alone is invincible. That virtue is a divine grace, an invincible weapon. With my courage I would indeed be invincible, I *was* the weapon. I'd also noticed an occasional lilac-coloured flower that looked uncannily similar to a thistle, the insignia for the Scottish queen. I was sure I was mistaken and had wrongly identified it; surely he would not be so stupid as to show his allegiance so openly? Two gentlemen I hadn't seen before were sitting with the duke at the top of the table.

Kate preferred to sit downstairs with the servants in case she found an opportunity to speak with Luke, but I could not allow that very often. As my companion as well as my maid she should be seated close by me in case I had need of her, and she went to sit a little further down the table as I made my way to my usual chair. When Philip was home he and his grandmother sat either side of the duke with me seated beside my husband. Now, although he was away and Lady Frances kept to her own rooms at mealtimes, I continued to sit one chair removed from the duke hoping he wouldn't engage me in conversation. I'd find it difficult to exchange pleasantries with him. Usually we ate in silence, but this day, as I approached my seat he and his guests half raised themselves from their seats and bowed towards me. I inclined my head a little in acknowledgement before slipping into my chair.

'Anne, let me introduce you to my guests who have recently arrived from Italy,' the duke said. That explained why both gentlemen had skin the colour of strong beer and black hair. Father Benedict had once brought with him a Jesuit priest from Rome, and he too had this dark colouring. 'This is Roberto Ridolfi, he is a banker and moneylender with whom I often do business, and this is Bishop Ross.' Thankfully neither of the gentlemen seemed remotely interested in me, barely nodding in acknowledgement of the introduction. The three of them continued to talk about mutual acquaintances and courtiers I hadn't heard of, although I wasn't expecting the duke to talk about anything of importance in front of myself or anyone else in listening distance.

The men finished eating and got up to leave the table without a word in my direction. I wouldn't have even noticed they'd left if it weren't for the fact that before they'd moved more than two yards, I heard Ridolfi in his heavily accented voice speak of a payment from the Pope. My head came up and I held my breath. I was adept at keeping my religion hidden, as was the duke, yet this man was speaking of His Holiness as though he were an acquaintance. Everyone in England knew the queen had been excommunicated, a ploy to persuade the clandestine

Catholics to rise up against her, and that even speaking of Rome was perilous. Immediately I was far more interested in exactly who he was and why he was here, especially as I saw my father-in-law's face darken as he pulled Ridolfi roughly by the sleeve and almost dragged him away. Clearly, he'd spoken of something which shouldn't have been mentioned where ears may be prying. And mine most certainly were.

Washing my fingers in a bowl of water left beside my trencher for that purpose, I wiped them on my napkin whilst I waited for the gentlemen to disappear down the stairs just beyond the chamber door, and then I was on my feet. Seeing me stand up, Kate also got to her feet and bidding good day to the duke's secretary, Barker, whom she was sitting beside, she followed me to the corridor leading to my rooms. As we entered my apartment she caught up with me.

'Are you feeling unwell?' she asked. 'You could not have eaten much dinner, we were only at the table for half of the hour. I saw the duke had guests, did they offend you?'

I was ignoring her questions as I scuttled around the room pulling on my old boots and finding a lamp and some spills with which to light it.

After a pause Kate added, her voice a little incredulous, 'What exactly are you doing?'

'Those guests, I believe they are worth investigating. One of them, the smaller man, is a banker called Roberto Ridolfi. As they left the table, I heard him say something about the Pope, and also of a payment. I am going to the secret passage, if they have gone to the duke's offices I may be able to listen in to their conversation. You can come with me or you can remain here. I do not care which, but either way you must make your mind up now, because I cannot wait.' I stood ready to go.

Kate shook her head slowly. 'This is madness,' she told me.

'You are putting yourself in grave danger because of some unreliable guesswork, with no evidence. You know what the duke does to people who get in his way.'

'I do, of course I do, nobody knows better than me. I am the person who should have protected my brother when he was in the way of the duke taking our father's estate for himself. I promise I shall not be caught, and somehow, I will put the duke back in the Tower, this time with no chance of a reprieve.' Lighting the lamp, my hand shook in time with my fast-beating heart. 'Are you coming?' I added.

'Yes, you know I cannot let you go alone.' Her face dark, she followed me out of the corridor and towards the adjacent wing.

This time we knew where we were going and within five minutes we paused in the dark passage beside the door we'd previously found. I couldn't be certain, but I hoped we were now either beside the office, or the privy chamber where my father-in-law received visitors. I could hear the deep rumble of male voices and I pressed my ear against the wood.

Disappointingly, most of what they were saying was muffled, other than the occasional phrase. I found the higher pitched tones of Ridolfi easier to hear, but his accent didn't help in deciphering what he was saying. I held my breath as though that may make it easier to listen to, my hand over my mouth. After a little while their voices faded away and I guessed they'd moved elsewhere but although I crept back and forth along the passage, I couldn't hear anything else. Turning back, we hurried along the passage towards the hidden door where we'd entered.

Within a few minutes we were in my rooms again and we brushed away dust and strings of cobwebs wreathed about our gowns and caps. Kate poured us both beakers of ale and I drank mine down immediately before holding it out to be replenished.

It felt as though I'd gritted my teeth and held my breath for the entire time we'd been gone from my rooms.

'Well then,' Kate said once we were sitting in front of the fire with our embroidery on our laps as if we'd been there all the time, 'what did you hear?'

'Not as much as I would have wished to,' I admitted. 'But I heard Ridolfi mention Queen Mary of Scotland, and later he spoke of gold.'

'But did you not say he is a banker, that was how he was introduced to you? If that is the case of course he will talk of gold, it is his currency, and the duke is a rich and important man.'

'He may be those things, but he's also supposedly a protestant so why would they be speaking of Queen Mary and the Pope? She is under lock and key on the orders of Queen Elizabeth. I confess at present I do not truly understand what is happening, but I shall continue to spy, already the passageways have proved useful.'

I leant back in my chair and mulled over this new information, a smile gradually creeping across my face. The day's activities had given me an advantage, however slight it might be. A little shift towards my oath to destroy my murdering father-in-law. In his eyes I was all but invisible, unseen. A pawn. But now I could be further concealed and in time he would learn the grave error of dismissing me thus.

The adults were laughing loudly as they watched Daddy carrying the big tyre down the garden, Sarah and Emily skipping beside him carrying a length of plastic coated bright blue rope. Sarah was so excited she'd already got her swimming costume on beneath her clothes. The water where the swing would be situated was shallow, only about three feet deep, but best to be prepared. The sun was already hot, so they'd soon dry out if they got wet.

Cordelia and Mummy had come to watch and offer advice, and it was all assembled in less than an hour. Daddy tested it first, swinging out over the clear water which rolled over the riverbed below.

'There you go,' he said as he landed back on the bank and rubbed his hands down his jeans. 'Who's going first?'

'Hold on, there are some rules to follow.' Mummy held her hand up as Emily pushed Sarah out of the way to ensure she could grab the rope. 'Emily, remember what I said, you can only use it if one of the grown-ups are here, you're too young to go on your own. Sarah, you don't have to, as you're a bit older. But please be sensible, both of you.'

Her announcement immediately provoked a wail of disagreement from Emily which fast descended into a tantrum and Sarah put her hands over her ears. As she'd known would happen, the rules were soon amended so Emily could use the swing if Sarah was with her. It was just as well she considered, given how little adult supervision they had during the holidays. Neither of their parents would accept spending hours sitting in the shade of the trees which overhung the riverbank whilst they played, and indeed after they'd watched the girls playing for five minutes and content they were safe the adults wandered back to the house, leaving instructions to be in for lunch within the hour.

Sarah knew better than to suggest she had a turn for the first twenty minutes as Emily repeatedly pushed herself off from the riverbank to swing out over the water with a squeal until finally she let go of the rope to fall into the pool of water below. They both shrieked with laughter as she jumped up, her clothes and hair plastered to her. Sarah grabbed the swing and joined in, until by the time she guessed it was lunchtime, she too let go of the rope and threw herself into the water, landing with a splash. She pulled her clothes on over her wet body before walking back to the house, her feet sliding in her neoprene beach shoes. Cordelia had suggested they wore them in case there were sharp pieces of stone on the riverbed.

They walked around to the side of the house where a back door led to an old musty boot room. Nobody seemed to care that they arrived at the lunch table soaking wet. Cordelia threw some kitchen towels at them to dry their hair so it wouldn't drip onto the food, and they dived into the usual bread, cheese and pâté which was the staple lunch for the entire summer. They ate in the kitchen; dinner was the only meal they were expected to eat in the dining room and that would require clean and dry clothes. Meals at home were far less formal because she and Emily didn't have dinner with their parents and would usually eat sitting in front of the television. Their diet mostly consisted of oven chips and something coated in bright orange breadcrumbs.

After lunch, Emily wanted to take her dolls outside to play on the terrace and Sarah grabbed the opportunity to collect a book and go and laze in the hammock. It was in the shade and she was thankful for it because none of the adults had thought to put any sunblock on her. She'd asked mummy if they'd brought any but had been met with a quizzical look as though she was asking for something ridiculous. Not like at school where they insisted on it, and now with her strawberry-blonde hair and pale skin, she was already peeling.

She read for a little while, the sound of Pete on the ride-on mower somewhere in the grounds creating a monotonous background noise. Above her in the tree, a dove was cooing and she could just hear Emily giving a running commentary on her game with all the dolls adopting various American accents. Eventually her voice stopped and screwing her eyes up against the sunlight, Sarah looked across to the terrace. The dolls were now abandoned, and Mummy, in her bikini, was laid on a sun lounger.

Making a quick decision, she left her book in the hammock and skirted along the line of trees on the same side of the garden until eventually she reached the big wooden shed where Pete kept his tools. The door was open but there was nobody there. She couldn't just run across the lawns to where she was heading, Mummy might lift her head up and spot her at any moment. Although they were allowed anywhere in the manicured part of the garden or the vegetable patch, she would be questioned if she was seen going into the woods. She regretted that morning's choice of a fluorescent yellow T-shirt but it was too late to change now, if she went inside she might encounter Emily, and then her plan would have to be postponed.

As soon as she reached the trees, she slipped in between them and began to run, her feet skimming across the deep layer of dried autumn leaves, acorns and spiky chestnut cases left from the previous year. The leaves crunched as she stepped on them, and she had to jump over fallen branches and roots that rose up out of the ground to trip her. For a moment she stopped, and bending down to catch her breath, she wondered whether this had been such a good idea. She only wanted to see Nero's grave and say hello to him; Cordelia's old black labrador had been dead for three years now, and Sarah missed him. She wasn't going into the nuns' resting place, Cordelia had made it plain that it wasn't to be disturbed.

Resolved, she carried on running until a few minutes later she arrived at the clearing behind the woods. It was the corner of Cordelia's land, where the stone walls which surrounded her garden met. There were dark iron railings, rusting in patches, behind which grew tall grasses, buttercups and big daisies, much bigger than the ones she and Emily made coronets from at home. Between the vegetation she could just see the tops of stones, bleached pale by centuries of sunlight and also two stone crosses, both leant at precarious angles. Despite the sunshine it felt darker here. Everything was muted, none of the colours were bright as they were in the garden.

In front of the railings was a much newer, small gravestone, etched neatly with the words 'Nero, gone home to rest'. She knelt down to tell him how much she missed him and his madly wagging tail, the way he'd lurk beneath the kitchen table when they ate lunch in hope of food falling to the floor. But the words were stuck in her mouth, she couldn't say them out loud, too conscious of the dead nuns. Were they listening too? She patted the top of the gravestone as if it were Nero's soft head. As she lowered her eyes, she was suddenly conscious of someone moving across the graveyard, and looking up sharply, she saw the shadow of a child flit across in front of a headstone. She turned around to look for Emily who must have followed her there, but there was no sound of feet on dry twigs or her sister's telltale giggle. She was always sneaking up on Sarah, but she lacked any subtlety. There was nothing, a profound silence, even the birds were quiet. Her heart now thumping so hard she thought it would burst out of her chest. She jumped to her feet and ran back through the woods to the edge of the lawn where the woods met the hedge around the tennis court.

Mummy was still sunbathing and, with her heart racing, Sarah went to the gap in the hedge where she could slip through to the tennis court behind. It was empty and sitting down on the wooden box which contained the rackets and balls, she waited for her heart to return to normal. Her face was sweating and she rubbed it with the hem of her T-shirt.

There had to be a simple explanation for what she thought she'd seen. Cordelia would doubtless have an answer, but then she'd have to admit where she'd been, the grown-ups would be angry and she might not be allowed the freedom she currently enjoyed. The thought of spending the summer with her fun curtailed, notwithstanding the amount of smug teasing she'd get from Emily, meant she'd have to keep quiet. It was probably a result of sunstroke she told herself; she wasn't wearing her baseball cap and the teachers at school were always going on about staying out of the sun, especially with her colouring. Just like with the sunblock, Mummy never seemed to be worried.

She remained where she was until Emily called her to wash

before dinner, by which time her legs had stopped shaking and her heart rate was almost back to normal.

'Have you been knocking a ball about?' Daddy called across from the terrace as she appeared from between the hedges again. 'I thought you were reading this afternoon.' He waved his hand in the direction of the hammock.

'I had enough,' she replied, before running around to the boot room. She and Emily weren't allowed through the terrace into the house with their shoes on, Cordelia said the rugs in the drawing room were old and delicate. Thank goodness Daddy didn't suspect where she'd actually been.

She didn't have much time to think about the afternoon's events until later. Dinner was fish and salad – which she hated, but thankfully it was followed by Eton mess – which she loved. Then she and Emily played Cluedo with Cordelia and she won easily because despite a lot of help, Emily couldn't remember anything from one room to the next. It had all ended, as most games did with Emily crying and running to find Mummy whilst she, Sarah, helped Cordelia put everything away. If there was a time to mention what she'd seen, or thought she had, she knew this was the time to do it.

'Cordelia,' she ventured, 'is this house haunted?'

'That's a funny question. Do you think Colonel Mustard will come and murder you with the lead piping tonight?' Despite her jokey tone, Sarah could tell Cordelia was being evasive and immediately her interest was piqued.

'No, silly.' Sarah forced a laugh. 'I was just thinking that this is an old house, so perhaps there are some ghosties.'

'Well, it is certainly old.' Cordelia went to put the game away in a tall mahogany cupboard and Sarah guessed she was stalling for time, just like her parents did when she asked questions they didn't want to answer. 'You know that the wing with the drawing room in is about two hundred years old, but this part where we are, is much, much older. It was a convent until the king at the time, Henry VIII, closed it down. Then it was converted to a house and some children lived here.'

'What were their names?' Sarah wanted to get the details right.

'I don't know all of them,' Cordelia confessed. 'But the youngest child was called George and he was about the same age as Emily, may be a little younger. He died here in a terrible accident, falling from his rocking horse. Although some say it may have been murder. He's supposed to haunt the bridges where the two rivers meet, riding his horse.'

'Could he be in other places too?' Sarah asked, thinking to herself that she'd never look out of her bedroom window at night again.

'Not that I've heard of,' Cordelia said. 'And I've never seen him, so I expect it was just some sort of made-up story by the local villagers to frighten each other. You don't need to worry about anything coming into the house, you're safe here.'

It wasn't the house she was worried about. Perhaps when George wasn't haunting the bridges, he'd taken up residence in the cemetery with the old nuns?

Her concerns were interrupted by Mummy calling to her to come and have a bath, so she left the subject and ran upstairs, but her mind was still turning the information over.

Later, she lay in bed and realised she'd left her library book outside. It was already dark and she wasn't going to get it, not now she knew about George. She couldn't ask Daddy either, from below she could hear raised voices and she knew it wasn't a good time to make herself known. At least it wasn't likely to rain and ruin the book, the weather forecast was set to continue fine for the foreseeable future, Cordelia had told her when they were playing earlier. She'd noticed Sarah's already sunburnt skin and freckles, and told her to wear a hat. She sounded just like a teacher.

Through the floorboards, she heard Mummy start yelling, and Sarah pulled the covers over her head. They may be on holiday, but some things never changed.

The Suitcase in the Attic

....

....

....

....

16

2025

'So, you did find some treasure then?' Cordelia was now sitting up and looking brighter than she had earlier. When Sarah arrived, clutching the package carefully in both hands excited to show her godmother, she'd discovered Cordelia had drifted off to sleep. Impatient to show someone, she'd gone to find Amanda and tell her, and now all three women were looking at the discovery where it was placed on the mahogany Victorian coffee table in the middle of the drawing room.

'I'm not sure we can call it that yet,' Sarah replied. 'It doesn't feel heavy enough to be a casket of gold. But it's something that was lost or hidden, so maybe I've inadvertently solved the family mystery.'

'Are you going to unwrap it?' Amanda asked as she glanced at her watch. 'Only I need to get the soup on, or lunch will be very late.'

Sarah nodded slowly. From the moment she'd discovered the package she'd felt unnerved, although she couldn't explain why. When she'd been at the graveyard and she'd thought there was someone unseen close by, the sensation had been fleeting and she'd convinced herself it was her overactive imagination just as it had been years before, but this time it hadn't gone away. She sensed something close by unseen, hovering, just out of her eyesight. However, despite her discomfort she wanted to know what she'd found.

Kneeling on the floor in front of the table she carefully unwrapped the fabric. Even though it appeared to be ancient, she could see that it had once been an embroidered silk, some of the threads still shimmering where they'd been left in the dark. In the folds it remained a dark green. Eventually it opened to reveal a small, slim book with a leather tooled cover. Scraps of gilt decoration still clung to the hollows. Cautiously, with her fingertips Sarah eased it open.

'There's writing in here, and it looks really old. The title of whatever it is has been decorated with coloured inks and tiny flowers and what looks like a teeny illustration of someone on a throne. Amazingly they don't appear to have faded much.' Sarah slowly slid the book around so that the others could see what she was looking at.

'It must've been in there for a long time then,' Cordelia said. 'That looks medieval or perhaps a little later. Are you able to transcribe it so we know what it says? Possibly it's a book of psalms or something left behind by a priest, given where it was.'

'I can have a go,' Sarah agreed, 'but I've no idea what to do. And, I also have a lot of other work to get done while I am here.' Her hopes of being able to escape from the house quickly were disappearing even faster. It was as though the ivy up the sides of the house was creeping in and binding her to it.

* * *

Once she'd returned to the library, the steps now firmly back in place, Sarah laid the book on the desk. The disquiet she'd felt downstairs had lifted, but she was certain that whatever was causing it hadn't gone far. A sadness still hung in the air, intertwined with her own. Whatever was in the house now had resurrected itself because of her. She'd disturbed it.

Opening the front cover again, she was engulfed in the now familiar scent of musty books. Grabbing the notebook in which she'd been listing everything found in the library, she carefully copied out the first two lines of the writing, following every loop and scribe. It was slow work and she swore under her breath as, just as she'd laid her pencil down and closed the book, she heard Amanda calling up the stairs to announce lunch was ready.

'And that's as far as I've got,' she explained to Jed who'd joined the women for lunch. He'd already finished his soup and was now eating cheese on toast. Despite the warmth outside, with all the physical work he was doing Amanda always made him a more substantial meal at midday.

'Will you be able to understand the writing?' he asked, 'if it's in "Olde English"?' He made quote marks in the air.

'I don't know yet,' Sarah admitted. 'It's not like anything I've ever done before but I'm going to have a try. Fingers crossed I can do some online research to help me. Who knows, perhaps I've found the thing that was lost and it will help me to unravel the strange family motto?'

17

1571

Before I could consider how I could use the information I was now in possession of, a messenger arrived at the house with an invitation for me to visit Ursula Walsingham. The letter explained that, in her capacity as one of the queen's ladies, it was considered prudent she should instruct me in the ways of propriety at court. Especially given that the queen was expecting me to return with a collection of poems. I'd been hoping the royal wish would have been forgotten, but it seemed it was not so. I quickly penned a reply accepting the invitation to Seething Lane the following afternoon and gave it to the messenger to take back.

'I must use this connection shrewdly,' I told Kate. 'It will be the closest I can get to Her Majesty other than through my father-in-law and I must not allow him to have any knowledge of my suspicions. If I am able to pass any information on then I hope, nay I will see that justice is done.'

Kate lay her sewing down and looked me in the eye. 'Please be careful, Anne. You do not know the Walsinghams well, remember how Lady Frances warned you that those at court do

not always show their true sides. Just as the duke conducts
himself, and we both know what he did to achieve his ambitions.
I do not want you to suffer the same fate as your brother. With
your sisters also to be wed to his sons, he needs only one of you
alive to ensure he keeps control of the Dacre riches and land.
You are putting yourself in grave danger.'

I shrugged my shoulders. She knew as well as I did that I
would not rest until I had exacted revenge. 'I promise I shall be
careful, but with every last breath in my body I will strive to
ensure the duke is brought down for what he has done.'

* * *

Preparations for my visit to Lady Walsingham took most of the
morning, just as it had when I visited court. Dinner was brought
up to my rooms on a tray and I picked at the roasted meat and
carp. I was too nervous to eat much, and I was also worried I
might accidentally drop meat fat on the glossy ribbed fabric of
my grosgrain gown. It was yet another new one, the fabric stiff
and heavy in a deep blue; a colour I'd never worn before. I had
pulled a face when I first saw it, declaring that it made me look
far older than my years, but Lady Frances took it from my press
and informed me it was entirely suitable to visit such an eminent
person. I was displeased with her self-appointed position as my
wardrobe mistress, but I knew better than to speak my thoughts
out loud.

The Walsingham's London residence in Seething Lane was
close to the Tower of London. It had originally been part of the
monastery of the Crutched Friars and was now converted into a
large comfortable dwelling, much as Howard House was. I
wondered idly whether this establishment also had a series of
secret passageways.

Alighting from the carriage I followed two guards, both wearing livery embroidered with an entwined FW insignia, as they led me across a courtyard and to the gatehouse of the Walsingham's home. It was built in the same grey stone and new red clay bricks as Howard House. Not like Barnhamcross, where the stone was combined with sections of pieces of flint, so familiar in Norfolk.

The men led me along corridors until finally we arrived at a small chamber, the walls covered with colourful tapestries depicting bible scenes. I was greeted by one of Lady Walsingham's waiting women who ushered me through to a much larger room where tall windows flooded the room with light. My host was sitting beside a round walnut wood table playing cards and immediately she put them down to greet me, hugging me as if I were an old friend. Before long we both had goblets of wine and relaxing, I found myself spilling out the sadness of what had happened at Barnhamcross.

'You poor child.' Ursula took my hands in hers. 'I know the pain of losing a loved one, two of my sons were killed in a fire and the hurt has never left me. How could it? And you must feel the same about George. We are kindred spirits in this and you must come to me if you ever feel unhappy.' Her face was wet with tears and I felt emboldened by her empathy to explain what I knew had really happened to my brother, that his fall had been no accident.

'My grandmother saw the deeds and papers pertaining to my brother's inheritance and his estates. Now all taken. They should have come to my sisters and me, but by arranging the marriages for each of us to his three sons, my father-in-law has ensured they are now his, just as he wished. My brother's blood is on his hands.'

If she was shocked by my words, Ursula didn't show it, and I wondered if I'd let my mouth run too free. Instead, in her turn she spoke of court and the undercurrents which swirled there constantly. How few people were as they initially appeared, just as Lady Frances had warned me.

'There are those who are close to the queen, very close, who cannot be trusted. And they are being watched. My husband's sources indicate there are missives between Thomas Howard and Mary Stuart implying that, despite all that happened previously, he still wishes to make her his next wife. If you are aware of men coming and going in a clandestine way to Howard House, you would do well to let Sir Francis know. I appreciate that for a young woman newly married, and your husband away, you are curtailed in what you may do, but please remember my words.' She looked long into my eyes until eventually, embarrassed, I looked away.

'It may be difficult for me to arrange an audience with Sir Francis if I need to speak with him,' I pointed out. 'Would it not seem strange? My father-in-law would immediately be suspicious.' I paused for a moment before continuing. An idea which had come to me previously, now felt potentially feasible. 'Although there may be a way. I am bade by Her Majesty to write some poetry to be read at court. I have written one already, I can show you if you wish. I brought my poetry book with me, I wondered if I may read it to you first and you might tell me if it is good enough to read to the queen? Perhaps in future if I were somehow able to include clues regarding anything untoward I overhear or see, you could relay these to your husband. They would need to be subtle so nobody else listening could pick up on them. If ever a trap is needed to be laid, then it must be undertaken silently.'

'That is an excellent idea! A cipher.' She nodded enthusiastically. 'Read out to me what you have composed so far.'

I opened the volume, its spine cracking as I pushed it wide so I could easily read what was there and read it out.

> *'Oh London fair and pretty, you welcome me so*
> *brightly,*
> *Beneath your majestic buildings, within your city*
> *walls I ride*
> *Amongst your subjects in their finery.*
> *I yearn still for my country past and the green*
> *pastures of home,*
> *Yet here I find a dancing wealth of beauty which hurts*
> *mine eyes,*
> *At our revered Queen's court my breath be taken, my*
> *voice subdued,*
> *By the magnitude and splendour, its rich abundance*
> *does overwhelm me.*
> *At its centre sits our most powerful majesty*
> *Who reigns over our beloved land,*
> *She keeps her subjects safe from those who would*
> *harm us*
> *Long live our most gracious queen.'*

At the end she clapped her hands and, leaning forwards, she kissed me on the cheek.

'Truly wonderful,' she enthused, 'and I do believe your idea may prove invaluable to Francis. I shall tell him to ensure he is informed whenever you attend court. William Cecil, the queen's secretary of state will know in advance and will not question being asked. If I can arrange to also be in attendance then I shall do so. Your position might be of extreme importance to the safety of the crown. Come, let us work out how you can write your poetry so I will understand the cipher.'

We put our heads together and worked solidly for two hours until we had devised a system that would hopefully work. The piece of parchment she had provided was covered in words, mostly crossed out, with the occasional one underlined, but eventually she leant back in her chair and nodded slowly.

'Yes, this is it. The third word of the third line followed by the third word of subsequent lines until the message is ended. And you shall use the word 'end' to indicate it is so. I do not know how you shall achieve all that, but I certainly believe you have the skill and cunning to do so. More than your father-in-law comprehends, without a doubt. At present we have no proof he is planning to commit treason once again, but his desire to sit on the throne is insatiable. And you, sweet child, have the motivation and, I believe, the ability to bring him down.'

'It may be difficult for me to indicate the beginning of every line as I am speaking them,' I warned, 'but I will take a deep breath as I start each one.' I demonstrated and we both laughed at my attempt to be subtle. 'I will also make a copy of each poem, and if it is possible I will pass that to you.'

As I travelled home in the carriage watching the vagaries of London life, I felt a trickle of foreboding crackle down my spine. What I had just agreed to, meant I had committed myself to uncovering any potential plots the duke might be involved in, even though nobody yet knew exactly what – if anything – was going to happen. If I were found to be watching and informing on him, I knew I would meet a swift end, just as my brother had. I clenched my fists tight. If the duke put a foot out of line, I would wreak retribution for my beloved George.

18

2025

Sarah tapped the end of her pencil against her teeth, as she examined the words she'd written for what felt like the hundredth time. Picking up her phone she tried googling medieval texts to see if she could get an idea of some of the letter shapes.

This proved a little more helpful and slowly she started to transcribe the easier bits, the ones she recognised. She barely noticed the time passing until Amanda popped her head around the door to say goodnight and Sarah realised it was almost dark outside, the shadows across the lawn lengthening.

'Sleep well.' She smiled as the older woman gave her a little wave and disappeared again. She'd spent the best part of three hours and so far only had two lines of the page partially transcribed. Determined to complete the next one with some of the letters now being easier she carried on and after a further thirty minutes she leant back, grinning. Not only had she been able to decipher the lines fairly accurately, but she could even read them as they described an arrival in London.

It was going to have to wait for another day though, the physical work she was doing left her exhausted and going to the windows she drew the curtains. The lamps she'd lit in the room made the outside appear darker, mirroring her in the glass. As she pulled the second curtain her eyes stopped looking out at the dark and instead focused on her own reflection. It was then that she realised the room was not empty. Behind her stood a person, also reflected in the window, its face cast in shadow. Letting go of the curtain Sarah spun around, but just as she already knew, she was the only person there. Looking back at the window now only her own reflection was there, her eyes wide and her face drained of all colour. Whatever she'd previously disturbed was now making its presence seen. And, she realised, it wasn't who she'd first believed it was. This wasn't her imagination, it felt too real for that. This wasn't like the shadows she'd seen that last summer.

Leaving her notebook on the table she quickly switched the lamps off and ran upstairs and along the corridor leading to her room, the shadows pressing in on her. The single bulb above her swung slightly from side to side and suddenly her bedroom felt like a safe haven as she hurried in to it.

* * *

The following morning Amanda informed her Cordelia felt unwell and was staying in bed. The doctor had been summoned.

Sarah felt her heart sink. She knew it was only a matter of time now for her godmother, but she'd hoped they'd at least have this one last summer together. And she'd decided, after her unsettling experience the previous evening to ask Cordelia if she had any more information about the boy ghost, because right now anything would be helpful. Now it seemed unlikely she'd get an opportunity to ask any questions today.

With Amanda taken up with nursing duties, Sarah went to find Jed. She wanted to tell someone what she'd transcribed and he'd seemed interested when she'd shown everyone the book. He was weeding around the edge of the terrace where the forget-me-nots had taken over.

'That's fascinating.' He pulled off his gardening gloves to take her notebook from her. 'And do you know what this means? The writing that you've translated.'

'Well,' Sarah said, 'the way that it's laid out, the lines, it seems to be a poem. I've looked at the other pages and they're all laid out like this. Now I need to continue with the transcribing and hope it starts to make sense the more I do.' She also wanted to tell Jed what had happened when she'd been closing the curtains, but he might think her unhinged. No doubt he knew the recent history of the house, what had happened here before, it would have been spoken of in the village for years. For all she knew, the rest of the household were on high alert waiting for her to have some sort of breakdown now she'd returned.

'Just out of interest,' she spoke hesitantly, 'are there any ghost stories associated with this house that you know of?'

'Well apart from young George Dacre riding his rocking horse over the bridges, I don't think so. You know about George?'

'Yes, my godmother told me about him when I was a child,' Sarah said. She hesitated for a moment before adding, 'I was wondering if there are tales of anyone haunting *inside* the house.'

Jed turned his head slightly and looked at her out of the corner of his eye. 'I've never seen anything, nor has Mum mentioned seeing or feeling anything unusual. What's happened?' He put his arm around her and she felt comforted.

'I don't know.' She shrugged and tried to give him a nonchalant smile but as she did so, her mouth wobbled a bit at the edges. Taking a deep breath to steady herself she said, 'It's my wild imagination I think. Seeing shadows in a house like this, it's hardly a surprise. The corners hold dark spaces.' As she said it, she realised that every time she'd felt something odd it was in the old hall, never in the newer Georgian part.

'You should get more sleep,' he told her giving her a squeeze and letting go. 'You've become too absorbed in what you're doing here. And you're carrying the stress of Cordelia's illness. How about coming out for a meal with me tonight, get away from here for a few hours?' Smiling he raised his eyebrows and she felt the shawl of gloom which swaddled her, lift slightly. His face was warm and open, his eyes crinkling and the thought of dinner with him suddenly seemed like an excellent idea.

'Thank you,' she heard herself say, 'that would be great.' Only weeks before she would have immediately shot such an idea down. What was this house doing to her?

* * *

At lunch Amanda explained the doctor was content Cordelia wasn't showing any signs of infection and that feeling tired was probably just a reaction to her medication. Although she wouldn't be getting out of bed, she was amenable to visitors and Sarah happily took up a plate of sandwiches and a cup of tea, finding the old woman propped up against a bank of pillows in pale blue linen covers. Her hair had been brushed back from her face and she looked tiny, like a little girl almost lost within the covers.

'You gave me a scare.' Sarah pulled her eyebrows down into a frown but smiled at the same time. 'I'm pleased there isn't anything too worrying going on. Best you stay where you are.'

'A couple of friends were supposed to be visiting this after-noon.' Cordelia shrugged. 'I've asked Amanda to put them off.'

It was the first time Sarah had heard mention of friends and she realised how little she knew of Cordelia's life in the years they hadn't seen each other.

'Local friends?' she asked.

'Members of a choir I used to sing with,' Cordelia explained. 'After everything that happened, I shut myself away for many years, I didn't want to see anyone. But eventually the loneliness stopped being a stick to beat myself with and I started getting out and about a little. Never very much, but the choir was a comfort to me and we all used to enjoy singing in the hall here with its great acoustics.'

Sarah could hear in her voice that talking was making Cordelia tired and changing the subject she said, 'I have an update.' She removed her notebook from beneath her arm, 'but I'm under strict instructions to make sure you eat lunch so I'm only going to talk if you eat at the same time.' She gave a little grin to take any harshness out of the words even though they'd been instigated by Amanda. Cordelia rolled her eyes.

'You don't need to tell me which dictator handed down that demand,' she grumbled even though she was smiling, and taking a small bite from her sandwich she added, 'I'm eating, so start talking.'

For the second time, Sarah explained what she'd managed to transcribe and her suspicion that it was actually some sort of poem.

'Perhaps you need to put yourself into the head of whoever wrote it?' Cordelia suggested. 'Are there any names in the book which give you a clue to the author?'

'I hadn't thought of that; if I knew who it was, I could do some research on them and see if that helps.' She paused for a moment before casually adding, 'and I asked Jed earlier so I'll ask you too, are there any ghosts here? I mean, apart from George Dacre.'

Cordelia put her sandwich down and looked Sarah in the eye. 'That's a strange question. Have you seen something? Although young George is well known about these parts there's nobody living who can say they've encountered him, nor anybody else to my knowledge.'

Sarah got the feeling that Cordelia knew more than she was letting on. She decided to play the same game and skirt around the truth.

'No, not really. Just a feeling that I've disturbed something.' She decided not to mention the shadow in the gallery, or she'd have to talk about her last visit to the hall out loud. The subject nobody spoke of.

19

2025

After lunch Sarah decided to get outside and enjoy some of the good weather. Inside the stable, climbing over several sacks of compost and piles of plastic plant pots – the musty, earthy smell from them indicating they'd been stored there for a long time – she managed to reach a lethal-looking scythe hanging on a bent nail. The small stone outbuilding and the dairy close by were as old as the hall and had been repaired repeatedly over the years. She wouldn't be going into the dairy though, that was a step too far.

Once she had hold of it, she walked to the graveyard. Her canvas bag containing her drawing equipment and camera was slung across her body, the familiar banging of it against her chest a comfort. High above the fields which lay beyond Barnham-cross Hall's land she could hear the shrill singing of a lark, whilst above her in the treetops, rooks squawked and rose in flight as she disturbed them. Beneath the cool canopy of leaves, butterflies rested and spread their wings in the sun where it filtered through.

The graveyard looked exactly as it had before. She could see in the distance that the wall she and Jed had repaired was still standing, which was a relief. Thankfully today she didn't feel weighed down with the remembrance of her father being there, perhaps she'd now let that particular memory go. If only she could do it to all of them, her mind would finally be at peace, but some were just impossible to revisit.

Kneeling down, she sketched the nettles surrounded by white butterflies, together with bees, grasses and poppies just visible in places where old stones peeped through, before abandoning her pad and pencils and starting on the scything.

Thankfully it seemed that Jed, or someone, had kept the blade sharpened and the shining steel sliced easily through the vegetation. Before long most of it lay flat; green and gold swathes of hay like brush strokes, woven with the splash of red poppies. Like blood.

Eventually she reached the back corner and stopped, turning around to survey with a smile of acknowledgement what she'd achieved. Using the back of her hand she pushed her damp fringe back from her face. The uneven rows of stones, totalling fourteen, now stood proud of the ground with just a circlet of grass around them which she couldn't get rid of with the scythe, she'd need to come back with the shears or a strimmer if there was such a thing here. The fifteenth stone was different and was standing away from the others, close to the corner in which she now stood. She remembered it from before, the memory of a sudden shadow rushing past her hadn't receded over the years and she wasn't sure if she wanted to approach it again.

'Don't be stupid,' she admonished herself, 'you were a kid with an overactive imagination.' Even if that were true, it didn't explain the strange episodes she'd experienced since she'd arrived back.

Stepping carefully over some still-vicious looking nettles, she stood in front of the stone, brushing the seeds and wisps of grass away from it. Unlike the others with their simple rounded tops and a single – now unreadable – inscription on them, this was tall and rectangular, with a design at the top. It looked like a crest, possibly a coat of arms. Why would a nun have a coat of arms? Crouching down she ran her fingers over the carved inscription. The words were weathered and indistinct, but this was a full name and what felt like additional words beneath.

Sarah recalled a history lesson at primary school which had involved taking sheets of paper and wax crayons and colouring gently with the paper against a rough surface so an indentation showed through. If she could do that here, she thought, she may be able to decipher what was on the stone. Her success with the volume of poetry had given her confidence a boost.

Standing up, she turned to go back to the house. She'd enjoyed spending a few hours outside, although she needed to remember why she was staying. It was understandable that Cordelia wanted her affairs in order, but it was a lot of work for one person with a time limit. She'd need to return to the grave-yard later.

* * *

Although the village pub served meals, having learned previously that she liked spicy food, Jed took Sarah to a curry house in Thetford. Over dinner, the table covered in small bowls of what appeared to be a dozen dishes, together with rice and naan bread, Jed began to get her to open up about her life a little. She suspected that the two beers she'd drunk were helping with the relaxation.

'There really isn't much to tell you,' she admitted. As she said the words, she realised how true they were, how small her world really was. 'I went to boarding school because my parents moved to Spain when I was eleven, my dad got a job teaching English out there.' She missed out the information that she'd been left entirely to her own devices when she'd visited during the holidays, and after she left university, she hadn't seen them since. How since that last summer her parents had somehow clung to each other and pulled up a drawbridge against the rest of the world. Including her. 'I studied fine art and now I make my living doing book illustrations. I also sell a few of my small works, mostly botanical, in local galleries.'

'In Cornwall?' Jed said.

'Yes, I went for a holiday after graduation and just stayed. My work is all remote, unless I need to visit London to meet with a client, and that doesn't happen often.'

'And no boyfriend, no string of broken hearts laying in the gutter?' He laughed as he said it.

'Not really.' She shrugged. *Not at all,* she thought. 'I keep myself to myself really. Now, tell me about your little girls.' It was a subject that she'd avoided so far, but she needed to face it. They weren't here, all was fine, she could cope with that.

He was more than happy to do so, and she could see by the way his eyes lit up how much he adored them. Despite everything she had told herself, taught herself to avoid, she couldn't help a tremble of attraction curl its way inside her chest as she listened to him, watched the animation on his face. He'd awoken feelings in her she didn't know existed.

20

2025

'Have you finished in the library yet?' Cordelia asked over lunch the following day. She was now out of bed, but once again she was making conversation to hide the fact she was barely picking at her food. Sarah had only been at the hall for a short while, but she could see her godmother looked paler and thinner, a small bird, its once bright plumage now fading fast, withering away.

'Not yet.' Sarah took a mouthful of the chicken pie and new potatoes that Amanda had cooked so she wouldn't have to admit she'd spent some of the previous day outside and that between what she'd discovered there and the book she was attempting to transcribe, she hadn't done as much in the house as she needed to. She'd have to work late into the night to catch up a bit.

As she promised herself, Sarah spent the rest of the day and most of the evening in the library, clearing further bookcases, dusting and briefly noting the books she thought may be of importance. A lot of what she was clearing seemed to be thrillers from the 1930s onwards, although she'd found a full set of Jeeves and Wooster and several battered Dickens which may have some value. Jed arrived with a mug of tea and some ginger biscuits at nine o'clock.

'Still here?' she'd asked him. Every time she saw him now, she could feel herself smiling a little bit wider, her face flushing warmer. She knew she needed to stop herself, that within a few months she'd be returning to her solitary life and yet she couldn't prevent the unbidden feelings.

'Mum had a few extra jobs for me,' he explained. 'She wanted the drawing room moving around because Cordelia said the sun shines in her eyes and it gives her a headache, so after she went to bed, I shifted her chair and the sofa. And by necessity we had to do a lot of vacuuming and dusting as we moved the furniture, so here I still am. I'm about to go home now, probably via the Duke. I reckon a cold beer will help get rid of all the dust in my throat.'

Sarah took a sip of her tea. 'I think a beer will be better than a cuppa, but this will do nicely, so thank you.'

'How much longer are you going to work?' Jed asked. He perched himself on the corner of the table.

'I want to finish all the shelves on this side of the room,' she said as she pointed to the longest wall. 'That's probably half of them all done then. I've still got a lot of other rooms to get through. And before I go to bed, I'd like to finish transcribing that first poem.'

'I spotted someone has cleared the grass in the old convent graveyard earlier, was that you?' he asked.

'Yes, I remembered that Cordelia always used to do it. She said it showed respect to those who lived and died here, and I wanted to keep it up. Have you noticed one of the graves is different to the others?'

'I can't say that I have, but I haven't paid much attention. There's an awful lot to get done over the summer whilst we have decent weather. And we've been very lucky so far.'

Sarah nodded. 'We have,' she agreed. Just like that summer years ago, day after day of clear skies and sunshine. It was as though the weather was mocking her for ever thinking she could return and lay her ghosts. It was impossible, already there was someone, something watching her. Haunting her.

After Jed left, Sarah drank the rest of her tea and opened her notebook once more, slowly making her way through the rest of the first poem. To her delight it went on to describe the author's visit to the court of Queen Elizabeth I.

'Well, that explains the little illustration of the queen at the top of the page,' Sarah muttered to herself. 'I wonder if she ever got to hear of this homage to her?' She put her notebook to one side so she could show Cordelia the next day.

Outside the sun had set but there was probably another hour of daylight left. She'd achieved a lot during the afternoon and evening and she decided to return to the graveyard. There was some copier paper in the butler's pantry and although she didn't have a handy pack of wax crayons, she did have a soft 4b pencil which, if she used the edge of it, may work okay.

Back at the cemetery, Sarah could hear the rooks still squabbling in the treetops as they settled for the night and the soft golden light of day threw long shadows as it fell away into dusk. The sun, now a shimmering golden disk, hovered on the horizon. A flock of swifts with their high-pitched calls wheeled above her before disappearing out of sight. Columns of dancing mosquitoes flickered in the cooling air. All was still.

She wished she'd changed into jeans to protect her legs from the ever-present nettles, but kneeling down carefully, she took a sheet of paper and held it against what she believed was a coat of arms and began shading across the engraving. It wasn't easy having to hold the paper with her right hand as she worked with her left, but she persevered and after three attempts she had a reasonable outline. It was definitely a crest of some sort, although the detail had been lost to the passage of time.

Now turning to what she hoped were words, she started again. These were slightly easier with less detail worn away and as she lightly drew the side of the pencil lead back and forth, she watched as words began to appear, emerging from history, from where they'd laid dormant.

George Dacre

9th Baron Greystoke

27 February 1561 – 17 May 1569

His spirit does not lie here truly, forever he shall ride over the waters where the two rivers meet.

Sitting back on her heels Sarah looked at the six sheets of paper she was holding, enough to capture everything that was previously unreadable. This was why the grave was different. It wasn't one of the nuns, but the young boy, George. No wonder there was a tale of him haunting the bridges given what was written here. In centuries past the villagers probably read this and whipped up hysteria. He was so young, it was hardly a surprise the house was so bleak, she could feel it in her very being. It howled silently for those who'd lost their lives and at the thought of them her eyes filled with tears. Time had dulled her emotions, but being back here had awakened them again, just as she'd known they would.

Collecting up the sheets of paper and sliding her pencil sharpener into her pocket, Sarah turned to go. As she'd been working, she hadn't realised how far twilight had fallen and although she could still see where she was going, it was fairly dark in the woods. She could see glimpses of brightness from the drawing room window of the house where she'd left the lights on. Walking quickly, she could hear her breath coming in short gasps, and as she did so she began to realise she could also hear someone else behind her. Breathing which wasn't hers, quieter and slower.

Stopping abruptly, she whipped around to confront whoever it was, ready to tell them they were trespassing, but there was no one there. Then a cool waft of air brushed the back of her neck and a twig close by cracked as if someone had stepped on it. Despite knowing she was alone, she turned and started to run towards the house.

Four weeks after my visit to court, something untoward occurred. Kate was helping me get undressed and into my night rail. It was late, perhaps a while after the clocks struck ten, we'd been entertained during the evening by a group of travelling mummers. For a house which so rarely had any sort of amusements this was a joyous occasion and everyone – servants, the duke who was now returned, Lady Frances and myself – enjoyed the performance. Kate was chattering on about the tumblers and their ability to traverse the great hall on first their feet and then their hands and I wasn't really paying attention.

In the courtyard beneath my window came the sound of horses' hooves on cobbles and low voices. I looked at Kate and raised my eyebrows.

'A little late for visitors,' I suggested.

'Surely it is just the mummers leaving?' she replied. I shook my head.

'I overheard Gilbert say they will stay tonight in the hay barn above the stables and be fed in the morning as part of their payment,' I said. Pointing to the window, I added, 'Extinguish the candles and I shall open the shutters as quietly as possible and perhaps see who is below.'

With a sigh Kate did as she was bid, but not before her face displayed her thoughts on my inquisitive nature, the inevitability of my getting involved in something dangerous.

'What can you see?' she whispered, even though the glass in the window meant it was unlikely they'd hear us.

'It is two men I do not recognise, and the duke's secretary, the older one they call William Barker.' I paused, watching where they went before adding, 'They have moved around the side of the building. Barker has his arm across the other man's back as though he is trying to hurry him along. A clandestine visitor then surely, otherwise he would enter into the porch and from there into the main hall. And who visits at this time of night when the household are all abed? Someone who wishes not to be seen, that is my guess. I must go to the passage, I may be able to listen in to what is being said if their destination is the duke's rooms.'

'That is madness,' Kate said, grabbing my arm as if I was about to dart out of the room immediately. She knew me too well. 'And it will take a while to put your kirtle on again.'

'I do not have time to change, I shall just wear my night-robe around me.' I indicated the silk gown which fastened around my waist. 'Will you come with me, or not? Either way you must decide in this moment.' As I spoke, I pulled a plain linen cap onto my head, for modesty. I looked across at Kate. 'Well?' I added.

'I have no wish to do something so reckless, and yet I cannot let you go on your own. Wait until I have lit the lamp again and we shall make haste.' Kate made no attempt to hide the anger in her voice as she hissed the words before silently re-lighting the lamp. We both hurried, lifting our hems as we almost trotted towards the door to the passage we'd previously investigated. The lamp flickered as we moved, at one point almost extinguishing itself.

We met no one and when we reached the tapestry we quickly slipped behind it, gently closing the door. The moment we were in the passage, I took the light from Kate and holding it up, I set off at a fast pace. It was dry in there but still cold, a sharp night-air breeze from somewhere cutting through us and I put my head down as I hurried.

Once we'd carefully traversed the curving stone staircase, I turned down the passage and within minutes we were once again beside the duke's apartment. I could hear voices in his office and I paused, turning and holding the lamp up so Kate could see my face, my eyebrows raised. I nodded to indicate that this time I could hear what was being said quite clearly.

There we both remained, perfectly still, hardly daring to breathe. Silently, I prayed neither of us would be affected by the dust in the close confines we were secreted in; a sneeze would immediately give us away and ruin any opportunity of my being able to prove the duke was involved in any wrongdoings. Because although I currently had no proof, I was certain his aspirations to be crowned king hadn't deserted him, despite his narrow escape from the executioners block not two years ago.

'I have the letters,' I heard someone say. Immediately I recognised the voice with its strong distinctive Italian accent as belonging to Master Ridolfi. Why was he now being brought into the house so secretly, when previously his visit had been completely open? 'See here, one to the Pope from yourself asking for gold to fund our conspiracy. And also, another from Queen Mary requesting ten thousand Spanish soldiers. These men will be provided by the Duke of Alva in the low countries and arrive at Harwich. Wherever that may be.' I could picture him shrugging.

'It is on the east coast of England,' the duke snapped. It occurred to me that whilst he may require the little Italian man to finance not only his own opulent lifestyle but likewise this dangerous treason, he did not hold him in high regard.

'I have spoken too with as many members of the nobility as I have been able, to ascertain their opinions on the outcome of what will happen. From these sixty-three men, six would declare themselves as enemies of yours, eighteen will not commit either way and thirty-nine are for you and Queen Mary.'

'Let me look,' the duke said. 'Lord Oxford, that is most interesting for he is a good friend of Walter Raleigh. It would help our cause if he too were standing by our side. Good, take these letters now to Europe with all speed.'

'My Lord, will you sign them?'

There was a pause during which I imagined the duke was doing exactly that, but then I heard him refuse. 'You do not need my signature when you are carrying out the wishes of our fair Queen of Scotland. Now, make haste to Dover and from there to France.'

Their voices faded into the distance and grimacing, I slowly flexed each limb, stiff from standing in one position for so long, especially with the cold in the passage penetrating my bones. I could no longer feel my hands and feet. I was about to usher Kate back so we could creep back to the entrance door to our hiding place when I heard the duke's voice again and I paused.

'I refused to sign the letters,' he was saying. 'Without my signature there is no way of proving my part in this plot should it be uncovered. I cannot be accused of treason again or it will certainly be the cause of my departure from this world.'

'Indeed, my Lord,' Barker murmured his agreement. Their voices faded as they walked through to another part of the apartment.

I turned and ushered Kate back along the way we'd come. I would ensure that his involvement in the plot was laid bare, signature or no signature.

22

2025

'I'm glad I've found you.' Cordelia walked into the drawing room leaning heavily on two sticks. It was late in the evening, past the hour at which Cordelia usually retired. Having finished in the library Sarah had spent the day in one of the spare bedrooms rummaging through trunks which contained yet more artifacts of Cordelia's travels, and now she was rewarding herself, sitting at the table, studying the second poem.

Jumping to her feet, she helped her godmother to her usual armchair where she sank into it, the bones in her spine cracking as she slumped against the back. 'Because you seem to be avoiding me,' Cordelia added.

'Avoiding you? How? We sit down for at least one meal a day together, with Amanda and Jed if he's about. I'm not hiding from you, I'm getting on with what you asked me to do. It needs to all be done by the end of the summer, because I do have to get back to my work.'

'It will need to be done by then, because it's highly unlikely I'll be here for much longer. But that's not why I wanted to talk to you. You're spending a lot of time with that book of poems, even now when I thought you were in here doing an inventory of my keepsakes from Japan.' She waved her hand towards a wide mahogany glass cabinet full of oriental china. 'Yes, I asked you here to undertake a job that needs to be done, but I was hoping you might also give more thought about what the family motto alludes to. And whatever you should be searching for it isn't that book, I'm certain. More importantly you need to face what happened the last time you were here because you aren't living your life to its full potential. The memory is permanently blighting your existence. Don't deny it.' She held her hand up as Sarah opened her mouth to interrupt. 'I'm not going to say any more. Stop allowing it to ruin your life.' Getting back to her feet she left the room.

Sarah watched her retreating back. She knew exactly why she'd been asked to return to Barnhamcross. Anyone could have compiled lists of what the house contained, it didn't need to be her. She'd been summoned to face her past, but whatever Cordelia said, she couldn't do it. Perhaps it was time her godmother accepted it too.

Blanking it all from her mind, something she was now very accomplished at, she returned to the poetry book and began the transcription. After the initial poem which spoke of a young girl's experiences and expectations of life in Elizabethan England, Sarah was unsure what to make of this one. At first reading it appeared light, but there was something incongruent about it. Something which didn't feel right. She recited it to herself several times over, at first thinking she was imagining something, but the more she went over it, the more she was certain that it was actually telling her something from within the lines. If only she could decipher it. After all, surely nobody concealed a book of poems unless it held something important, or dangerous, between its covers, otherwise, it would have just been on the shelves with the others.

She laid it down carefully. Having been hidden in the dark for so long it was in remarkably good condition, and she wanted to donate it to a museum when she'd finished reading it. Technically it still belonged to Cordelia, but she was sure her godmother wouldn't mind where it ended up.

Another oddity was that less than half of the book had been used, the remaining sheets of cream coloured parchment stiff and thick. She could see tiny pockmarks from the fine layer of animal skin it had been made from. How someone may have excitedly sharpened their quill in readiness to write. The world was very different these days, few people wrote in long hand other than a shopping list, in fact Sarah couldn't remember the last time she'd needed to put pen to paper, not when there was her laptop or phone readily to hand. She felt a pang of envy at the pleasure this book must have given its author.

As she finished running her fingertips across the blank pages she reached the back cover, admiring how the leather binding had been so exquisitely fitted around the wooden covers and the tooled gold design. Looking closer as she examined it, she noticed for the first time that the back cover wasn't as well finished as the front. She could see there was just the slightest crinkle in the leather, not as flat and smooth beneath her fingers. Switching on her phone torch she shone it against the crease where the cover met the back spine and realised that there was the thinnest of cuts there. A narrow slice. Unless you were looking extremely closely, you'd miss it, as indeed she had done until that moment.

She ran her fingertips back and forth over the area, feeling a slight undulation as though something had been inserted beneath the binding. It would need something very gentle to lift it out and she smiled to herself before hurrying from the room. The day before, she'd been disparaging of the drawers of stamp collecting albums and equipment in the library, but there was a set of thin philately tweezers and they'd be just right for what she needed.

Returning to the dining room with them, together with what appeared to be a set of fine ended forceps and also an Angle-poise lamp, she carefully laid everything out as though about to undertake a surgical procedure. She needed as much light as possible for what would be a delicate operation. She looked at the cut in the leather again. She didn't want to stretch it with the tools she had, she just had to hope that if there was indeed anything there, she'd be able to remove it with minimal disturbance.

Sliding the tips of the instruments beneath the leather she laid her head on the table so she could look sideways into the gap. As she'd suspected, there was a slip of something in there and delicately gripping it with the pincers she pulled it out gently, millimetre by millimetre, finally dropping it onto the table and letting her breath out slowly.

She'd executed everything far too slowly to have created any sort of disturbance in the air, and yet as she watched, the piece of paper lifted slightly and glided across the table. Not away from her, but towards her.

* * *

'I've got something to tell you.' Sarah was already in the kitchen with a cup of tea and her breakfast when Jed arrived. She was so excited she'd set her alarm early. The night before she'd decided not to start transcribing the hidden page, it was already late and she was uncertain if its importance outweighed the rest of the poems, or indeed if it had anything to do with them. He raised his eyebrows as he flicked the kettle on and took the egg box from the fridge.

'Come on then, spill the beans,' he said as he started to whisk some eggs in a jug. For a moment Sarah was distracted with how his biceps bulged as he worked, and she gave a start as she realised that he was waiting for a reply. Quickly she explained how she'd realised that the back of the book had been tampered with, and what she'd subsequently discovered.

'Before you ask,' she continued, 'I haven't even started trying to work out what it says yet, I just had the briefest look. It appears to be in the same hand as the poems, so hopefully written by the same person. Perhaps it's a secret confession, or a love letter. Do you want to come and see?' Jed, who by now was forking steaming scrambled eggs into his mouth, nodded.

'Where are your table manners?' Amanda squawked from the door as she arrived with Cordelia's breakfast tray. Jed gave her a grin and muttered an apology before picking up a knife and returning his fork to his left hand. Sarah looked down so he couldn't see she was laughing. Nobody ever escaped a mother's all-seeing eagle eyes. Unless of course your mother and father had distanced themselves so far from your upbringing it was possible to go months, or even years, without encountering each other. Sometimes she wondered if they'd even realised when she was no longer there at all.

'Yes, I do want to,' Jed replied as he finished eating. 'But first I need to get some bits finished outside that I started yesterday. Shall we meet up after lunch?' Sarah agreed and after washing and drying her dishes – despite what Amanda had said, she would not just leave them for the other woman to do – she went and collected her laptop.

23

1571

I could feel my heart was thumping so forcefully I thought it may burst. I'd been summoned to recite some of my poetry to the queen, and there was much importance on what I was about to do. One of the poems also contained a message and I hoped Lady Ursula would be present, so she could explain it to Sir Francis later. It seemed we were about to find out if our arrangement would work or not. I was certain my voice would just dry up and come out as a squeaky croak, and I'd miss my opportunity. Slipping the poetry book into the pocket of my gown, I walked downstairs to find the duke seated in the waiting carriage.

The court was still at Greenwich and I followed him through the same corridors and chambers, the halberdiers with their pikes topped with shining steel curved blades standing to one side, their backs straight as we walked past. The queen had a lot of protection, but she needed it. What I already believed to be true proved that.

Once we arrived at the privy chamber, this time not waiting in the outer room, my eyes hastily scanned the others present. I was relieved to see Sir Francis although he barely glanced our way as he continued his conversation with another courtier. Ursula, on the other hand, looked up from her embroidery and smiled encouragingly. I breathed a little easier; at least I had one friend in there with me.

'Anne, you have brought me poetry?' the queen asked, her voice carrying across the room, filling it.

'I have, Your Majesty,' I replied. Until that moment it hadn't occurred to me that the queen may decide to read them to herself, which would have been of no help to Ursula because I needed to pause to denote the breaks between the lines, but thankfully I was bid to read them out. The ladies-in-waiting and those noblemen close by went quiet to listen and once again my legs quivered with nerves.

'I have only written two.' My voice wobbled and squeaked and I cleared my throat before I began to read out the first of my poems, the one that I had shown to Ursula. Out of the corner of my eye I could see her nod and smile and I heard my voice begin to strengthen. Then at the end I turned the page and stood up a little straighter before I began the second poem, the one with the message hidden in the third word of the third line, and on every line thereafter. As I began to speak, I kept my eyes on the parchment in front of me and deliberately didn't look towards either of the Walsinghams.

> *'My family who remain still in Norfolk,*
> *How my breaking heart yearns and longs for them,*
> *From London letters fly often*
> *those I send to my dear sisters there,*
> *They return requests for all this city holds,*
> *Silks from Europe the finest there are with,*
> *Threads of gold, crimson and forest green*

emeralds, pearls and rubies, so much would they want,
Carried by soldiers ten thousand of them,
To this end I must say no to their childish wishes,
And send my fondest love always to those that I miss.'

At the end of my recitation the queen clapped her hands, and everyone else duly followed suit. I could feel my face burning and I kept my eyes trained on my feet hoping fervently that the duke hadn't been listening or have any notion of the dangerous thing I'd just done. I felt as though I might be sick at any moment.

'That was most entertaining,' the queen said. 'You must continue to write, you have an aptitude for it. Norfolk,' she turned to the duke, 'bring this girl to me again. We move to Westminster later this week, come and visit me there.' Turning to me she added, 'I look forward to hearing more of your works next time we meet.' With that she got to her feet and left the room whilst everyone present sank to one knee.

The moment she'd gone, the duke appeared by my side and informed me the guards would accompany me back to the carriage so I could return home. He had people to speak with and so wouldn't be travelling with me. I bit my lower lip with frustration, this would mean I couldn't pass the copied poem to Ursula.

'Are you leaving immediately?' As I walked from the room someone's voice stopped me and I smiled when I realised it was Sir Francis.

'I am, I have been instructed to do so by my father-in-law. He says he has meetings to attend before he can return home.'

'Indeed, I have just witnessed him leaving with the Spanish ambassador. There cannot be any good reason why he would speak with him again; the queen tolerates the ambassador at best, but we all know there is no love between the English and the Spanish. Come, let me accompany you downstairs and we can talk as we go.' Sir Francis held his arm out, elbow bent so I could lay my own forearm on his and together we walked back through the rooms towards the gatehouse.

Not wanting anyone to overhear anything untoward, I said, 'I hope you enjoyed my recitation, Sir Francis? I take great pleasure in writing my poems and I am most pleased the queen requests more.'

'They were delightful,' he replied. 'Hearing how much you miss your childhood home and your sisters and their long list of desires.' He laughed before adding, 'My own daughter is much the same and is perhaps indulged too often. I think she would like to read your works.'

I looked up to catch his eyes and he nodded, almost imperceivably. I knew he'd understood what I was trying to convey. With the barest movement of my hand and his, a copy of the poem I'd scribed was handed over.

Down in the cavernous hall, Sir Francis bade me goodbye.

'We both hope you will visit Ursula again soon,' he said. 'She very much enjoyed your company last time.'

'Of course, I would be delighted to.' I smiled as I curtsied to him and with his face straight, he dipped his shoulders and head in kind.

24

2025

Sarah was finishing the final shelves in the library and enjoying the fact that, with its thick stone walls and smaller windows, it was much cooler in there than the drawing room. She heard the now familiar thud of Jed's footfall on the stairs and he arrived in the room waving his phone.

'Excellent news,' he announced, a grin spreading across his face, 'I've just had a chat with my ex and she's agreed Poppy and Skye can stay this weekend. I'm going home now to tidy the house and get their bedroom ready. I'll borrow Mum's car to collect them.'

Before she could even open her mouth to tell him how pleased she was for him, he'd enveloped her in a hug and squeezed the air from her lungs. His hard, muscular chest and arms felt so welcoming that she couldn't help relaxing against him, her own arms going around him as she breathed in the scent of his aftershave mixed with the fresh smell of the outside: warm sunshine mixed with plants baked in the heat. He made her heart beat faster as a warmth stole down inside. She didn't want to let him go, but eventually he stepped away.

'That's fantastic,' she told him. 'I bet you'll have a brilliant weekend.'

'Of course we will, and I hope you're going to join in. I was thinking if it's okay with Cordelia, I'll bring them over here tomorrow. Otherwise, Mum won't see much of them now she's working here. And the girls will love running about in the grounds. I can collect them after school so I'm leaving now and we'll see you tomorrow.' He kissed her cheek and for a moment paused and Sarah thought he was going to kiss her lips as his eyes looked into her own, but then just as quickly, the moment had gone, and so had he. Rubbing her hands against her arms she tried to quell the disappointment which washed over her.

The room felt emptier once he'd left and Sarah sank into a chair. When he'd first told her about his daughters, she hadn't considered there was any chance she might meet them. They were a big part of his life, of course they were, but she didn't do small children and she wasn't sure how she could avoid Poppy and Skye if they were at the house.

Taking her notebook and pen she went to see if Cordelia was now up and about and sure enough, she found her godmother in the drawing room. Although she had a paperback on her lap, her eyes were closed and Sarah stopped in the doorway ready to back out of the room and leave her in peace.

'It's okay, I'm not asleep.' Cordelia's voice called out and Sarah walked across and flopped down on the sofa. The heat in the room felt stifling after the library.

'I just thought I'd sit with you and pick your brains about something I found in the poetry book, hidden inside the binding at the back.' Sitting down next to Cordelia, she showed her what she'd done so far and explained how she matched words and letters with those she'd already done.

'And what is this other poem you found hidden?'

'Ah no, I don't think this is a poem. It's really odd, constantly referring to the number three. Look here.' She showed Cordelia her notebook. She read it out to save the other woman from having to put her reading glasses on. 'From the third, and three again until it does end. It sounds a bit like a code, doesn't it?'

'It does indeed, but why the number three? There are more than three poems in the book aren't there? Is there something special about the third one?'

'I don't know, so far I've only transcribed two. The second one is a bit strange actually. Didn't you do anything to do with spying at the Foreign Office? I was hoping you'd tell me you're a dab hand at codes.'

'Ha.' Cordelia gave a shout of laughter. 'I fear you have glamorised my working life far too much. I mostly dealt with British nationals who had found themselves on the wrong side of the law and needed assistance with a lawyer or translator. It wasn't remotely exciting.'

'Oh well, looks like I'll have to muddle through on my own then,' Sarah smiled as she turned back to her notebook. 'Let me read out what this second one says.' She recited what she'd transcribed. Pursing her lips she tapped the end of her pencil against them as she looked at the page in front of her.

'Hang on.' She held her hand up, a grin spreading across her face. 'It's just come to me, I think I've got it. Look here.' She placed her notebook on Cordelia's lap. 'If I apply the rule of three or whatever that piece of paper is referring to, it makes a different sentence.' She paused as she read the poem through again under her breath. 'Now it reads "Letters. Send. Requests. Europe. Gold. And. Soldiers. End." Possibly the word "end" is like the old fashioned "stop" instead of a full stop in a telegram? Do you think this poem was warning someone?'

'Or they are requesting those things so they can carry something dangerous out,' Cordelia suggested. 'Try your theory with the first poem you translated.' She leant her head back and closed her eyes and Sarah apologised for tiring her.

'You don't need to say sorry.' Cordelia opened one eye. 'I won't be here much longer and I'm enjoying being a part of what you're doing even if I'm not much help.'

Sarah decided that she needed to speak with her godmother about what was pressing on her mind before she completely exhausted the other woman. Abruptly changing the subject she blurted out, 'Did you know that Jed is having his girls for the weekend?'

'Amanda did mention it when she brought my coffee,' Cordelia replied. 'In fact, more than mention it, there was little else she could talk about. She's very excited.' This time she opened both eyes and turned her head slightly towards Sarah. 'So how do you feel about it? Two little girls running around the place again.' She'd gone straight to the heart of Sarah's concern.

'I don't know,' she admitted. 'Scared. Sick. Horrified. I thought coming back here was the worst thing I could ever do, but this actually makes it even more stomach churning. Maybe I'll go out tomorrow, do some shopping in Norwich.' Even as she said it, she knew she couldn't. Jed would be so disappointed and she'd have a lot of explaining to do, and that was the last thing she wanted.

'It's fine.' She slapped her hands down on her thighs as if emphasising the point. 'I've got lots to keep me busy, I'm sure I'll barely notice that they're here.' Picking up her notebook, she got to her feet. Perhaps she'd work in the lofts which were as far from the gardens and ground floor as it was possible to be. Somewhere to hide.

Just two weeks after my visit to court I was invited once again to visit Ursula and as previously I sat and allowed Kate and other maids to prepare my attire until I could barely move in the stiff gown and ruff I had been dressed in. I would rather have worn the less formal clothing I favoured when at home but visiting one of the queen's ladies necessitated a level of elegance and a nod to the courtly fashions.

I picked up my poetry book. Everyone knew about my writing for the queen so it wasn't questioned and hopefully it would prove to be the way to fool the duke right beneath the nose on his face. It now contained dangerous coded allegations and I did not dare allow it out of my sight.

This time the Walsinghams were residing at their other home at Mortlake, a longer trip along the Thames, and when I arrived, I was surprised to also find Sir Francis waiting with his wife.

I curtsied to them both. 'My Lord, I was not expecting to see you here as well.'

'Court is moving to Westminster at present. I am here though because, thanks to the information divulged in the poem you read out at court, we have been able to apprehend two men at Dover coming from France. One of them, Charles Baillee, is a servant of Bishop Ross, who we have reason to believe is a conspirator with Mary Stuart. He was carrying prohibited books and strapped to his back, letters written in code. All due to your observation and warning, which meant we knew to look for them.'

'I have met Bishop Ross,' I exclaimed. 'He was visiting the duke with the Spanish ambassador. I am so pleased I have been able to assist,' I said. 'Does this now mean the duke and his cohort will be arrested?'

'No, not yet. At present we do not have enough evidence to accuse him of his part in the plot. And unfortunately, we cannot now decipher the letters we have taken. They are with Lord William Cobham at his home in Blackfriars and Baillee is currently residing in Marshalsea Gaol.'

I smiled to myself. I remembered the duke pointing out Cobham's residence to me when we travelled along the river to Greenwich that first time, perhaps he hadn't realised that the man was assisting Sir Francis.

'What do you wish me to do?' I asked. 'I assume that is why I am invited here, and you know I will help in any way I am able.'

'Somewhere, there must be a code, a way we can decipher these letters and I believe it is hidden at Howard House. We need you to find it. A parchment sheet, perhaps more than one with numbers and letters on.'

I frowned as I considered how I could undertake such a request. 'I am not sure I can,' I admitted. 'I cannot be found prying in the duke's rooms and it is highly unlikely to be spoken of around the rest of the household. Unless,' I held my finger up as an idea came to me, 'my maid, Kate, can befriend a member of the duke's staff. It is just possible they might know of its where-abouts and perhaps can be tricked into spilling any secrets.'

'Please try with whatever means you are able. Until we are able decipher these letters, we will not know what is being plot-ted. This is potentially the crucial point upon which our investi-gations are balanced.'

'I will try,' I promised, although I knew I sounded a lot more confident than I was feeling.

The remainder of my visit was spent pleasantly with Ursula as she told me about the best merchants to visit in London: those who sold the finest jewellery, the softest gloves and slippers and silks freshly arrived from the far east.

* * *

As soon as I had returned home, I explained to Kate what Sir Francis had asked of me.

'How can you possibly undertake such a task?' she exclaimed. 'You are taking far too many risks in your quest to bring the duke down. Have you not considered that his demise may mean his title and estates are confiscated and Philip will be an heir to nothing? You would lose your right to live in this fine house, and access to his riches.'

'Then I should be very happy,' I replied, holding my hands out to each side as though throwing the riches away. 'I could return to Norfolk and live with my sisters again. I do not care what may become of me, I only care that the one responsibility I did have I failed at, and now I wish justice to be meted out.'

Kate was trying to unlace the stiff ruff around my neck but I kept trying to turn around to speak to her as we could only speak in whispers.

'Please stand still,' she admonished, 'or you will be encompassed in this forever.' I waited until she eventually removed it and helped me out of the gown. But once I was seated beside the fire with a goblet of small beer and a plate of sweetmeats, I continued planning as though she hadn't tried to persuade me otherwise, her words falling on ears that were not listening.

'We need to go and search for the cipher,' I explained, 'or Walsingham will not be able to prevent the plot from continuing. He is depending on me.'

'Then he is wrong to do so,' Kate said. 'It is all very well Walsingham giving out orders, but it is not he who must put themselves in harm's way.'

'He has no other option, for he has told me I am the only person in this house he knows he can trust, and I believe him. We both wish for the same end, for the duke to be stopped in his plot. Do not worry, I shall ensure I am never in any danger,' I reassured her.

'And how exactly do you intend to do this?' she demanded. Clearly, she was not mollified by my assurance.

'I intend to use one of the duke's secretaries to lead me to the papers I seek. They are the closest people to him, whatever he does I am certain they will know of it.'

'That is impossible,' Kate said. 'They will not speak with you in any intimacy, because of your position in this house.'

'I was not thinking of myself,' I admitted, feeling myself blush at the request I was about to make. 'I was thinking of you. Maid and companion to the heir's wife is equal in status to one of the duke's men. You are perfect for the task.'

'No, no, no.' Kate put both hands up as she shook her head vehemently. 'You know that I am sweet on Luke, and I am certain my feelings are reciprocated. What will he think if I suddenly start talking with another man? He and I will have no future before anything has begun!'

'But it is the most obvious solution, can you not see that?' I said. 'And above everything in this world, I want to bring down the man who murdered my brother. Please, you must help me, If I could think of an alternative plan then I would do so.'

Kate sighed, shaking her head slowly. Her eyes were brimming with unshed tears. 'You know I cannot say no to you, mistress, I love you and I mourn little George as if he were my own family. Yes, I will do it even if it means my own life may be torn apart.'

I threw my arms around her. 'Thank you,' I whispered. 'I promise I will explain to Luke afterwards it was at my request you behaved as you did.' I pulled back my shoulders. 'We have no time to waste. If either of the men are at dinner today then you must sit with them and engage them in conversation. Try and discover what you are able.'

'They are hardly likely to reveal all whilst I chatter on about the weather and the number of rabbits I have seen on the cloisters lawn. I have no conversation to use, our lives are so insular here,' Kate said. 'What man will be interested in my embroidery, or how many times I have beaten you at Primero?'

'Talk to them about how old this building is,' I suggested. 'And that we previously lived in something similar. Ask about the spirits of dead monks which wander the halls. Try, if you are able, to encourage them to talk about the layout of the duke's offices, for that is surely where the ciphers are hidden.'

'That may take many weeks,' Kate said, 'and you have already spoken of the urgency Walsingham emphasised. I fear this plan is destined to fail.'

'It will fail if we do not even try. And at present it is all I have.' I looked at the clock on the mantle about the fire. 'And it is now just about time for supper. Instead of having it here in my rooms, let us go and take our places in the great chamber. There is no time to waste.'

I had to admit to myself that my approach was weak at best and would probably bring forth nothing, but taking my seat close to the duke, I watched as Kate placed herself a little further down the table opposite William Barker. The other secretary, Robert Higford, had not appeared.

'Gilbert tells me you visited Ursula Walsingham again.' The duke didn't stop eating as he addressed me, tiny particles of food being sprayed across the table as he spoke. I wasn't sure how to answer, whether he knew of my previous conversation with her husband and he was intending to expose me. Playing with me, as a cat toys with a mouse before it is killed.

'Yes, I was invited to visit. She is instructing me in the ways of the ladies at court. She says I will need to know these things when my husband is duke. Not that I am expecting your demise any time soon,' I added, even though that was my dearest wish. I hoped he could not hear the insincerity in my voice.

'My mother can tell you all you need to know. Do not visit the Walsingham's again.' His voice was sharp and for a moment I looked up at him. He was clearly more tense than he was showing.

'But Lady Ursula is my friend,' I protested. 'It would be rude of me to decline an invitation.' And it would be difficult to pass information on if I was solely reliant on reading my coded poetry at court, I could never be certain when my next invitation would come.

'Do as I bid,' he said, 'or you will be sent to the country and see no one.' At that I kept my head down and did not speak again. If I were sent away, I would have no chance to complete my plan.

From then I ate in silence, trying not to look sideways and see what was happening between Kate and Barker. The duke was often taciturn at meals and this day he was more so than usual and, it seemed, agitated as he kept rubbing one side of his face, his leg bouncing up and down at great speed. Eventually he placed his hand on his knee as though to physically stop the leg from jumping. He waved away servants as they went to place more food in front of him and then abruptly left the meal halfway through. Barker got to his feet to follow, but the duke held his hand up to indicate that the man should sit back down.

'Eat first, then come to my office,' he said. I felt my chest lighten as Barker sat back down and continued his conversation with Kate. They did at least seem to be talking quite freely.

Eventually when I knew I could not delay returning to my rooms without raising suspicion as to why I was just sitting and slowly cutting an apple into smaller and smaller pieces, I got to my feet and Kate followed suit.

Once back I pulled her with both hands into my chamber.

'Pray tell me if you were able to glean any useful information,' I said. Kate nodded her head slowly.

'Not as much as you would wish for,' she warned, 'but he was quite loose with his tongue considering he barely knows me, once I laden my words with sugar and let him believe I am but a silly girl. When my hand was upon his arm, making my eyes grow bigger it was easy to tease information from him. He is a foolish man, and I played upon my strength. As you suggested, it seems my position being close to you means that I, as yourself, am above suspicion. Of course he did not direct me to the papers you want, but he did say that he has been tasked with hiding things which would cause the greatest danger for the duke if they were uncovered, and they may cause great turmoil in the country. But he said they were in such a place that they will never be found prostrated before the whole of England's lands. I have no idea what that means, nor do I believe you have any chance of finding them.'

'Well at least we know that they do exist and are being kept here, although it is frustrating he did not give you any more of a clue,' I said. 'Perhaps they have been buried somewhere, maybe beneath the floor? I need to go and search for myself. Sir Francis impressed on me the importance in the undertaking he gave to me.'

'You cannot do that whilst the duke is at home, they are always occupied either by him or his staff. Barker complained to me about the amount of work he is being given, letter after letter to be scribed. That is why Higford was not at supper, he must work late into the night.'

'Then I shall watch and wait, for in the dead of night there will surely be a time when his offices are empty, then I shall make my move. An unwatched pawn creeping out of sight across the checkered board.'

26

2025

Saturday dawned as bright and sunny as every other day since Sarah had arrived, even though she could feel a dark cloud of worry hovering over her. In the kitchen she found Amanda once again singing along with the radio as she mixed something in a large bowl.

'Mmm, that looks delicious,' Sarah said. 'What are you making?'

'Cake, of course,' came the reply. 'A big cake for my lovely granddaughters. I haven't seen them for months and I fully intend to spoil them rotten, whatever Jed says about how he'll pay the price at bedtime when they're hyperactive from all the sugar they've been fed.' She giggled to herself. 'Thankfully Cordelia seems to be having a good day, I was worried she'd be feeling rough, and we'd have to keep the girls quiet; it's not one of their specialities. Jed could just take them out, but I want us to have a family day and there's lots of space here for them to run around in.'

Sarah swallowed hard. She knew Amanda had no idea how painful her words were to hear, and she had no intention of saying anything. The other woman was brimming with excitement.

'Well, I'm certainly looking forward to meeting them,' she said. If she said it often enough, she could persuade herself it was true.

After breakfast she decided to sit and work on the poetry book until she heard Jed arrive. She was now working on the third poem and carefully she transcribed the letters waiting for each word to reveal itself.

Eventually the slam of a car door alerted her of their arrival and getting to her feet she looked out of the window. She heard Poppy and Skye before she saw them, the sound of young, high-pitched voices calling across the garden, occasionally punctuated by Jed's voice remonstrating. She closed her eyes and leant her head on the glass. The sound took her straight back to then, running across the brown, sun-baked, straw-like lawn with Emily, their voices carrying in the peace of the countryside. The laughter, the arguments, so many arguments, now just a series of memories; little stills, monochrome snapshots of how it was back then, the colour leached out.

As she stood with her eyes closed, she remembered the other noises, the awful background sound punctuating each day, the sniping and shouting of her parents arguing. Every day they rose at lunchtime, looking far more dishevelled than they usually did at home, as though the holiday was an excuse to stop being Mummy and Daddy, instead leaving the role to Cordelia and as the hours progressed towards evening their raised voices would start again. They were usually still at it when she and Emily went to bed. Only Cordelia kept some order and ensured the two girls were supervised and fed properly.

Jed's voice calling up the stairs interrupted her musing and reluctantly she walked to the doorway and down the steps to the landing.

'Hello.' She smiled as she saw him looking up at her. His hair was looking dishevelled but his eyes were bright and he had a wide grin spread across his face. She felt her heartbeat shift up a gear.

'Come and have some cake and meet the girls,' he said. 'You'd better be quick before they've scoffed the lot.'

'Let me just grab my phone and I'll be right down,' she replied. With a nod, his face disappeared and she slowly made her way back to where she'd been, sifting through her memories, lost in another summer, a time gone by. There was no way she could avoid the girls, Jed was so keen for her to meet them. And why wouldn't he, she knew how proud of them he was, and she liked that about him.

As she approached the kitchen the babbling of voices grew louder, but as she entered the room fell silent. Two pairs of green eyes, mini replicas of Jed's beneath auburn fringes, turned to look at her. The table was scattered with cake crumbs. Sarah took a deep breath.

'Hello everyone.' She tried to sound bright, but to her ears her voice sounded brittle and forced. Thankfully nobody else seemed to notice, as Amanda offered her a coffee and Jed went to get an extra plate for some cake.

'I wasn't sure if there'd be any left,' she said to the girls as she sat down. 'Your daddy told me that you had eaten it all!'

'We haven't.' The smaller girl, Skye, pointed to the cake stand on which was half of a chocolate sponge, its top dusted with icing sugar. 'We asked for big pieces but Daddy said no or there won't be any left for later.'

'I promise I'll only have a teeny slice,' Sarah reassured her. 'So there will be lots for tea time.' In her head she'd built up this meeting into a huge monster, but talking to Skye felt okay and her heart rate slowly returned to normal.

Beside her, Poppy sat quietly. The eldest, the sensible child persona in comparison to the noisy gregarious younger sibling, Sarah recognised it immediately. Sure enough, Skye proceeded to chatter away to Jed barely pausing to take a breath or to gulp down some of the orange squash in front of her which had spilled in small puddles on the wooden tabletop. Amanda, usually fastidious about her kitchen being kept clean seemed oblivious to the mess.

'So, you're Poppy?' Sarah turned to the girl beside her and spoke softly. She suspected if Skye realised the attention wasn't on her she'd interrupt and try and rectify the problem.

'Yes,' she whispered, Sarah barely able to hear her.

'I think you've chosen a good weekend to visit Daddy,' Sarah continued. Her lack of experience with small children meant she had no idea what to say. 'It's lovely weather so you can play in the garden. Maybe you can have a picnic. What sorts of things to do you like to do at home?'

'I play football,' Poppy replied. 'But not at the moment, now it's stopped for the summer. And I like reading, and drawing.' Sarah latched onto the one thing that she could talk about, given that she'd never played football and her choice of books would be a bit mature for the little girl.

'I love drawing too,' she said. 'It's what I do for a job, drawing pictures for books. Probably ones that are more for Skye's age than yours.' On hearing her name, the younger girl looked up.

'Me?' she asked. Sarah explained what she'd said, and as she got to the end to her surprise Poppy slipped her hand into Sarah's.

'Drawing,' she said. 'Sarah does drawing and so do I. We're like sisters. Can we do some today please?' She turned to look at

Sarah with such hope in her eyes that all thought of the work to be done in the rest of the house was forgotten.

'Of course, if it's okay with Daddy?' She looked across at Jed who looked delighted that Poppy had taken to her so well, and Sarah realised how pleased she was too, if a little surprised.

'Only if we aren't taking you away from your other work,' he replied as he explained to Poppy that she was busy with tasks in the house.

'It's fine,' she reassured him, 'I can do some later when you and the girls have gone home. Come along then,' she got to her feet, 'I brought my pencils and paints with me, they're up in my room. Let's go and get them and some paper, and we'll find something in the garden to draw.' With a quick 'see you later', she followed Poppy out of the room.

Behind her she heard Skye begin to complain and Amanda say, 'You'll get some special time with Daddy, and Poppy can have some attention all to herself.' Clearly despite being a besotted grandmother, Amanda could see how the older girl was being overshadowed by her little sister. She heard Skye agree, immediately informing Jed of a game they could play.

Sarah and Poppy sat in the shade on garden chairs, both of them drawing some slightly tired and wilting roses. Everything in the garden was drooping under the relentless heat and Amanda had announced at dinner the previous day there was now a hosepipe ban, so they wouldn't be able to revive the plants. Beneath the drawing she was doing she sketched in the petals, brown around the edges now laid on the ground.

Poppy was chattier away from the noise of her sister, whom they could still hear somewhere in the house. She talked of school and how well her football team was doing, and then a long tale about how difficult it had been to buy her new kit. Sarah hardly noticed the time passing until she heard Amanda calling them in for lunch and she sent Poppy ahead whilst she tidied up their work. The little girl's drawings were very good for her age, she certainly had a natural creative talent.

Jed and his girls ate once again in the kitchen, but Sarah chose to eat with Cordelia.

'How are you doing?' Cordelia asked. Sarah had barely sat down but she appreciated her godmother knowing instinctively how difficult the situation would be for her.

'I'm okay.' Sarah nodded as she helped herself to some of the ham, pickles and seeded bread on the table. 'Honestly,' she added as she realised that Cordelia wasn't eating, but instead watching her. 'I thought it would be difficult, two little girls here, but I've just spent a couple of hours drawing with Poppy and I'm feeling a lot less stressed now. More importantly, how are you?'

'Well despite the heat I'm feeling reasonably well today, thank you. Like yourself I was expecting having the girls here to be very difficult, but hearing their voices outside has been nice. Some young blood around the house. This place needs children in it, I don't know when there were last any living here.'

'Perhaps since George and his rocking horse,' Sarah suggested. It had been several days since she'd thought about him but now the memory of a sweeping shadow, the feeling that someone was standing behind her made her shiver.

'He was centuries ago,' Cordelia pointed out. 'There will have been children since then.'

They were still eating when they heard the sound of Poppy and Skye whispering outside the door, followed by Jed telling them to be quiet and wait where they were. He appeared in the doorway.

'When you've finished lunch, Sarah, the girls would like to know if you want to come with us. We're going to paddle in the river as it's so warm.'

Sarah dropped her cutlery making it clatter on her plate. 'No,' she said, her voice rising. She struggled to stop herself shouting at him. 'No, you mustn't. They mustn't. Don't take them to the river, please Jed.' He was frowning at her but although her mouth was still open no more words were coming out. It was though she had become paralysed with horror. He looked at Cordelia.

'It's okay,' Cordelia told him. 'You go with the girls, the river must be really low now and I know you'll be with them.' He looked across at Sarah again and she could feel her face wet with tears even though she hadn't realised that she had started crying. He disappeared and she could hear him ushering the girls away, his voice low.

'Why would you tell him that?' Sarah stuttered, lifting up the hem of her T-shirt and wiping her face. 'It's not safe. Not at all.'

'Because he's with them and, although I'm sure you haven't been to look since you arrived and I no longer can, I know that after a hot summer the river will be low. It's perfectly safe. Your fears cannot colour what other people do. And they shouldn't still be affecting you either, after all these years.'

'How can they not?' Sarah asked. 'How can they not after all that happened? After everything I caused?'

Cordelia sighed. 'I keep telling you that none of it was your fault. The responsibility was not yours and your parents were wrong to let you believe that. I carry as much weight of culpability as you, in fact more. You were just a child.'

'And there we will have to continue to disagree,' Sarah said getting to her feet and collecting up the dishes. 'I'll take these through to Amanda given she's got twice the work today. Would you like a hot drink?'

'No thank you, can you tell Amanda I'm going for a lie down please?'

Immediately Sarah felt the weight of guilt grow heavier. She was burdening her godmother with her own issues, when the woman only had months, if that, to live.

'I'm sorry for my outburst,' she apologised. 'You don't need to hear all this again. It was just a shock, Jed saying he was taking the girls to the river. I'm sure, like you say, they'll be fine. I'll pass your message on and then head up to the loft to have a look at what needs sorting up there. Perhaps I'll find some sort of clue to whatever it is I'm supposed to be searching for, whatever that family motto, *"Search for that which you desire, for here it awaits you, and it shall be yours. Courage alone is invincible."* means.' She kissed Cordelia's dry, papery cheek and carried the crockery out of the room. Her heart was still racing and the plates were knocking together where her hands were shaking. The day could not have gone any more disastrously wrong, and she was saddened that she'd let it happen.

27

1571

I was satisfied with my latest poem and keen to read it at court, where hopefully Sir Francis or Lady Ursula would be there to hear it, and they'd understand what I was trying to say. Then we could talk more privately, if that could be arranged without seeming untoward, given that I'd been instructed not to visit Mortlake or Seething Lane.

My wishes were granted when, as though my desire had created an opportunity, I was invited to court once more and again, I succumbed to the primping and tweaking and pinning that was required to bring me to a standard that was acceptable to be at when in the company of the queen.

I was surprised when the duke arrived in my parlour as I was sitting having my hair decorated with a string of pearls which had been presented to me recently for my birthday from Philip. He hadn't returned from Cambridge with them; instead a messenger arrived, together with a sweet letter of apology that he was unable to visit and wishing me felicitations. I was grateful for his thoughts though, as only Kate had otherwise remembered the date and she gave me a handkerchief of finest soft lawn embroidered with yellow daisies. She also requested of the cook a cake decorated with marchpane and comfits; it was finer than any I had been presented with on my birthday before, and I was delighted.

'I have just been informed you are visiting court,' he said. The look on his face showed his annoyance – nay, anger – that I was going when he hadn't instigated the visit. I could see a fine sheen of sweat across his brow which was creased up. Was he looking worried? Were the winds of his deceit starting to rise? The thought of it made me want to laugh at his obvious discomfort. I put my fingers over my mouth and bit on the inside of my cheek to stop me doing so.

'I was invited by Lady Walsingham,' I replied. 'My *friend* Ursula whom I am most fond of, to read more of my poetry to the ladies. I do not know if the queen will be present.' His face paled as I mentioned her name once again. He may have forbidden me from visiting her home, but he couldn't stop me attending court if I was invited and I was enjoying demonstrating that I always managed to get my own way.

'It is not suitable for a young girl such as yourself to travel there on your own. I have stayed the carriage for thirty minutes whilst I change, and I shall accompany you.'

'Of course.' I smiled although I could feel that my face barely moved given how tight my mouth was, before giving a quick nod and turning back to the mirror I was in front of. In the reflection I watched his back straight and stiff, his fists closed in tight balls as he left the room. Perhaps he wondered whether he'd been deliberately left out of the invitation, if the queen's men were closing in. He had no idea exactly how close they were crawling silently towards him, I thought.

Because of him, our departure was delayed by almost an hour and I was becoming increasingly concerned that our late arrival at court would cause anger. Whilst I didn't know if the queen would be present, I'd heard of her legendary temper and I had no desire to witness it for myself. Eventually he arrived in the great hall where I was waiting, drumming my fingers on the arm of the settle I was perched on. It was impossible to relax in the stiff court attire; I was forced to sit completely upright and straight. I noted he had certainly made an effort, resplendent in a black, velvet doublet criss-crossed with embroidered gold thread creating a quilted effect.

The market was in full swing at West Smithfield and, to add to the chaos, a horse had been startled and was running amok, scattering people who were screaming and shouting as they tried to grab the rope attached to its bridle. An old man had been knocked down and lay on the ground with a hoof-sized puncture in his chest, which was bleeding profusely. I looked away as we clattered past. Despite the mayhem, nothing prevented the duke from passing through, and although I could not see him on his horse, I imagined he would simply ride at people so they moved out of his way or risked ending up like the man I had just witnessed.

Negotiating the steps at the river was every bit as precarious as before. It had rained overnight and they were wet and slippery, the barge rocking on the choppy water and increasing my fear that at any moment I might fall into the river where my heavy gown would drag me to its depths. I was holding my poetry book tightly, ostensibly the reason I was visiting court. If I wasn't treading so carefully, I would have laughed out loud at the fact that the duke cared not one jot about it even though it contained information specifically written, line by line, intended to bring about his downfall. I may not have enough information yet, but I was steadily collating it. Every word, every line was one step closer to his final demise and here it was right before his eyes, his life in my hands.

Thankfully, despite the rough water, the journey to Westminster was far shorter than the one to Greenwich and did not require us to travel beneath London Bridge. Instead, we moved upriver where the city streets with its crowded, dark toppling buildings soon gave way to lawns rolling down from huge houses, past the old Bridewell Palace, which was now a house of correction and also, I'd been told, a place where orphaned children could gain an apprenticeship. That was probably preferable to being married off to your stepbrothers. We continued past the Inns of Court where the lawyers who frequented the Old Bailey resided, and then onto the palace at Westminster.

Here, the jetty was easier to navigate and I followed the duke towards the great hall; a huge chamber with a vaulted ceiling, which welcomed everyone visiting the palace.

Groups of men stood in little huddles talking, although their voices were lost in the cavernous space. It would be easy to talk of plots and subterfuge here and not even appear suspicious, I thought. The duke didn't acknowledge anyone, even though various men turned and bowed their shoulders towards him as though they would have liked to claim an acquaintance. Such was the high position he held as cousin to the queen, whilst all other men climbed upon each other's shoulders to ascend the structure of those surrounding the monarch.

I hurried after him across the stone slabs towards some steps which led up to another, smaller hall, this doorway guarded.

As at Greenwich I followed him down long echoing corridors, the floor beneath our feet worn smooth with the passage of time, the footsteps of kings who'd trodden them before us. The rooms being used here were smaller than at Greenwich, with only two courtiers in the privy chamber together with three of Her Majesty's ladies. I was relieved to see Ursula and I managed to catch her eye before I curtsied to the queen and opened my poetry book in readiness to recite. I hoped Ursula could hear clearly what I was about to say, even though it was just the fact that I had no definite answers yet.

'On dark days when my heart is heavy and sadness
    looms,
When all around me feels empty and lonely
And when I sense a cloak of despondency close,
Then I have to take my mind to a golden
    meadow with
Sunshine and no dark clouds, where brilliant flowers
    bloom,
That do answer me with their smiles when I call to
    them,
And so today and every day I choose to shun,
The dark end within which captures the day and
Always turn my face to the sun.'

At the end the queen clapped and immediately the others in the room applauded too. I noticed the duke was making the smallest of efforts, even though his face didn't reflect any of the felicitation, his gesture was supposedly giving. In fact, he bore the worried look I'd observed when he first entered my chamber earlier that morning and throughout the journey to Westminster as though his thoughts were elsewhere. He obviously hadn't been able to decipher what I'd just read out, and I hoped it was not too subtle for Ursula to understand.

The queen bade us to stay and drink some wine and I was thankful when the duke began to talk with her and I could go and sit with the other ladies present. Almost immediately, Ursula moved to perch beside me on the velvet cushioned chair I was sitting on.

'I have missed you,' she whispered to me whilst keeping her eyes trained on the book she was reading. 'I gather that your father-in-law has forbidden you to visit me again?'

'Yes, this is true.' I tried not to nod knowing that despite talking with the queen, the duke was conscious of my every move. He was watching me and I knew what I was doing for Sir Francis was placing me in grave danger. 'I believe he is wary of your husband finding out about the comings and goings at Howard House. I now know that the ciphers are indeed hidden there but have not yet been able to search for them.' In order to appear to be having an innocent conversation, I got the book out and began to point at passages and Ursula followed suit with the book she was reading as though we were comparing the two.

'Fear not little friend,' she reassured me, 'I understood what you were saying. You are very clever, very astute. I shall relay what you have said to my husband when I see him this evening. Please continue to try and discover where they are, time hastens on and this is now of the utmost urgency. You may well be the key which unlocks the conspiracy.' Hidden by our skirts she held my fingers and squeezed them. Looking over I realised that the duke's audience with the queen was over, and he was walking towards us, his eyes trained on my own.

Getting to my feet as quickly as I was able in my heavy voluminous skirts, I spoke loudly. 'Thank you, Lady Ursula, you are correct, the lines would flow better if I do as you suggest.' I hoped the duke would be satisfied we'd been talking about poetry and not ask any further questions, and thankfully he did appear to. He held his arm out and I lay mine on it and with a quick smile over my shoulder towards my friend, now whispering in the queen's ear, I left with him. But not before, just momentarily, the queen caught my eye and stared at me for a moment. I wondered if she knew of what I was doing with my works. From being initially horrified I would have to recite them at court, I was now thankful I had the potential to help bring down the duke with my words.

I thought we'd leave immediately, but to my surprise, once again the duke paused to speak with the Spanish ambassador. He was becoming careless in his behaviour; this time instead of scurrying away to whisper in dark corners he hailed the ambassador from along the corridor. He didn't tell me to wait, so brazenly I followed him at a little distance. Just occasionally, being considered to have no sense simply because I was a girl played in my favour. I strolled along looking at the paintings on the wall, my ears pricked as I listened to their conversation.

'Good day to you.' They greeted each other like old friends, despite supposedly being adversaries.

'Do you have news I may be interested in?' the duke asked. 'Does anything happen of which we should know in England?'

I tried to read between the lines because I didn't understand what he was actually asking. Was there an update on the invasion by Alva which I had overheard Ridolfi speak of? If there was, I needed to inform Sir Francis immediately – that could not wait for a coded poem. Or perhaps what he was saying would lead me to the ciphers.

'They have our men, Cobham and Baillee. And the letters they were carrying,' the ambassador said in a low voice. 'Someone knew the men were arriving from France, but we have hoodwinked them yet again. Burghley is a fool, for all that he has the ear of the queen. Whilst Lord Cobham was in possession of the letters, the Bishop of Ross managed to exchange two of them for others containing nothing of interest. So now Walsingham and Burghley and their cohorts are attempting to decipher missives which hold no information pertaining to that which shall shortly happen.'

'That is a relief.' The duke laughed loudly before turning around to see if he was being overheard by anyone. A little bit late for that, I thought. His eyes skimmed over me as though I were not there, and I had to stop a smile from spreading across my face. If only he knew how hard I was striving to bring about his demise.

'Young Cobham is now residing with his brother, but Baillee is in the Marshalsea. Somehow, we need to free him, but that will not be simple. And if they take him to the Tower, there is every danger he will shout from the rooftops of all that he knows,' the ambassador admitted.

The duke let his breath hiss out through his top teeth. 'We must get to him first. Pay someone to knife him whilst he is incarcerated. There are plenty of villains in there who will do it for a handful of groats. They all know they are bound for the gallows anyway, so it makes no odds to them and some money for ale or hard liquor to make the time pass more palatably is a good incentive.'

'You will have to arrange it,' the ambassador said. 'I have no jurisdiction to organise such a thing.'

'Leave it with me,' the duke said. 'And in the meantime, I shall pay a visit to Lord Cobham and see if I can discover anything with regards to his younger brother.'

The two men bowed and as they did so I wandered back towards where I had been abandoned ten minutes previously, still looking at the portraits on the wall, hoping to give the inference that I hadn't even noticed their clandestine conversation.

'Come, we must leave.' The duke swept past me as though I were Blade waiting for him. Biting my lip, my eyes narrowed, I followed him.

* * *

Once back at home, having endured the return journey along the Thames, I couldn't wait to tell Kate what I needed to undertake at Ursula's request.

'She has urged me again to find the ciphers, they are now imperative to the investigation. Thankfully she was able to read between the lines of my poetry and understand what I was trying to convey. I am determined to uncover them.'

'And how do you propose to do that?' Kate demanded, her hands on her hips. 'You still have almost no information to give you any indication as to where they are.'

I knew she wouldn't approve of my plan, but I cared little for her opinion in this matter. She could be stubborn, I had witnessed that previously, but I was more headstrong and determined than she, and she should know by now I would get what I wanted, one way or another. Just as the duke would find out in due course.

'I shall search my father-in-law's offices when they are empty. What might it mean, "in such a place that they will never be found, prostrated before the whole of England's land" because from what you said about Barker chuckling to himself, I do not believe this was a simple statement. You must ask Luke to tell us when the duke is going away. Luke often goes with him, does he not? Once they are gone, I shall search the apartment.'

Kate huffed. 'This is a most ridiculous plan, are you sure you do not have a fever?'

She moved as though to put her hand on my forehead and I

batted her away impatiently. 'Of course I do not, I am not ill. I am, however, now a vital player within those who shall bring the duke down, to expose his plot wherein he will topple the white queen and leave the last piece, the king, on the board. Himself together with his black queen, Mary Stuart. Let the game begin, and may the scaffold be built on Tower Hill.'

28

2025

After the girls returned home, the house felt much emptier than just the subtraction of two small people should have evoked, and Sarah was surprised by how much she missed the background noise of their chatter. Nothing further was spoken about her outburst when she'd joined them for tea.

She started on the next poem which was easier to decipher, as Sarah recognised more and more words that had been used before. As she finished, she sat back in the chair picking up her notebook and reading through the coded lines.

'I. Have. No. Answer. Today.'

If her thoughts about the cipher were correct, then the author was telling someone that they didn't have anything to report. She went to find Cordelia.

'Do you know if there are any books or paperwork about who lived here previously?' she asked. 'Because whoever hid the book must have had a close connection to this house, to know there was a priest hole and where it was located. Although the first poem refers to the queen and I'm almost certain the author visited court.'

'Goodness knows. You already know the house was originally a convent before the Duke of Norfolk had it converted into a house. A lot of courtiers were given properties after the dissolution of the monasteries, perhaps you could research that and maybe try and move forward? I don't think it's ever been sold, just passed down through various, sometimes random, relatives. So, somewhere way back when, I suppose we must have been related to the Norfolks, which is pretty cool, no? Possibly there's a family tree if anyone has previously researched, or maybe a bible with names somewhere in the house, which would be a start. Mind you the place was an awful mess when I moved in, and when I was working, I was absent for a lot of the time. Once I retired, I tackled the worst of the chaos but after a while, I simply became accustomed to how it is, and stopped noticing. I suppose I always thought I'd have plenty of time to get it in order, and now I don't. Never put things off Sarah, because one day time runs out and all those things you promised yourself you'd do, haven't been done.'

Sarah leant down and clutched Cordelia's bony hand. 'I know you're right. And I'm going to try, I promise.' She left the room and returned to the library, which was fast becoming her haven. But there was nothing else to search through here, if there were any family records, they were either in the loft, or possibly the old desk in the butler's pantry. She'd put money on Cordelia having never been through all the drawers and boxes in there, although, so far, her own rummaging had turned up nothing of any note.

Two hours later Sarah flopped down in the captain's chair in the butler's pantry and pushed her hair, damp with sweat, off her forehead where it stuck up like a cock's comb. She'd found receipts and old letters going back for over a century, even a copy of the will detailing that Cordelia was to inherit Barnhamcross, but nothing further back than that. She'd have to look in the loft next.

If she thought it was warm downstairs, it was nothing compared to the heat in the roof space. The small wooden dormer window frames hadn't seen a paintbrush for goodness knew how long, and she didn't dare try to open them for fear that the whole lot would crash to the ground below. The wood was split and as she prodded it with her fingertips, small shards flaked away. That would be another job which would have to be done. Thankfully when the place was sold it wouldn't be her problem. Perhaps as well as going through the contents of the house, she should be doing an inventory of repairs as well. Though she suspected this was too specialised a job to ask Jed to take a look.

She surveyed the numerous cardboard boxes, packing crates and old broken or discarded pieces of furniture stacked up and seemingly disappearing into the distance. The lofts ran along the whole length of the old part of the house and Sarah suspected it was going to take her weeks to make her way through it all. She'd only poked her nose in a couple of boxes close to the entrance so far, the ones left there most recently.

As she stood with her hands on her hips surveying every-thing around her, she slowly became aware that the hairs along her arms were lifting to stand on edge and the heat in the space had dropped away. It had been sucked out, replaced with a cold so sharp it made Sarah gasp. She stood perfectly still, too fright-ened to move. A cool breeze brushed her cheek as though a door somewhere had been slammed shut, wafting the air towards her, but she knew that nothing had moved around her. Nothing that she could see, anyway.

'Hello?' she whispered. 'Who's there?' There was no reply, but the cold intensified even further until she didn't dare to breathe in. A jagged prickle crawled slowly down her spine and it was then that she spotted a shadow close to the floor – the outline of someone crouched down. Whatever it was didn't seem to know she was there, they were in another world, another time. But then as the shadow began to fade it moved, as though turning towards her, and Sarah threw her hands over her face, too afraid of what she may see next. Slowly the heat returned to the room and when she took her hands away, she was once again on her own.

Every instinct in her body told her to run back downstairs and abandon the loft, but something was telling her she was exactly where she needed to be. Walking to where she'd seen the spectre or whatever it was, she knelt down. There was an ancient-looking tarpaulin on the floor and she tugged at it with both hands, having to stand up to get some purchase on the floor. Eventually she pulled away enough to see what was beneath and her stomach turned to liquid as she realised that in front of her lay a sizeable wooden horse, its back legs attached to long wooden rockers.

Her hands over her mouth she stepped backwards, unsure if she'd really found what she thought she had, when she heard her name being called from the bottom of the stairs leading to where she was.

'Are you up there?' Jed called. She managed to shout back to confirm that she was, although her voice came out in a croak. A moment later he appeared, clad in just a pair of khaki shorts, his upper body tanned and shining from all his outdoor work. 'Lunch is served, my lady,' he bowed whilst flourishing his arm. 'I've just been told off for being inside the house semi-naked and told to put a shirt on before I can eat.' He rolled his eyes and added, 'My mother, bless her, has house rules even when it isn't her house.'

Sarah wanted to say that it was a shame he would have to cover up because from where she was standing the view was very nice indeed, but she was still so shaky she could only smile and nod. At least he had a mother who cared, she thought to herself as she followed him down to the kitchen, where he pulled on a vest which still barely covered him, and she washed her hands.

'How did your morning go, anything interesting turn up?' Cordelia asked as soon as they were all seated around the dining table and Amanda had handed round bowls of fragrant smelling asparagus and watercress risotto. Sarah wasn't sure what she wanted to divulge, and adding some parmesan to her bowl she quickly ate a couple of mouthfuls before she answered.

'Not yet,' she replied. 'But I still have what looks like about a hundred other boxes, and several old tea chests, so lots more to wade through.' Turning to Amanda and Jed, she explained that she was currently searching for anything which may be a family tree or indication of who'd previously lived in the house and might have owned the poetry book.

'Good luck with that,' Jed said. 'This house is enormous. Are you going to search the whole place?'

Sarah pulled a face. 'Well as I'm supposed to be going through it all anyway, the answer to your question is quite possibly yes. Then maybe I'll also find whatever the answer is to that wretched motto. Have any of you spent any time up in the loft?' She wondered if she should mention the horse and she was hoping that someone else would say something first.

'Only when I used to dump boxes of things I no longer wanted downstairs,' Cordelia admitted. 'For which I now apologise, as you have to go through it all. I never thought I wouldn't have the time to do it myself.'

'There was a fleeting moment, an uncomfortable atmosphere in there...' Sarah started to say. She wasn't sure she wanted to admit what had happened, but she was hoping Cordelia would say that she'd previously felt something too. At the last moment she decided not to mention the other strange things she'd experienced. This was enough of a confession to start with.

'Perhaps the heat has got to your head,' her godmother suggested. It seemed that she didn't know what Sarah was talking about. 'Maybe only work up there early mornings and evenings when it's cooler.'

Sarah agreed although she was certain that what she'd seen, felt, would still be there waiting, whatever time of day she went there.

29

1571

I'd been concentrating so hard on what I had been tasked to do and the potential outcome of my undertaking that I hadn't noticed what had been happening within the confines of my own limited circle.

The day after I attended court, I felt weary and sat resting in my parlour. My poetry book was open on the desk, but the page was blank. Instead, I was staring out of the window whilst my mind drifted away to Norfolk.

The spring showers had now given way to warm weather and I shunned my heavy gowns in favour of ones made from fine wool. They felt far more comfortable to move about in, and I was reminded of happier days playing outside in the grounds of Barnhamcross, warm summer days when we'd take our supper and sit on the grass beside the rivers. Not a pastime considered suitable for me now, but our childhood was much freer, despite who our stepfather was. We were only required to behave as the highest nobility, dependants of the great Duke of Norfolk, on his rare visits. What I wouldn't give to be there now with my sisters.

I was interrupted from my musing by Kate. She cleared her

throat and looking back from the window, I realised she was standing just inside the door, with Luke. Both of them with shy smiles on their faces. I had suspected for a couple of months that they were becoming closer and there had been no doubting the delight on Kate's face whenever she saw him. He was a nice-looking boy, taller than her, with dark hair and a wide, open smile.

'Hello,' I said, looking from one to the other. 'Is there a problem?'

'No, not at all,' Kate said hastily, 'we wished to speak with you if we may. Both of us together.'

'Of course.' I pointed towards the chair that she usually sat in, and a carved wooden seat with tapestry cushions that I liked to use beside the fire. 'Come and sit down or I shall get a pain in my neck looking up at you.'

Kate, with a look of relief, sank down as if her legs wouldn't hold her up for much longer. Luke, his own face somewhat pallid, perched on the edge of the chair and rubbed his hands along his breeches. I looked at them both with my eyebrows raised, waiting for one of them to speak. Eventually Kate cleared her throat and said, 'Luke and I have fallen in love and we wish to marry. Will you please give your consent?' The words came out in a rush, as though she couldn't have contained them a moment longer.

I was very happy for them both, if not a little surprised at how quickly they had decided they wished to be husband and wife. Unless there was a more urgent requirement.

'I would be delighted to,' I said, 'although once you are married Kate, at some point you will have to leave my employ. If I may make a request, please do not be too hasty to go. Or do you have to be married as a matter of necessity?'

There was a pause whilst Kate worked out what I was thinking. 'Oh no,' she reassured me, her face flushing, 'there is no reason for us to be wed quickly, except that we are in love. And I am sure Luke will not mind waiting until you have chosen and trained a new maid.'

I looked across at Luke, who had lost his previous pale countenance now they had my blessing.

'Of course, I am happy to wait as long as needed,' he said. Taking Kate's hand, he looked at her and added, 'As long as ever I have to, for I have found my true love.'

'And have you also asked permission, Luke?' I enquired. 'Must you ask Gilbert?'

'Yes, we have yet to speak to him, however with your blessing, I believe it will be easier to gain his agreement,' Luke said.

'And if he forbids it, we shall send him to you,' Kate said, her mouth pouting. 'He cannot refuse something which you have consented to.'

I wasn't as certain as Kate that my standing in the house, married to the heir to the dukedom or not, was as powerful as she believed it to be. Time would tell though if Luke did not meet with the response they wished from Gilbert. They asked permission to go and find the steward immediately and I gave it. I knew I wouldn't get much sense from Kate until she had the permission she desired.

After they left, I returned to gazing out of the window, feeling even more morose than I had when they arrived. Kate was the one link in London with my home. When she eventually left my service, I'd have nobody with which to reminisce about Norfolk. No one who remembered my brother.

Kate was the daughter of our head groom at Barnhamcross and had been working in the house since she was six years old. She was only a year older than me and after my betrothal to Philip when my grandmother decided I should have my own maid and companion, I had known immediately who I wanted, and I had never once regretted that decision. Kate was kind, and funny, able to mimic most of the older members of staff – which vastly entertained me – and she was my best friend within weeks of starting her new role.

I couldn't prevent her from getting married and having a happy life with Luke, and nor would I want to. I was pleased for her, indeed for them both. But she was my confidante and also my ally in my current clandestine undertakings, so I needed her with me at least until I had achieved all that I wished to. Somehow, I couldn't imagine any other maid agreeing – even grudgingly – to creep along dark, potentially verminous passages with barely a word of protest. No, I corrected myself, plenty of words of protest, yet accompanying me anyway. I wondered how much of my gambit she'd told Luke, if she'd told him at all. It was too late now; I was in too deep and I would just have to rely on him to keep his lips locked.

* * *

Kate's excitement about her nuptials, even though they wouldn't happen for months, were palpable and I had to remind her on more than one occasion that there were far more pressing concerns to be dealt with first. The ciphers needed to be found, and soon. Each day that passed, I became increasingly restless, and one night when I knew the duke and his men were to be away from home, I informed Kate we were going searching and I would not brook any argument.

I knew it was extremely unlikely the steward Gilbert would be prowling the house at night, especially given how much mead I watched him consume every evening as he sat beside the fire playing cards after supper.

'I am sure you were hoping I had forgotten about the duty I have been directed to fulfil,' I said, 'but I must search tonight, whilst my father-in-law is away from home. I shall use the passageways so nobody sees us prowling the corridors outside the duke's apartment, which would be difficult to explain. And I would prefer it if you came with me.' Silently I sighed with relief as she nodded her head in agreement.

'I cannot allow you to put yourself in danger without being there to help if you get into difficulties,' she said. 'At the very least I can listen for any movements which may indicate someone is coming.' It was a good idea, and one I hadn't even thought of, and I told her so. Her face creased up as she smiled. I would miss her when she was no longer with me every day.

We waited in my chamber, dozing on and off, until we heard the bells ring out across the city to tell all it was two in the morning. I sincerely hoped we wouldn't meet the monk's ghost on his way to ghostly Lauds. With no sound from other parts of the building I decided it was a good moment to go. Giving a nod to Kate, I opened the door to my apartment, as she lifted the already lit lamp and followed me into the dark corridor. Here, the candles in sconces on the walls were now extinguished, so holding the light up high, Kate led the way along the corridors until we reached the door we needed.

'Let us do this,' I whispered, my voice echoing in the silence before it drifted away. The door swung open, and I stepped through, standing to one side so that Kate could use the light to see where she was walking. Suddenly she gave a squeak of shock followed by an angry huff and before I could remind her that we were supposed to be as quiet as the dead, I saw what had startled her. Blade, who must have been beside the fire downstairs and heard our movements above him, pushed his way past her to nuzzle his face into my body, his tail batting from side to side, displaying his obvious delight in finding me. I sighed audibly.

'No, no, you cannot be with me now. Go and find your bed.' I tried to drag him back by the scruff of his hairy neck towards the door, but with his size and weight it was impossible to do. He just kept twisting and turning until I gave up. It would be daylight before we got to our destination if we wasted any more time. He'd have to come with us, and I told Kate so, reminding her to shut the passage door.

'Surely you are jesting with me?' she exclaimed in a voice that was far too loud. I pushed my face closer to her to shush her. 'We simply cannot let him accompany us,' she continued in a whisper, 'if he barks he will alert anyone who is awake to the hidden passages.'

'He rarely makes a sound unless he wants the food someone is eating. We cannot leave him behind now, we must push on with all haste before we have no time left. Come, he will not be any trouble.' I walked away with the lamp and Blade at my heels, knowing that Kate would have to follow, which indeed she did.

Once we were behind the door which led into the duke's apartment, I paused with my ear against the wooden planks, listening for any indication that someone was in there, but I heard nothing. Beside me, Blade stood stock still and cocked his head on one side as though he were listening too.

I held my hand over the latch as I slowly pressed on the top to open it as quietly as possible before slipping through pushing the arras to one side and gaining access to the room, followed by Blade, and then Kate. It was cold, despite the warmth we now enjoyed during the day. Without a fire lit in the grate the rooms soon became cool at night and this one hadn't been warm for days. Which boded well because if the duke were due home, the fire would be lit for a day to take the chill off the room.

Using a flint rasp I found on the fireplace, I struck a spark and lit two of the candelabras which were on side tables.

'Is that wise?' Kate asked. 'The light may be seen by the guards outside.'

'Do you honestly think they are awake and doing their duty whilst my father-in-law is away? I certainly do not. They will be in their cups for certain, I am confident nobody will notice. Now, what we are searching for will doubtless be on slips of parchment small enough to be hidden in the narrowest of spaces. And all we have is the clue you were able to glean. If indeed they are still there and as I have no idea what it means, we must search everywhere.'

I walked over to a bookcase and began to go through each book hunting for anything hidden between the pages or within the bindings, and I heard Kate start to shuffle through desk drawers. It all seemed too obvious though, and I still couldn't tie anything up with what Barker had told her.

An hour later and we'd exhausted all the most likely hiding places, and several unlikely ones.

'There is nothing here,' Kate said as she flopped down in the chair behind the duke's desk. I tried to imagine his furious reaction if he knew one of the servants was sprawling in his chair. If she put her feet on his desk, even though such an idea would not enter her head as it had mine, the image would be perfect.

'There has to be, we just have not found it yet. Let us try his parlour.' I blew out all the candles and taking the lamp we walked onto the gallery from which we could access the other rooms.

We approached the door, Blade still close to my hip as though he had been stuck there with horse hoof glue. I looked around at this lavish space, once again furious that such luxurious surroundings, thick carpets and heavy arris which stopped draughts had been afforded, whilst Barnhamcross had been left bereft of any comfort. Despite that though, I still yearned for home and I always would. We crept along the gallery to the parlour and Kate entered first.

As I paused for a moment while she quickly checked the room for occupants we may not have heard, I glanced up at the framed painting above my head, over the door. It was a map of England.

'Kate, come back here with the lamp,' I hissed. She reappeared immediately, her eyes wide open and her hand on her chest.

'Is someone coming?' she gasped.

'No. But see here, I have possibly found a clue. Look,' I pointed above my head, 'a map of England, could they be around here? Prostrated before the whole of England's lands?'

It was at that point I realised Blade was snuffling at the mat which lay in front of the doorway where we were now standing.

'What have you found?' I asked ruffling his head and encouraging him to follow me. He would not though and continued to worry at the space with one of his giant hairy paws. 'Is there some food spilled on here?' I asked, picking up the mat to shake out whatever he was after. Beneath it, squashed flat, were several pieces of parchment tied with ribbon.

Despite how she'd felt in the loft, Sarah knew she needed to return and take a proper look at the rocking horse. It was almost impossible to believe it was the one which had once belonged to George Dacre, the boy in the folklore who supposedly haunted the three bridges. Only by examining it would she know for certain.

Climbing the stairs, her legs felt wobbly and, as she slowly moved along the loft space towards the horse, she was alert this time to any change in the stifling temperature. But it remained just as hot and close as when she'd first opened the door and been hit with a wall of heat.

Once she arrived at the horse, she dragged away the rest of the tarpaulin creating a cloud of dust which wafted into the air before coming down to rest on the surrounding area. Although she put the back of her hand against her mouth it wasn't sufficient to prevent the dust from entering her lungs and making her cough. Eventually after pausing to wipe her eyes, she was able to examine what she'd uncovered.

She pulled a couple of smaller pieces of wood to one side

until eventually she realised that what she'd found was indeed the body and legs of a large rocking horse which when properly set up would have probably been the size of a small pony. The rockers, the curved pieces of wood were in her estimation about six feet long. The back two legs together with the torso were still attached to the rockers, but one leg was loose and the other, she realised, was in two pieces – the ones she'd just moved. She couldn't see the head at all though. She searched around behind and within the boxes nearby, but it was nowhere to be seen.

Pulling out an old duster she'd brought from the kitchen from her back pocket, she set about wiping it down. The wood was now split in places where it had dried out, but she could still see the red, blue and yellow painted decorations even though they were faded. As she ran her hand over the rump her fingers snagged on what she thought was splintered wood, but then looking closer she could see that there was something roughly scratched into the surface. It was too small and rough to read but taking a photo, she was then able to enlarge it on her phone. She screwed her eyes up but it did no good, she couldn't work out what it was except it looked similar to the old letters in her poetry book. Examining the rest of the horse for anything more, she found nothing. She'd need Jed's help to turn it over and look at the other side, the main body was too heavy and cumbersome for her to manage on her own.

Somewhere below her she could hear the steady thwack of an axe on wood and guessed she'd find him at the woodshed alongside the kitchen garden and she ran down to the ground floor and past Amanda in the kitchen who just had time to ask, 'Where's the fire?' before Sarah raced past her.

'Can you just give me a hand, please?' Sarah was out of breath and had to explain her discovery between puffs of breath. Jed rested the axe on the chopping block and waited until she'd finished before indicating the heap of logs he was splitting into more manageable pieces.

'Can it wait?' he asked. 'I want to get this done by lunchtime because I've got to go into Norwich this afternoon and collect something for Mum. You could come with me if you want?'

Sarah thought for a moment. She was torn between her desire to know if there were any other engravings on the horse and the chance to spend time with Jed. Her attraction to him was definitely growing stronger and although she'd thought at times perhaps it was reciprocated, other times she thought he just considered her a friend, thrown together by their circumstances of being in the same place at the same time.

'Yes, thank you, I'd like that.' She said the words before she could change her mind. The horse would still be there when she got back and if they weren't too long then Jed may still have time to help her.

Leaving him to finish his work she went inside to find Cordelia and update her with the photos she'd taken.

'Goodness,' Cordelia slowly shook her head. 'In all the time I've lived here I never found a rocking horse up there. How old does it look, is there a possibility it's George's? Wouldn't that be incredible.'

'I don't know,' Sarah admitted. 'It seems almost impossible that his horse may have been up in the loft for over four hundred years, although other people must have found it before I did and just not been interested as I am. And I don't understand why the head is missing. One of the front legs isn't attached to the rockers though, which does correlate with the story of how the accident happened, that the horse collapsed whilst George was sitting on it.'

'Let me see the photos again please.' Sarah handed her phone over and showed Cordelia how to zoom in. 'It does look very old,' she agreed. 'And thick and heavy. I imagine it would have been made of solid oak, if it really is sixteenth century. No wonder you couldn't move it.'

'What about these words scratched in it though?' Sarah said. 'Can you tell me what you think they say?'

'Don't ask me,' Cordelia laughed. 'You're our resident translator, I'll leave that up to you.' Sarah took the phone back and looked at the words again. This would be more difficult to work out, some of the letters now split apart by the ageing wood.

* * *

After a quick shower in Cordelia's wet room and a change of clothes he'd brought with him, Jed announced he was ready to leave. It was still only eleven thirty and he suggested they found somewhere for lunch on their way to Norwich. Sarah was happy to agree and within minutes they were driving through Thetford towards the A11.

'How about here?' Jed asked as he slowed down and pulled into the car park of a pub. There was only one space left and he reversed into it, his left arm resting along the top of Sarah's seat, making her catch her breath as the warmth of his skin brushed against her neck. He clearly had no idea of the effect he was having on her, she mused, and once the engine was off he jumped out and stood waiting for her to do the same.

'Have you been here before?' she asked as they walked into the cool interior of the building. Despite its small appearance at the front, she could see that the bar and tables stretched through to another large room at the back.

'Nope,' he replied. 'But the car park is full which usually means it's popular with the locals. Even on a weekday lunchtime like now.'

Within fifteen minutes they both had glasses of sparkling water and a large board with charcuterie and cheeses, bread, crackers and chutney in front of them.

'I didn't realise how hungry I was,' Sarah admitted fifteen minutes later as she finally sat back and put her napkin on her plate.

'Are you sure you've had enough?' Jed asked. 'Because all that wood chopping has worked up an appetite and I could easily finish this off.'

'Be my guest, I'm stuffed.'

'Well, while I eat, you can tell me about this horse you've found,' Jed told her as he piled a cracker up with a large piece of blue cheese. Sarah explained everything as she'd done to Cordelia whilst showing him the photos on her phone.

'I just need to check the other side of the horse to see if there are any other markings,' she said. 'Later when we get home, I'm going to see if I can decipher any of these etched words.'

Within an hour they were in Norwich and having never been before Sarah was happy for Jed to show her around some of the sights. Looking around the medieval buildings and streets, she couldn't help thinking about the fact that they'd been there while the author of her poetry volume had been writing in it. It put into perspective exactly how old the book was.

As they approached Jarrolds, the large department store, to collect Amanda's purchase they walked along the ancient, cobbled streets and wearing her flip flops, Sarah felt her feet slip from beneath her. Instantly, Jed caught her arm to stop her falling and after she laughed and apologised, he held her hand as they continued walking. The close proximity to him and the ease with which he'd ensured she didn't stumble again just made her warm to him even more. She tried to admonish herself and remind herself there was a reason why she didn't get close to other people, but now she just couldn't help it, no one had ever made her feel this way before. Her tightly woven life was starting to unravel.

'What on earth is that?' she asked as he reappeared from the online orders collection point carrying an enormous paper carrier bag.

'Lego,' Jed replied, holding the bag out so she could see. 'Mum decided that we should have some toys at her house for when the girls visit. I told her she didn't need to buy something so large, but my mother will not be deterred when it comes to the girls. She's the original doting grandmother.'

Taking her hand again, Jed led them back to the car. Sarah was surprised at how disappointed she was that the afternoon together was almost at an end. It was not an emotion she could ever remember encountering and it hit her hard. Was she beginning to fall for him? She needed to put some space between them; once the house was sorted she'd be returning to Cornwall and Jed would remain somewhere in East Anglia, close to his daughters. Even if either of them wanted anything to happen, and she was sure he was just being friendly, it wasn't going to. The time had come to put up her barriers again.

'Sarah, can we play a game?' Emily had found her in the hammock, already onto her last library book, but still with another two weeks of holiday left. She'd asked Cordelia if there was anything she could borrow from the library here in the house, but she'd been told no and reminded of the fact that the room was out of bounds.

'I suppose so,' she answered, putting her book down and swinging her legs onto the ground. It would make a change from Emily constantly asking to go on the rope swing; they'd spent at least an hour if not more on it every day since they'd arrived. 'Do you want to play with your dolls? We could make them go on a jungle adventure through the trees?'

Emily shook her head. 'No, I want to play inside. Not with my dolls, they're all having a rest. Come with me, I have a good idea.' She ran off to the back door and Sarah picked up her book and followed. She'd been told off for leaving it outside the day when she thought she'd seen George, so she'd been careful to make sure she didn't do it again. Mummy had threatened to stop taking her to the library, and that would be an absolute disaster.

They darted through the stiflingly hot kitchen, where Cordelia was baking bread whilst also preparing a custard tart for later, and along the corridor to the entrance hall. This was the coolest part of the house and Sarah flopped down on the wooden settle which stood against one wall. The rest of the house was silent, Mummy and Daddy had driven to the super-market and Sarah hoped they may think to buy her a book whilst they were there. She'd hinted but considered it doubtful.

'So, what do you want to play?' she asked.

'Hide and seek,' Emily grinned, jumping up and down on the spot in delight. It was the one game she was really good at; her lithe, small frame was able to slip into tiny spaces, and this was a big house with a lot of hiding places. Sarah was surprised it was the first time she'd asked that summer.

'Okay, I'll count,' she said, putting her hands over her eyes. 'One, two, three,' she heard the scamper of Emily's feet as she ran off upstairs and judging by the thumping overhead she'd gone into the newer wing of the building where their parents' room and other spare bedrooms were. They weren't supposed to go there, but as ever, Emily ignored the rules, knowing she'd be forgiven if she was discovered.

As soon as she reached one hundred, Sarah ran after her sister and crept through the bedrooms for ten minutes, wrinkling her nose at the smell of stale tobacco in her parents' room, even though she knew Daddy had been asked not to smoke in the house. The dressing table was scattered with make-up, a dusting of face powder covered everything. And their bed wasn't made, she noted with disapproval, given that she was told to make hers every day. She was beginning to wonder if she'd find Emily when she realised that the door to a small anteroom was slightly ajar. The room, just big enough for a single bed, led to yet another bedroom. Cordelia had explained once it had been a room for the gentleman of the house to use for his clothes and to get dressed in, and he may have had a bed or sofa in there to sleep on if he'd been thrown out of bed for snoring. Now it just contained a vacuum cleaner and storage boxes, which was where Sarah finally found Emily, crouched down in a corner behind a box which said 'bedding' on it.

'Found you!' she shouted. As Emily began to climb back out Sarah added, 'My turn!' before running back downstairs. She knew from experience that unless she acted quickly Emily would start whining to be allowed a second go, and she heard her sister begin to count from above her. Pausing in the hall, she wondered where to go. In previous years she'd hidden behind the long, floor-length curtains in the drawing room and another time stood behind the dining room door from where she'd eventually had to reveal herself. Her eyes scanned the hall until she remembered the library. Emily would never find her in there, because she'd never believe Sarah would dare to go in. Nobody expected her to misbehave and with a spark of rebellion she usually kept suppressed, she darted back to the small flight of steps which lead up to it.

Thinking it would be locked, she turned the worn and slightly dented brass doorknob, cold in her hand, surprised when she heard a click and it opened. For a moment she just stood there, but then with a quick look over her shoulder to make sure she wasn't being watched, and a double check that Emily was still counting, her voice now a blur of numbers as she got faster and faster, Sarah slipped inside.

The room was murky, the only light coming from around the heavy drapes at the windows, casting just enough illumination to catch on the edges of the furniture and show the walls lined with bookcases rearing up around her like castle walls. She hadn't yet heard Emily run across the landing above her head, so she hurried to a curtain and opened it a crack and peeped outside. The library was at the rear of the old part of the house, Cordelia had told her that it was originally the private sitting room of the abbess. Perhaps one of the ones buried beneath a headstone in the cemetery. The hairs on the back of her neck still stood up when she thought about what had happened there that day; she hadn't been back since.

The windows were at a right angle to the drawing room and terrace which continued around the corner in front of the library too. If she was going to open some of the curtains and have a proper look at the room, she needed to check there was nobody outside who might see the movement. She was in luck, Mummy and Daddy must still be out shopping and she already knew Cordelia was in the kitchen.

Having created a small amount of light she was now able to look around the room properly. She was certain that Emily wouldn't even think to open the door, she had at least ten minutes whilst her sister searched the rest of the house.

The floor to ceiling shelves were full of old books, their dark ridged spines and gold lettering too faded to read. Some of them were behind glass and the ones which weren't were covered in a layer of dust.

They were squashed together so there was no space left and on a table in the middle of the room were stacks of more modern books, the kind of thing she'd seen Cordelia reading. A few dining chairs stood around the edges of the room and the only other furniture was a battered looking sofa, the sort you could lie on all day reading, if you were allowed access to the room. Perhaps that was what Cordelia did when they weren't visiting.

One wall was devoid of bookcases; it was instead panelled in dark wood in thin vertical ridges and in the middle stood a vast stone fireplace similar to but larger than the ones in the dining room and kitchen. The kitchen one now housed a big, cream coloured oven which also apparently ran the heating and Cordelia had to shovel coal into if she wanted to use it, although when they were visiting in the summer she said there was no need and she just used a normal cooker and a microwave like Mummy did. There was a dark sooty stain up the middle of the stone surrounds.

She was quite disappointed with the room. It was full of books as she'd expected, and there were few things she liked more than reading, but these weren't like the ones she read. They weren't even similar to the textbooks she used at school – those had colourful pictures. She'd bet all her pocket money, currently at two pounds and seventy-two pence after she'd bought some new hair slides, that none of these books had pictures. Why had Cordelia been so assertive about she and Emily not going in, when there was nothing she'd remotely want to touch anyway? She couldn't ask though, despite her curiosity, because then it would be known she'd been in there, and all hell would break loose.

From outside the room, she heard the thump of Emily's feet running past and down the rest of the stairs, and quickly replacing the curtains exactly as they'd been before, she slipped back out. Emily was nowhere to be seen and Sarah sat on the settle in the hall until she heard Emily and Cordelia talking as they walked from the kitchen. Quickly she lay down and pretended to be asleep.

'How did you get there?' Emily shrieked as she threw herself on top of Sarah who burst out laughing.

'I've been here all the time,' she said. 'You obviously aren't very good at looking if you ran past me. I've had a lovely doze.'

'You're a liar!' Emily's voice changed in a moment from amused to annoyed. Sarah should have guessed she wouldn't take kindly to being tricked. Luckily Cordelia was used to diverting tantrums, much better than Mummy in fact.

'It's lunchtime,' she announced, clapping her hands together, 'Mummy and Daddy will be back soon but I'm hungry now so let's go and tuck in. I've got some raspberry ripple ice cream too; we can go out in the garden after lunch with some cones, is that a good idea?'

Immediately Emily's scowl disappeared and with a smile, she trotted back towards the kitchen. As she went to follow, Cordelia turned and gave the merest hint of a grin, and instantly Sarah loved her godmother even more than she had before. She was an ally, and other than Daddy, Sarah had few of those.

They were sitting on the sun loungers eating their ice creams, Emily humming to herself in enjoyment, when Mummy and Daddy returned. The area where the cars parked was at the front of the house on a large gravel patch but even with the distance between them Sarah flinched as she heard the car door being slammed shut loudly, followed by her mother shouting, 'Don't even speak to me, I've had enough!'

Sarah slid her eyes towards Cordelia to see if she'd also heard. Emily was still burbling away totally oblivious, but her godmother had paused from eating her ice cream for a moment. Then, without a word and without looking at either of them, she just continued as if there'd been no interruption. Sarah wanted her to say something, to acknowledge what was going on, but she guessed that it was a subject not to be spoken of. Her parents had always argued, but this holiday had been far, far worse than usual. No wonder Daddy kept sliding off for a quiet cigarette – he needed some respite from Mummy's constant sniping comments.

The back door slammed, and then there was silence. Still Cordelia remained where she was and Sarah sat holding her

breath with her ice cream dripping down her hand, waiting for
what would come next.

Five minutes later Daddy stepped out from the French
windows behind them and onto the terrace, tapping the end of a
cigarette on the box. There was no sign of Mummy.

'I've put the shopping in the fridge,' he told Cordelia, 'but I
don't know where the tins and packets go. Alright chicken?' he
said to Sarah as he winked at her. She smiled and nodded and
without another word he walked away down the garden, lighting
his cigarette and typing with one finger on his fancy mobile
phone at the same time. Cordelia got up and disappeared inside,
and although she really wanted to follow, Sarah guessed that it
was probably better if she didn't. Nobody wanted to inadvertently come across Mummy if she was still in one of her unpre-
dictable moods, no wonder Daddy had escaped.

'Rope swing?' Emily interrupted her musing. It seemed that
for once she'd picked up on the underlying tension and had
harnessed a previously unseen prudence. Sarah nodded, and
quickly finishing her ice cream and wiping her sticky fingers on
her shorts, she followed Emily as she ran towards the river. This
holiday was carrying an increasing burden of worry, an oppres-
sive atmosphere that previous ones had not.

32

2025

Sarah was already drinking coffee and waiting for Jed when he arrived at the hall the following morning.

'You're up early,' he said as he took a bowl from the cupboard and filled it with muesli and milk.

'I wanted to grab you before you go outside and start work,' she explained. 'I was hoping we could try to shift the rocking horse first thing, before it gets too hot in the loft.'

'Okay,' Jed nodded. 'Let me just eat this.'

Thankfully she only had to wait for a short while until he'd finished and he led the way up the stairs two at a time. Sarah followed more slowly wondering if there would be any change in the atmosphere this time, waiting to see if he noticed anything. It seemed not though, when she arrived he was already beside the horse and lifting pieces up as though trying to fit them together.

'I can't see the head,' he said. 'Have you moved that some-where else?'

'No, it seems to be missing. If I pick up the neck, can you hold the rump, and we'll try and turn it over? You can see where

I swept the dust away and found the scratching at the top of that leg,' Sarah said.

Jed bent closer rubbing his fingers over it. 'And what does it say?' he asked.

'I haven't attempted to decipher it yet, that's what I'm going to do before I start on the next poem. And after I finish sorting out up here a bit.' She bent her knees to take the weight and began to lift the horse's neck and quickly Jed grabbed the other end and between them they were able to roll it over so it was laid on the other side. Immediately they both started to wipe the dust off to see if they could find any more etchings, but soon realised there was nothing there.

'That's a shame,' Sarah said. 'I was hoping I might get some more clues. The paintwork on this side is brighter though, so it must've been laid there for a very long time.'

'Given the obvious connection between this house and a rocking horse, do you think that this was George Dacre's?' Jed asked.

'I don't know for certain, but it does seem likely, doesn't it? Maybe the head became detached when he fell off. Given that the rumours say some of the wooden pegs were removed, causing the horse to collapse so the head may have come off too.'

'That's what I was told,' Jed agreed. 'Now, do you need me for anything else?'

'Sorry, I shouldn't have hijacked you,' Sarah apologised. 'But thank you for your help.'

'Honestly, it's fine, I'm as interested as you. I hope you're going to work out what the etching says.'

'I will, but I should really get on with some of Cordelia's trinkets first. It's what I came here to do but I've got behind because the poetry sidelined me.' Getting to her feet Sarah followed Jed down to the floor below, relieved that she hadn't experienced any other visitors whilst they were up there.

* * *

'Aha, I'm pleased to find you in here sorting out my bits and bobs.' Cordelia made Sarah jump and almost drop a china vase as she arrived in the drawing room.

'The library is now complete,' Sarah said. 'And there's nothing really in the bedrooms. I've had a quick scout through the loft, but it looks like you said, to be boxes of junk which nobody wanted to throw away and most will likely end up in a skip at some point.'

'Apart from the rocking horse, that sounds as though it may be valuable.'

'I think it's value is probably to this house,' Sarah said. 'Perhaps it can be renovated at some point and if we can't find the head another could be made. It could sit on the gallery where it is reputed to have been before.' Instantly she thought of the dark shadow pitching forward; she knew exactly where the horse had stood.

After lunch and with many of the oriental artifacts now listed, Sarah took herself to the library to try and decipher the words she'd found scratched on the horse.

Slowly, just as she had done at first with the other writing, she copied each letter out, trying to simply work out where one word ended and the next began, which in itself wasn't easy. Eventually she thought she'd worked out where the first six words were and she examined each letter, recognising some and guessing others until she'd deciphered them. Once she'd got those six words though, she slumped back in her chair, her hands over her mouth is silent shock. '*Search for that which you desire.'* She didn't really need to decipher any more, because she knew what the message was, but she carried on anyway. Except when she got to the end the last words were different. *'Search for that which you desire, for here it awaits you, and it shall be yours. Sola Virtus Invicta.'*

Her knowledge of Latin was non-existent but entering the words in her search engine immediately told her what they were, and then everything began to become a tiny bit clearer. 'Courage alone is invincible.' Part of the family motto and apparently it was also the maxim of the fourth Duke of Norfolk.

Flipping back through her notebook she found where she'd decrypted George's gravestone. He'd died in 1569 and grabbing her phone she quickly Googled before giving a little punch to the air and hissing 'yes' through her teeth. 1569 was when Elizabeth 1st was on the throne and there was a picture and mention of her in the first poem. Whoever her poet was, they'd coincided timewise with George, and given that she found the book here at Barnhamcross, had her author once lived here too? Were they related to George, or to the Duke of Norfolk? The fact that whoever it was could read and write presumably meant they were a member of the nobility, not a servant.

Frantically she started to look online for other connections to George. Her shock intensified as she worked. He'd had three sisters, all married off by their stepfather, the fourth Duke of Norfolk, to his three sons. And the eldest Anne, a talented poet, had spent some years in London. She was married to Philip, the Norfolk heir, so it was not a stretch of the imagination to think she may have been at court. It didn't explain though why she was writing coded poems if indeed she was the author, but the use of the Norfolk motto made her a strong possibility.

Running downstairs, she looked for someone to tell, but Cordelia was having an after-lunch doze and Amanda had left a note on the kitchen table to say that she'd popped to the village for milk. That only left Jed.

He was in the stables and she took some coffees with her, perching on the edge of an old table with a wobbly leg and told him what she'd just discovered.

'Well, that sounds like a massive step forward,' he said. She nodded in agreement, before looking around her.

'Such a load of old junk,' she said. 'It looks like everything that's ever been thrown out of the house has either ended up in the loft, or in here.'

'That's about right,' Jed agreed as he pulled a length of rope out from beneath a wheelbarrow which no longer had its wheel. 'When you've finished searching inside the house you should probably come and look in here and in the dairy too, it's also stuffed full of goodness knows what.' He took a mouthful of his coffee and raised his eyebrows. 'Do you want to come and see, or have you already risked opening the door and looking?'

Sarah felt her face flush and for a moment she thought she was going to choke on the coffee she'd just swallowed. Once again, she was having to face the past, an invitation to go into the one section of the outbuildings which she simply couldn't enter. Somewhere where the memories were too close to the surface, and always would be. Perhaps going inside with Jed for the first time would make it easier.

'No, I haven't,' she admitted.

'Come on then, let's have a look, no time like the present.' Jed got to his feet and headed off towards the dairy. It was more ramshackle than the stables, which had received some rudimentary repairs over the years. The dairy, however, had been left to fall down or be consumed by the ivy that now crawled all over it, suffocating it. The best thing to happen, Sarah thought.

After a not-insubstantial amount of tugging at the door,

tightly wedged in the frame and warped with years of Norfolk weather, eventually Jed gave it a hard wrench and it opened just wide enough for an adult to slip inside. Stepping back, he held his arm out and said, 'After you.'

'No thanks,' Sarah said, her voice wobbling. 'You go in first.' She wasn't sure she was even going to be able to step in through the gap Jed had created. Her head was buzzing loudly as though there was a swarm of bees stuck in there and in her ears she heard the whispers of children creeping into a place they'd been forbidden to enter. A deluge of rain which had drenched them, somewhere to shelter in the hope it would start to lessen.

Jed didn't seem to notice how her reply wavered as he pushed his body sideways through the gap. From where she was standing, she saw the darkness light up as he switched on the torch on his phone.

'Blimey, there's some rubbish in here.' His voice drifted out of the door, 'Come and see.' He leant out through the door and held his hand out to her. She had no option but to place hers in his and let him pull her in. She stepped forward carefully, lifting her legs over the bramble cables which tracked across the ground stealthily waiting to trip the unaware.

The first thing that hit her was the smell. Musty, dark, centuries old vegetation. A space for dark secrets and murmured threats.

'It does look like a lot of stuff,' Sarah said, her voice sounding croaky as she cleared her throat. It looked no fuller than last time she'd been in there. Nothing exciting, just items small children shouldn't be playing around with. Old furniture and broken garden tools. Over in one corner she could see the old armchair, its horsehair stuffing still poking out. The place where they'd argued.

'It's quite large, isn't it. For somewhere to just make cheese and butter,' Jed said.

'Probably when the house was in its heyday, there were a lot of people to feed. If the Duke of Norfolk visited, he must have had a big entourage. Maybe this was built when the house was converted from a convent, I can't imagine the nuns had many cows, perhaps just one or two for milk.' She turned around on the spot as if surveying the contents. Her eyes were seeing nothing yet seeing everything. They snagged on a coiled-up piece of blue plastic rope in one corner, and at that point she'd seen enough.

'I doubt there's anything in here of any interest and it's very dirty, shall we head back to the house?' As she spoke, she was already edging her way back out, where she let her breath out in a long shaky stream of relief to be away from the memories. Despite her best efforts since she arrived, they were starting to spill out, pour from where she'd locked them away all those years ago. She was having trouble holding them back, a deluge. Just like that night and the terrible thing that had happened.

She waited for Jed to reappear, switching his torch off as he did so. The moment he was out, she began to walk back towards the house using every bit of her willpower not to break into a run. She was obviously moving swiftly as she heard Jed call out.

'Hold up.' He laughed as he caught up with her and put his arm across her shoulders. 'I think we need to investigate in there properly, when we have time to have a good rummage. Let me get rid of the ivy so some light can get in through the gaps where there used to be windows and sort out the door so it opens properly, then we can spend a day in there. What do you think?'

Sarah had no intention of ever going back, whatever it contained. 'I expect Cordelia looked at some point,' she replied. 'It wasn't always overgrown like that. The door used to open easily.' As she spoke the words, she put her hand to her mouth, horrified at what she'd just let slip. She thought Jed hadn't noticed, but his next words showed she was mistaken.

'Have you been in before?' he asked. By this point they'd reached the kitchen and moving away from him Sarah took a glass from the cupboard and filled it from the tap before drinking half of it down as her brain frantically turned over a number of responses like the pages of a book flipping quickly beneath her thumb. Her glass was trembling in her hand, the water shimmering like the river outside skipping over the stones in the shallows below.

'Not since I visited as a child,' she opted for a shortened version of the truth, 'but it was forbidden so I didn't tell anyone. In fact, it was only when I got inside, I remembered I'd been there before. Anyway,' she quickly changed the subject, 'all that dust, I'm going to jump in the bath. See you later.'

If Jed was surprised at her sudden termination of their conversation, he didn't say so, finishing his own drink and going back outside.

Lowering herself down onto a chair Sarah leant her elbows on the kitchen table and put her face in her hands. She'd hoped to avoid going back into the dairy, and just as she'd imagined it would, she felt the past pressing against her in there. The coiled rope and the stench of guilt.

33

1571

Pushing Blade out of the way I bent down and grabbed the papers before they disappeared into his voluminous mouth. Even by the light of the lamp it was impossible to read them and grabbing Kate's hand I hurried back towards the door to the passage, the light she was carrying dipping and swaying as she trotted beside me. Blade loped along too as if it were a huge game. He had no idea what he'd done, undoubtedly saving the queen's life.

We squeezed back through the door, Kate going in front so she could illuminate the way. Before I could stop him, once again Blade pushed his way in front of me trapping him in the small space with us. Ineffectually I tried to encourage him back hoping to leave him in the duke's apartment, but once again I was no contest for the heavy-set brute so eventually I just let him accompany us. As we approached the place where we ascended the steps to the upper floor, Blade suddenly stopped and I almost fell over him. He was staring into the dark towards the other passage, the one we hadn't explored, growling low in his throat.

'He can see the ghost,' Kate yelped as she put her hand over her mouth. I had to admit that had been my first thought too, everyone knew that dogs could see spirits when they returned to revisit those left behind.

'Well if he can, I am not waiting to see it too,' I announced and giving her a little push we both ran up the steep steps holding onto the icy stone wall to stop us tumbling backwards. After a minute I felt the hot panting breath of the dog on my arm and I knew he was behind us.

I held the papers tight against my chest until we were back in my apartment. My plan had been executed perfectly. Apart from the addition of Blade, but in fact he'd proved to be the most useful member of our little group. He settled in front of the embers still glowing in my fireplace, clearly intent on going nowhere. Kate threw some small pieces of kindling and another log on, making bright sparks dance up the chimney.

Once the candles in the room were all lit and the fire was blazing, I sat at my desk and opened out the parchments. Kate watched over my shoulder.

'They are just random letters and symbols,' she exclaimed. The disappointment was evident in her voice. I wondered what exactly she was expecting to see and had to stop myself from tutting.

'They cannot be easy to solve,' I pointed out. 'That is the whole reasoning of writing in ciphers. But these pretty papers,' I tapped them with the back of my fingers, 'will ensure Sir Francis and his cohorts can prevent my father-in-law's plot from going ahead.'

'How will you pass these on?' Kate asked. I cursed myself silently. I hadn't even thought of how I may be able to do that given that the duke was away and I had no idea how I could contrive an invitation to visit court.

'I shall do it the only way I know,' I replied, 'by including the information of what I now possess in a poem.'

With such an urgent requirement to speak with Ursula, I had no option but to risk sending her a message requesting a meeting. I needed an excuse which would not be questioned and with no other option I wrote a note saying that I wished to speak with her about a delicate illness. I grimaced as I sealed the letter, but I knew it wouldn't be questioned. Within hours I received an invitation to attend her at court where she was currently residing and my heart plummeted. It would be much harder to pass on the papers I was in possession of in full view of the courtiers there. The duke's corrupt friends would most certainly pass a message back to him if they suspected I was prying in his affairs.

With just a day in which to not only write a poem to relay that I now had the ciphers but also copy them out I spent all the daylight hours and several with the candles slowly burning down until I was happy with what I'd composed. If Lady Ursula – or her husband if he were present – didn't understand I possessed that which Sir Francis needed, I may miss the opportunity to hand over the copied sheets.

Once at the palace I found myself as before taken quickly through the great hall, populated with pairs and small groups of men, their heads together whilst at the same time their eyes roving around at everyone moving through. So much business and so much potential treachery being laid down here. As a female, their eyes swept over me unseeing and finally my sex held an advantage for me. Too uneducated, too small, too immaterial to be of any concern. If only they knew.

When I stepped inside the privy chamber, the ciphers hidden within a pocket hastily sewn into the sleeve of my gown by Kate, there were only few people there. But I was horrified to see not only the Spanish ambassador whom I knew was involved in Ridolfi's plot, but my father-in-law. I had no idea he was back in London; he hadn't yet been to Howard House. Where was he staying? He gave me a tight smile which didn't reach his eyes, and I felt in more danger than I had ever been before. I tried not to instinctively put my hand against the hidden pocket, certain that guilt was writ large on my face. This was a man who killed my brother without a qualm, and if he discovered what I was doing, the same would happen to me. I felt the cold trickle of approaching danger crawl down my spine.

34

1571

I could not fathom why the duke was at court, with everything he was plotting I would have thought it more sensible for him to stay away. Reading the poem with all it concealed within its lines made my heart race. If the duke guessed what I was reciting, it would be not only the end of me but probably also my sisters. I had to trust my instincts that he was too confident and superior to bother paying attention to me. I cleared my throat. 'For my Philip,' I announced.

> 'As night beckons and the bed drapes fall,
> I drift into a dark world of dreams so fierce,
> In which I run through passages dark,
> Scared I have no way to find my way home.
> And then what did happen to me, I prayed my
> Love that you should find and rescue me, for you are
> All I need in my life and I wish for our
> Lives to end with us forever surrounded by our
> Loving family if we are so blessed.'

As I spoke the final words I looked around at those who had stopped talking to listen, relieved to see Lady Ursula was watching me as she caught my eye. I knew in that moment she'd understood and I breathed a sigh of relief. Looking over to see if the duke had picked up on anything I could see him talking to Cecil Burghley, completely ignoring my recitation. Silently I said a prayer of thanks. But now I needed to pass the hidden parchments to Lady Ursula without being seen. She beckoned me over to sit with her, and after the queen gave her assent with a regal nod of the head I did as I was bid.

'We must leave the chamber,' Ursula whispered as she picked up the embroidery she had been doing and showed it to me. I held it up to the light flooding in through the tall stone mullioned windows with their tiny diamond panes of glass and nodded as I examined the exquisite black needle work around the sleeves of a man's shift. I had previously noticed how fine Sir Francis's white cuffs were and now I knew who was responsible for them. I wondered if one day I would sit and do something similar for my own husband.

For a moment my thoughts halted where they were meandering, and I reminded myself that after the duke was exposed, his titles, which should be passed down to my husband, would probably be confiscated. Philip may lose everything including his own Earl of Surrey title, and all the estates. We could find ourselves living in poverty. Did I care, I asked myself? The answer was no. I felt sorry for my husband, innocent of all that was happening here in London, but his father deserved to lose everything, all he'd obtained through treachery and murder. The memory of George hardened my soul. When the time came, I would go home to Norfolk, and there was nothing I wanted more.

'Follow me, and do as I do,' Ursula whispered. She got to her feet and immediately curtsied to the queen. I copied her even though I had no idea what was happening. Ursula whispered in the queen's ear and without even turning to acknowledge us she nodded before continuing her conversation with the Earl of Leicester. A good-looking man with dark features and a ready smile, he'd been in attendance previously when I had visited court. Ursula caught my hand and led me round behind the throne to a door elaborately carved with Tudor roses. A guard opened the door and Ursula swept through with me so close behind I was almost standing on the hem of her gown.

The corridor here was lined with linen fold panelling shining in the light from the numerous beeswax candles along the walls. They were dripping wax onto the floorboards which were as glossy as the wooden panels and I wondered about the poor servants on their hands and knees having to scrape the floor every morning.

Ursula was walking quickly and I almost tripped in my attempt to keep up. I was still unused to the shoes I was expected to wear to court. She stopped beside a door and opening it, she peered round before slipping inside and pulling my hand to follow. We were in a small chamber containing no furniture other than a settle beside the fire, which was not lit.

'Where are we?' I asked. Ursula shrugged.

'There are many rooms such as this in the palace. In all of the royal palaces. It may have had a purpose at one time and perhaps it will again. But now, it is empty and unobtrusive and perfect for what we required. I told the queen you wished to use the garderobe; she was hardly going to refuse you.' Ursula giggled at her subterfuge and not for the first time I considered that with her mischievous nature, she was the perfect wife, a foil for the very sensible Sir Francis.

'Here, take these quickly.' I pulled the papers from their

hiding place and passed them to her and she slipped them into
her bodice. 'They are copies. I am guessing you understood the
message in my poetry. I was afraid I had not made it explicit
enough, because I had to weave my words so carefully.'

'I understood it all.' She leant forward and hugged me close,
I could feel the sharp edges of the parchment against my breast.
'However did you find them?'

I explained briefly about the passages I'd discovered, and
how we found the ciphers casually placed under the mat
beneath the map of England. Then I told her about Blade
joining us and him growling at a dark corner in which we could
see nothing.

'The buildings that were originally monasteries are full of
lost spirits who cannot lie,' she said. 'Those who were turned
away from their religion by a man who wanted complete power
even over the church. Of course they are not silent. Listen in the
dark and you will hear them whisper their woes. I have experienced similar at Seething Lane.'

I shuddered at the thought and changed the subject. 'What
else can I do now to help expose the plot,' I said. 'You know I am
your servant and will do anything that is asked of me.' I was
certain things were beginning to gain momentum, and I wanted
to assist in any way I might.

'I am sure when my husband needs you, he will let you know.
He will be most pleased with what you have brought today. Can
you return the original ciphers so nobody knows we have sight
of them?'

'They are already back where I found them,' I reassured her.
'I went to my father-in-law's apartment and left the ciphers upon
a desk whilst I had his secretary searching for a silver letter
opener I knew was not there. When they are discovered
everyone will doubtless blame each other for not concealing

them correctly.' I gave her a small smile and giggled at my duplicity.

'You are so clever.' She squeezed both of my hands in her own. 'Now Francis also has letters from Baillee addressed to your father-in-law, smuggled out of Marshalsea by a man called Herne. He is what my husband calls a turncoat. He tells one person that he is a friend, and then he turns his coat and is a friend of the man's enemies. And now Baillee resides in the Tower, in Little Ease.'

'Little Ease?' I questioned.

'It is a small cell in the Tower. Barely four feet in dimension with no air nor light, the walls running with water. There are few who are able to keep their lives after being incarcerated in there.'

I shuddered at the thought of it. The way people were treated if they were traitorous made me question, not for the first time, why the duke would risk everything to attempt to place himself and Mary Stuart on the throne as husband and wife. It seemed men would stop at nothing to achieve greatness.

'Will he be tortured?' I asked.

'Not if he tells Lord Burghley everything he knows. Then he can go to Tyburn with his body intact. Even if he does not speak freely he will still eventually divulge his secrets, but he will be a pile of broken bones held together by his skin as they place the rope around his neck,' Ursula replied. 'Now, let me take you back to the gatehouse. Her Majesty will not notice if I am gone for the remainder of the day, so I shall return home to find Francis who is residing at Seething Lane at present. He will be delighted with what I am going to give him. Would you like to come with me so he can give his thanks personally?'

'No, thank you.' I held my hands up. 'I do not know if the duke is returning to Howard House today so I must go back just in case, given that he has already forbidden me to visit you.

There was a look of surprise when he saw me in the queen's privy chamber and then I left with you. He may wish to speak with me, so I must be available just in case.'

We arrived at the gatehouse and my guards who'd been waiting walked with me towards the river. To my consternation I heard the tramp of heavy boots and from the gardens the duke appeared, also heading towards the jetty. I clenched my fists. The last thing I wanted was to have to explain why I was attending court without him, but I guessed that would be the topic of conversation.

I quickly said goodbye to Ursula and stepped down into the boat which was bobbing quite violently on the water. A brisk wind had blown up since I arrived, the sky was a steel grey and the river was squally and angry, the choppy waves growing larger. I doubted we'd get home without being caught in heavy rain. I tucked my poetry book further into my sleeve, almost catching the corner on the secret pocket.

The duke jumped down beside me, making the vessel rock precariously from side to side. I put my hand out to stop myself falling with the sudden jolt and the duke grabbed it pressing so tightly I feared he'd break my fingers. As the first droplets of rain began to fall I hurried over to the seats beneath the canopy. Although once again the canvas sides had been added to protect us from the worst of the weather, the rain was being blown from all directions including the open front. I pulled my gown around me as best I could.

I had hoped the bad weather would keep away so the duke would stand, as was his wont, at the front of the boat, but he too was sheltering within the scant protection provided. As he sat down beside me, I was surreptitiously stretching and rubbing at my hand which was still hurting.

'I was most surprised to see you at the palace this morning.'

He had barely settled himself before he spoke. We were now out in the middle of the river, rocking from side to side as the oarsmen fought valiantly against the weather. I was holding tight to the arms of my seat thankful it was nailed down before it tipped over.

'I was invited once again by Lady Ursula,' I replied. 'I can hardly refuse my friends, can I? She said the queen had been melancholy and needed some entertainment. Apparently my poetry has that effect, and I was happy to help.'

'And then you seemed to excuse yourself, I did not see you leave,' he said.

I wanted to point out that he was talking so fervently with Lord Burghley he would not have noticed anything, but instead I gave the same excuse Ursula had.

'I needed to deal with something... personal and Ursula assisted me.' I knew he would enquire no further after an answer like that and indeed his face paling at the subject change he said nothing more, turning to look out at the rain bouncing off the river in tiny momentary hollows.

Eventually we arrived back at Blackfriars, and I was relieved to step from the barge, which was still dancing from side to side, and climb into the carriage which had been awaiting my return. With no horse waiting for him, the duke got in beside me. The rain was hammering so loudly onto the carriage roof it precluded any talking, and the minute we arrived in the courtyard at Howard House he jumped down without waiting for the steps and strode into the house calling for Gilbert as he went. His shoulders were hunched up and to my mind he appeared to be a man with worries beginning to heap themselves upon him. A small tremor of hope danced through me.

I followed the duke from the carriage at a more sedate pace and found Kate waiting in the great hall for me.

'I am very wet,' I said laughing. 'Come please and help me change.' I started up the stairs with her behind me, and walking with me my now ever-present shadow, Blade. I knew she wouldn't question me until we were back in my rooms, but I could see upon her face the shock at seeing the duke alight from the carriage before me.

Once I was dressed in a simple wool gown with a shawl wrapped around my shoulders, I was finally able to speak. I kept my voice low.

'I was able to read my poem to the queen,' I told her, 'and gave the other missive to Ursula. She was pleased with such a gift.' We both knew that I couldn't mention, even when we were supposedly on our own, what I'd really done, so had agreed previously to pretend everything was poetry and gifts.

'And the duke was also at court?' she asked. 'Not long after you left, his secretaries Barker and Higford arrived, and I overheard them saying he'd gone directly to see Her Majesty. I was afeared it could make your visit more difficult.' She was choosing her words carefully.

'Yes, I was most surprised to see him, but for the most part he was speaking with Lord Burghley.'

Kate raised her eyebrows. 'I am sure he has many other friends at court though whom he may wish to converse with.'

'Indeed, he is a powerful man with many friends. Those who bask in his power and wish to harness it.' I knew I needed to say no more.

35

2025

Sarah's worry about returning to the dairy and its dark memories were wiped from her thoughts the following morning. She was taking a break and drinking a cup of coffee when Amanda arrived in the kitchen saying that Cordelia was asking for her.

'Is she okay?' Sarah put her cup down and was immediately on her feet, fearing the worst.

'She's fine. Well, I don't think that's true, something has arrived in the post and upset her. After reading it she asked for you. Take your coffee,' Amanda called as Sarah ran out. In the drawing room Cordelia was sitting with her feet up on the sofa, her legs covered with a blanket. Amanda was right she looked even paler, if that were possible.

'You wanted me?' Sarah asked, pulling a footstool over and perching beside her.

'I've had a letter.' Cordelia waved a piece of thick crisp paper in the air. Sarah could see it was handwritten. 'You can read it, but the gist of it is that it's from your parents. Well, your father mostly, and they're coming to visit. In fact, they're probably on

their way now. He considers the matter important enough not
only to get his fountain pen out but to present his argument in
person. Let's face it, he must be pretty riled up to come here of all
places, and your mother too.' She passed the paper to Sarah and
leant back, closing her eyes. The effort to have said so much was
written in the lines on her face.

Even without reading it, Sarah felt sick. She'd had nothing to
do with her parents for over a decade. There was no way she
could be there with them in the same house. This house. She
scanned the words quickly, hearing every word being spoken in
her father's voice.

It would appear that, being the honest and upright person
she was, Cordelia had felt obliged to let him know she wouldn't
be leaving Barnhamcross Hall to him. Bizarrely, despite everything that had happened, it seemed he'd still believed himself to
be the heir and was now beyond furious – the tone of the letter
would suggest incandescent – that Cordelia had chosen to leave
it all to Sarah. They were on their way to contest everything.

Carefully folding the letter up and sliding it back into the
envelope she placed it beside Cordelia's untouched cup of coffee.
'I seem to have thrown a cat into a large flock of pigeons,'
Cordelia said. 'Or more like, introduced a tiger to Trafalgar
Square. I admit I hadn't realised my decision would cause quite
such a violent reaction, but don't worry, I'm not changing my
mind so they're coming quite unnecessarily. I asked Amanda to
call them and say all this, but apparently she spoke to a cleaner
and they've already left. Bloody people. Amanda will make up
the pink room for them. I'm sorry; if I thought they'd do this I
wouldn't have written to him. Me and my stupid sense of duty.
Although I sincerely wish I could smooth everything between
you all before I go.'

'Don't apologise, you weren't to know Dad would be so

angry,' Sarah told her. 'But you instrumenting some kind of *Entente Cordiale* is impossible, it's way too late for that. I'll find a hotel in Thetford to stay in whilst they're here.'

'What? No.' Cordelia pushed herself into a more upright position and opened her eyes properly. 'You are going nowhere, my darling. You're here for a reason and they are not, as ever, pushing you out. You have a right to be here and they don't.'

'I'm struggling with being back here as it is, I can't cope with them too. Please don't ask me to.' Abruptly getting to her feet she ran out of the room and up to her bedroom where she sat on the edge of her bed, hot tears of self-pity, of anger and regret running down her face to drip off her chin. The ghosts of that summer were crowding in on her, lining themselves up, one by one.

Ten minutes later there was a sharp rap at the door. 'It's just me, Amanda,' came the voice. 'May I come in?' Sniffing and quickly running her palms down her face, Sarah called back giving her permission.

'Cordelia's told me you don't want to stay here whilst your parents are. Why don't you sleep at my house? You can return here when they've left.'

'But what about Jed, isn't he staying in your spare room?' Sarah asked.

'Yes, but you can use my bedroom, given that I'm now living here full time,' Amanda said. 'It's not very big, but it's clean and tidy. And you can travel back and forth with Jed each day.'

The thought of staying in such close proximity to Jed and how he was beginning to make her feel made Sarah stall her answer for a moment. The offer was infinitely better than having to move out to a hotel though, so she thanked Amanda and agreed that, with no idea when her parents would arrive, she'd pack her suitcase and move into the cottage that evening. It wasn't much of a solution because she still needed to be at the hall during the day and there was going to be a huge argument when her parents confronted her, but they couldn't say anything more than they'd said before. Everything she'd told herself time and time again. It was all true and despite the pain they'd dredge up for everyone, she had no doubt they'd repeat it all again.

36

1571

It was a full month before anything else occurred and I grew increasingly agitated as I wondered what, if anything, was happening. Every day felt agonisingly long, each hour dragging as I listened out for visitors, or for a message boy with a letter from Ursula. Patience was not a behaviour I found easy to practise.

It was now high summer and London smelled rank. The Fleet ditch where all manner of residue from the fishmongers and butchers was thrown, along with rotting vegetables and the contents of people's soil buckets, emitted a stench which spread like an unseen cloud over the city.

The queen was progressing around the country visiting friends as she did each summer when the heat arrived, and I assumed the duke was accompanying her as he hadn't been seen at Howard House for several weeks. I was furious that he'd just left me behind to suffer the unpleasantness of the hot, foul-smelling city. Even Lady Frances was still in situ, the poor woman.

One hot afternoon Kate and I were walking in the shade of

the duke's cloisters where it was thankfully a little cooler. The grass in the centre was now a pale straw colour. In the distance, I could hear shouting coming from the tennis court although I had no idea who was playing. My hair beneath my linen coif was left undressed in a dark ripple down my back.

'When will this heat ever stop?' Kate complained. 'My hair is sticking to the back of my neck. We cannot even venture into the city for entertainment or shopping because of the risk of disease. And I can smell Smithfield market from here.' She held up a lavender filled pomander I had loaned her to her nose. My own was hanging from my girdle, banging against my thigh as I walked.

Her constant moaning was starting to irritate me, and it was exacerbated because the duke had taken Luke with him, wherever they were. It was an honour for the young man, but there was always a risk that he may be told to remain at another of the duke's properties and not return to London. Kate fretted about it constantly and even though I understood her worry it was beginning to grate. I was opening my mouth to suggest we return to my apartment when at the same moment we both spotted activity through the windows in the duke's gallery as two yeomen marched in, followed by his two secretaries and the unmistakable silhouette of Ridolfi. His diminutive size and his profile were immediately recognisable, especially as he'd now visited several times.

Kate looked at me for a moment and I started to walk again so as not to draw attention to the fact that we were now scrutinising what was going on. Slowly we strolled to the door which led from the cloisters into the library, and from there to the stairs leading back to my rooms, all without saying a word.

Once there I closed the windows so I could speak freely, but there was no wind to cool us anyway. The air was still, as though awaiting something huge to happen, the city holding its breath.

'Who was that?' Kate said. 'I am guessing you recognised him. Although I wonder why the duke has a visitor when he is away from home.'

'It is Ridolfi,' I said. 'And perhaps he does not know the duke is not here, although given the time of year he might surely have guessed it. Now I suspect a messenger is flying as fast as his horse can go to wherever my father-in-law is currently residing asking him if he wishes to return to see his banker. I would wager a gold noble he will be here by tomorrow morn.'

Kate clapped her hands. 'Then perhaps Luke may return,' she said with pleasure. I hoped for her sake and for mine that he would, but I was far more interested in why Ridolfi was visiting again, and this time seemingly without an invitation.

37

2025

As Amanda had warned, her room wasn't big, but Sarah was so grateful it could have been the penthouse at the Ritz and it wouldn't have been any more wonderful. She'd had dinner with Cordelia and Amanda, Jed having gone into Thetford on an errand and she was now sitting in the living room at the cottage with a cup of tea and a crime drama she wasn't following on the television. With so much turning over in her head she was simply grateful for some noise in the background whilst she tried to go over what had happened, and more importantly, what was about to happen.

She'd messaged Jed to warn him she'd be there when he returned, and it was nine thirty when she heard him call out hello as the back door opened.

'In here,' she shouted back. He appeared in the doorway.

'Sorry, I would have come straight home, Mum didn't tell me you were here until about thirty minutes ago. I'd arranged to meet an old uni friend for a drink after I'd been into town. She filled me in a bit on why you're staying, do you want another brew and we can talk about it?'

She knew he was being kind, but the last thing she wanted to do was talk about it. There was nothing to be said, the truth was hers to carry.

'It's fine, thanks.' She got to her feet and took her cup into the kitchen. 'There really isn't anything to discuss. For reasons best not spoken about, I haven't seen my parents for many years, and nor do I wish to. It seems that my father, despite saying he never wanted to return to Barnhamcross didn't intend that decision to extend to his inheriting the place. Apparently, he's en route with my mother to persuade Cordelia to change her mind.'

'Good luck to him with that then,' Jed said. 'I may not have known Cordelia for very long, but she doesn't strike me as the sort of person to be dissuaded from decisions she's made.'

'No, that's true.' Sarah managed a smile before giving Jed a hug. She was about to turn to head towards the stairs when he pulled her closer with one arm and taking her head with his other hand, he brushed her lips softly with his own. For a moment she paused. They'd been getting closer, although she had wondered if he was just being friendly, but it seemed the attraction she felt wasn't just one sided, and she kissed him back.

Eventually she pulled away. 'I wasn't sure you felt the same way as I feel about you,' she admitted.

'It's not easy is it, with Mum watching our every move. At least she isn't here, unless she's got CCTV set up.'

'I hope not,' Sarah laughed. 'I also wasn't sure, what with the situation with Laurie and the girls, if you were steering clear of anything vaguely romantic.'

'That's all fine, I'm over the marriage break-up and I felt an attraction to you from the moment you agreed to do some drystone walling with me. The way you wielded a lump hammer was very sexy,' he replied.

'Well, anyway, it's been a hectic day.' Sarah felt the need to put some space between them. She wasn't sure at that point if her emotional waters could be muddied much further. With another lengthy kiss goodnight, she ran upstairs to her room. Now, whatever happened, she knew Jed was there for her.

* * *

Her parents arrived late the following afternoon. Sarah had taken herself to the solitude of the library where she was transcribing the next poem, although she was constantly alert to the sound of a car arriving. When she finally heard the crunch of tyres on gravel, she knew immediately who it was.

Holding her breath, she paused and waited for what she guessed was coming. Within seconds came the snapping tones of her mother instructing her father about the suitcases in the boot of the car. Her voice didn't sound as strident as it once had, but it was still familiar. Sarah assumed her father answered, although she didn't hear him. Once upon a time he'd been her hero, but he abandoned her both emotionally and physically, and that above everything hurt the most. Would she be able to control herself when she saw him? Was she still yearning for him to hug her and tell her everything would be okay as he had so many times in her childhood? Except when she'd needed him the most he wasn't there.

The banging of the door knocker echoed through the hall. Several sharp raps as though the perpetrator thought to knock the door down if they hit it with enough force. They'd be hard pushed to do so, it had been standing there for five hundred, possibly more, years. And had doubtless withstood all attacks, until Henry VIII had sent in his heavies to close it down; there was no barricading themselves in when Thomas Cromwell came calling.

Getting up from her chair she crept towards the library door, pulling it open a little so she could listen to what was being said in the hall below. There was the low murmur of Amanda's voice and the clack of heels on the stone slabs. She caught the words 'room' and 'now' and she could just imagine her mother giving out a string of demands. Did they even know she was there? Sarah had forgotten to ask Cordelia if she'd told them. If not, it was going to be a big shock for them.

She heard the sound of footsteps coming up the stairs and, thankful that the door was only slightly open, she quickly stepped behind it and held her breath. They continued past and up onto the landing, their voices fading. Amanda must have been taking them to their bedroom.

Shutting the door completely in the hope she wouldn't be disturbed, Sarah slumped back down in her chair. There was no avoiding them; at some point she was going to have to show her face, and undoubtedly there would be a huge, dreadful, ugly confrontation.

She'd remained a wraith at the periphery of their lives, and she could imagine their sighs of relief when university ended and she'd sent an email informing them that she'd secured work and somewhere to live in England. They hadn't replied, not even to ask for her address. That was ten years ago and there had been nothing during that time. No birthday messages, no invitation for Christmas, instead she'd mostly spent the celebrations on her own. Despite the occasional offer, she couldn't face someone else's family festivities, excited children and general bonhomie.

Looking down at her notebook she turned the pages back, slowly reading what she'd just deciphered. If she was listening to a recitation, even she wouldn't notice it hugely because the lines moved on, but now she understood the code she could tell there was a discord in the cadence that only a reader who understood would know it was telling a story.

'I have what you need.' Sarah repeated the coded lines out loud. If she'd been in any doubt about having worked out the code before, now she was certain she was correct. But what did the author have, and who needed it?

Still lost in thought she gave a jump as there was a small knock at the door and it opened slightly. Jed peered round and gave her a grin.

'I thought you might be hiding in here,' he said, slipping through the gap and closing the door behind him.

At the sound of the knock Sarah's heart had begun to race and she put her hand against her chest feeling it beating hard. 'I'm so on edge,' she confessed, pulling a wry smile. 'I almost jumped out of my skin.'

'Sorry, I just thought you may be in need of a hug?'

'Thanks, I really am.' Sarah got to her feet and let Jed squeeze her so tightly that once again she was in danger of expiring. With a start she realised that her own demonstrations of affection, so rarely given, were probably woeful having received no parental hugs or physical contact for so many years of her childhood. No closeness to any other human for about a decade. Yes, she'd had boyfriends, few and far between, but not until university. One of them had told her as he broke up with her that she was cold and unyielding. At the time she'd thought he was making up some pathetic excuse because he'd found someone else, but maybe he was right, and she was broken inside.

'I'm actually here to tell you dinner's in fifteen minutes,' he said as he let Sarah go. 'Cordelia has requested your presence. And she said to tell you she hasn't informed your parents you are also here, so expect fireworks. Those were her exact words.'

'I feared as much,' Sarah said. 'Thank goodness I can escape with you when I've had enough.'

'Absolutely, I am your knight on a white charger. Mum and I won't eat with you this evening, but I'll be in the kitchen and if it gets really heated and I can hear shouting, I'll come and intervene. So, you have both Cordelia and us looking out for you. It will be fine.'

It will be anything but, Sarah thought. She looked down at her dusty jeans, T-shirt and canvas pumps, brushing her palms down her jeans as if they'd suddenly look more respectable. What was she doing? Worrying about how she would appear to her parents who'd ignored her for years. Not just as an adult but as a child as well. There was no point trying to improve matters now if there was going to be one unholy row, so she may as well go and face it. Their criticising of her appearance was the least of her worries, she doubted they'd even get to that with so many other accusations to sling at her.

Jed disappeared back to the kitchen closing the library door behind him and Sarah remained where she was. Ten minutes later as she'd suspected she would, she heard the sound of footfall on the stairs, the creak on the half landing where the steps up to the library joined the main staircase before they became more distant as they disappeared downstairs. She took her hands from the edge of the table where she'd been gripping it, her knuckles white. There was no way of avoiding this, and a fine sheen of sweat prickled across her forehead. Beside her she felt the air stir and shift slightly, and as she turned her head she caught a glimpse of a shadow against the table, despite there being nothing to cause it. Whatever presence was occupying the hall, it was as disturbed as she about the change in the atmosphere her parents' arrival had caused.

'Please God don't let it be her, not now,' she whispered,

pulling her eyes away and walking out of the room and downstairs, breathing quickly and hoping that nothing was following
her. On wobbling legs, as though she was walking through water
which threatened to pull her under, she made her way to where
she could hear voices in the drawing room.

Seeing them sitting on the sofa was such a shock that for a
moment Sarah found herself unable to speak. For some inane
reason she'd been expecting them to look just as they had the
last time she'd seen them, the summer before she left for university. The intervening years had not been kind to them. Suddenly
they both looked much older than their sixties, with lined faces
from the hot Spanish sun and grey hair. Both of them looked
haggard, tired, old. As though the vagrancies and harshness of
their lives had suddenly caught up with them and for a moment,
she felt sorry for them. Although that sentiment was immediately wiped from her mind as they both got to their feet, their
faces both bearing the same look of fury.

'What are you even doing here?' Her mother sounded
incredulous. 'I cannot believe you have the nerve to come back
here and take what is rightfully your father's!'

'I'm here at Cordelia's request,' Sarah answered. She still
hadn't moved from the doorway.

'I will fight you through the courts if I have to.' Now her
father had joined in, hearing his voice, now less strident as it
once was, reminding her of the time when it was full of love for
her, and Sarah swallowed hard. 'You have no right to this house,
it should be mine.'

'Get out of our way.' Her mother strode towards her. 'We will
eat dinner in our room, assuming that housekeeper can cook.'

Sarah stepped out of the way as they swept out of the room.

'That went well,' came a dry voice from Cordelia's chair.

38

1571

We didn't see Barker until dinner the following day. He was looking very tense, picking up items of food and placing them on his trencher but not actually eating any of it. He did however drain three beakers of ale, one after the other.

Kate sat next to him a couple of seats down from me, but she kept looking down at her food, and eventually I got annoyed with her lack of engagement. 'William, we have not seen you at Howard House for several weeks and now here you are and looking tired,' I called out. 'Are you not sleeping well? I have heard owls these past nights that are keeping me awake, have you also heard them?' I hadn't been kept awake, but that did not matter.

'No mistress, it is not that,' he replied. 'I have a lot to do for the duke at present and he is keeping me working long into the night.' I felt my heart jump at the possibility that I may glean further useful information.

'I notice that although you have returned, my father-in-law is not present,' I nodded towards his empty chair. 'Is he still away from the city?'

'I have received word today he is on his way back to London, that there is a delivery he has been impatient for arriving here tonight.'

The minute the words left his lips Barker's face flushed and his eyes snaked around the room as though looking to see who may have overheard. He had let slip something that was not to be spoken of, I was now more certain than ever that something big, something dangerous, was soon to happen. It appeared nobody had heard him and I watched as he exhaled slowly. I was barely able to contain my laughter. He was telling me because he believed me to be totally innocent, that I was the one person in the hall who had no understanding of why a delivery would be clandestine. Although in fact, I was the very person who was most interested, most invested.

'And what is it?' I raised my eyebrows and opened my eyes wide, hoping I appeared as naive and innocent as he believed me to be. 'A gift for someone? Me perhaps? Might it be a puppy? I love Blade but I would so love a dog of my own!' I squeezed my hands into fists beneath my chin.

'No, my lady, it is something being conveyed to the duke from Italy. It will be brought late tonight. I am told I must wait up for it. And with the duke also arriving, there will be more upheaval.' He sighed and placing his palms on the table he pushed himself to his feet. Bowing to me, he walked slowly across the great chamber towards the duke's apartment, the weight of his responsibilities as heavy as the robe on his shoulders.

The moment he disappeared from view I placed my cloth on the table to indicate to the servants standing behind me I had finished and paused as a footman stepped forward and pulled my chair back so I could stand. I tapped my foot on the floor impatiently as I waited for Kate to join me. Eventually she followed me back to my rooms where, once the door was closed,

I told her everything I had just been told. She had clearly not been listening.

'Does this mean that Luke will return if the duke is?' she said.

'At present that is not of importance,' I snapped, cross that she did not realise the significance of what I had just relayed. 'Something is coming from Italy. Surely it must be being brought by Ridolfi with that Italian connection and I need to know what it is. I intend to watch from my window and when the visitors arrive, I shall go immediately to where I can listen to them.'

'You must not,' Kate put her hand on my arm as if she could stay me. 'This is becoming too dangerous. I cannot let harm come to you. I promised your grandmother I would ensure this.'

This was the first time I had heard of such an agreement, and it made my eyes well up that my grandmother had cared so much. But in reality, it mattered not. I hadn't protected my brother and he'd paid the ultimate price for my inadequacy, despite being only twelve years old at the time, little more than a child myself. Now I fervently hoped the duke would shortly get all that he deserved and I would relish in playing my part in it. It was imperative I knew what was being brought to Howard House, so I could alert Sir Francis. He could do nothing without the information I could provide, and I realised just how important my part in the exposure of the plot had become. Already, lines of verse were beginning to form in my head. Taking my now familiar seat by my open window, I sat down to wait.

An hour later there was a knock at the door to my parlour. Kate's face paled and turned to mine, her eyes wide, her mouth open. I frowned a little and shook my head before calling 'Enter.' The door opened to reveal one of the maids carrying a bowl of steaming scented water, followed by another carrying drying cloths. Smiling, I said thank you, hearing the nervous wobble in my voice. Hot water was brought to my room every evening but in my worry, the air in the room like a sharp knife, I'd completely forgotten. As soon as they'd left the room, I let my breath out as a long hissing sigh.

'You are like a crouching cat ready to pounce, but twice as nervous,' Kate said. 'I still implore you to rethink your decision.'

'And I reply again that nothing will deter me from helping to play my part, be it big or small, in what shall come to pass.' I turned away from her and looked down to the gatehouse beneath the archway, into the courtyard where everyone entering the house must pass.

My surveillance was soon rewarded as within the hour my father-in-law arrived, accompanied as usual by an entourage of guards and servants. They all disappeared as though by magic leaving just the duke, two yeomen and one man – who from my vantage point looked like the duke's secretary, Higford – to follow him inside. The chess master had arrived and now we awaited the other pieces in his game. Already the queen, and the bishop in the shape of Bishop Ross were assembled on the chequered board, and himself as he was doubtless imagining himself king. The rest of us were pawns who could if required be eliminated at a moment's notice.

Two full hours later and I was still at my place awaiting the arrival of whatever Barker had spoken of. Kate was clearly tired and exasperated at my stubbornness as every few minutes she yawned loudly. Several times she got up and walked around the apartment stretching her back. I could feel her eyes on me, but I ignored her. I too wanted to get to my feet and stretch my limbs, however if I moved from my vantage point I may miss something.

When it eventually happened, I was correct in my surmising. Two men arrived from the gatehouse on foot accompanied by four guards. One of the men seemed to be struggling with a heavy pair of horse panniers whilst the other, wrapped in a large dark cloak despite the warm night air, was small. Just as Ridolfi was. I saw his now familiar profile as he scanned the windows across this front façade of the house and I leapt away hoping I hadn't been seen.

Once again, the front door opened, although from the narrow strip of candlelight that fell across the ground it seemed only just wide enough to let the two men slip in. There was the smallest of thuds as the heavy door was pressed home. I had no time to lose.

'Now I shall discover what this secrecy is about,' I said to Kate, who was already opening her mouth to remonstrate, her brows drawn down over her eyes and her hands on her hips. 'Stay here,' I added and picking up a candle, its wick burned low, I swept out of the room before she could utter a word, and I was relieved when I realised she hadn't followed me. This would be easier when I only needed to worry about myself.

Thankfully I met no one as I hurried to the passage. The hour was late and even the servants had retired for the night. Blade was nowhere to be seen and I guessed he was either asleep beside the fire in the kitchen or if he'd been in the main hall, had followed the men to the duke's offices.

There was no time to waste and holding the candlestick up I rushed to the end of the passage and down the stone steps, almost slipping on one in my haste. I paused for a moment and waited for my beating heart to slow down a little before stepping more carefully down the rest and walking to where I now knew I could hear anyone in the duke's office, or his gallery. The candle flame flickered in the draught I was making as I hurried to the door. The grumbling of low voices confirmed I was in the correct place. Holding my breath, I pressed my ear against the wood and listened.

'Is it all here?' The duke's voice was deep and sounded muffled.

'Yes, yes it is. Count it if you do not believe me.' Ridolfi's Italian accent immediately identified him. 'Six hundred gold nobles.'

I put my hand over my mouth to stop myself from gasping out loud. From the other side of the door, I heard the telltale jangle of money being run through fingers.

'Barker, Higford, you have your instructions. Everything is organised, you will ride at first light to Shrewsbury.'

'Yes sire,' Barker answered. I'd had no idea they were in there and such an integral part of the subterfuge, although I imagined they were just following his instructions. 'When we arrive in Shrewsbury, we shall visit the shop of the draper Thomas Browne and hand over the gold.'

'That is correct, and he will in his turn pass it forwards to my man Bannister. He has not been alerted as to what he will be carrying, so do not tell him. He is merely a go-between. The plot is almost at fruition, that gold will finance our rebellion, Queen Mary will take her place as the Queen of England with me by her side as her king, and my cousin Elizabeth shall be executed. Now help me put it in the safe until you leave.'

There was the sound of men grunting as they lifted the heavy coins before a soft bark indicated that Blade had indeed followed the men – and was getting in their way by all accounts as the duke snapped at the dog, telling him to move.

To my alarm, Blade must have relocated closer to the tapestry concealing the door as, giving two small joyful barks, the sort he made when he greeted me, he began to sniff along the bottom of the wall hanging. I willed him to go away before he alerted them to my presence.

'What is that dog doing?' I heard the duke say. 'Has he found something?' There was a pause and then I heard him let his breath out in a hiss from between his teeth. 'No, I know what is bothering him. Hurry up with that gold and get out of here, all of you.'

There was scuffling and some sort of remonstration in Italian but within seconds all was silent in the room, other than Blade still snuffling on the ground.

'I am coming for you,' the duke announced and for a moment I had no idea what he was talking about, but then I realised and my heart leapt into my mouth. He too knew of these passages and within seconds he would be in there with me.

39

2004

The fierce summer weather continued with no sign of abating. Sarah was spending most of her time in the hammock; she'd long since finished her library books and she and Emily had persuaded Daddy to take them to the supermarket. Mummy had just raised an eyebrow and said nothing. She rarely took them shopping if she could help it, but Daddy was far easier to get around, especially when Emily was there. Sure enough, her sister had returned with a comic and two new Barbie dolls, and Sarah had found a wonderful box set of seven books about a wild horse called Roanie. It didn't look a lot compared to Emily's haul, but she was delighted.

There was only one week of the holiday left. The uncomfortable atmosphere in the house had increased, like a balloon being slowly blown up until it filled every space, every crevice of the building. They were all breathing it in and out, their lungs filled with discomfort. Mummy didn't seem to be speaking to Daddy, dinners being eaten in silence, and the rest of the time Daddy found any excuse to disappear to different parts of the garden where he'd smoke and gaze into the distance. Sarah had found more than one cigarette butt down at the rope swing. She was certain that at some point the taut skin of the balloon would burst and something terrible would come screaming out.

In the middle of their final week, she came back from the river, standing in the empty kitchen, her clothes dripping on the floor. There was no one to tell her off about not taking a towel with her. Emily was on the terrace with Cordelia, she'd seen them as she'd emerged from the kitchen garden, and as usual there was no sign of her parents. Tiptoeing across the tiled floor, hoping her footprints would dry before they were spotted, she walked towards the entrance hall, realising as she did that she could hear from upstairs her parents were – once again – arguing. Thankfully they were in their bedroom so she could head up and get dried without encountering them. Mummy's wrath wasn't something to get in the firing line of if it could be avoided. Poor Daddy, he should have escaped outside straight after lunch, instead of announcing he was going for a lie down. Mummy had made a snipe about the fact he'd been drinking with lunch, but Sarah had silently observed he wasn't the only one.

She'd just wrapped herself in her towel, still damp from where she'd left it on the floor after her bath the previous evening, when the raised voices were paused by the sound of a loud crash of china hitting the floor and splintering into a thousand pieces. There was a moment of silence before a door along the landing opened and footsteps strode away and then faded as someone – it sounded like Daddy – ran downstairs. Probably to fetch a dustpan and brush, Sarah surmised, perhaps he wanted to hide what had happened from Cordelia. At home she herself had occasionally concealed broken objects if she thought she'd be in trouble, because if anyone believed Emily was the perpetrator there wouldn't be a telling off. Win-win.

She got dressed quickly. From below she could hear Emily

still chatting to Cordelia, oblivious to the drama unfolding above their heads. Or perhaps so used to it that they hadn't even noticed. And now with no noise from her parents' room Sarah had a quick look around the gallery to ensure nobody was about before she headed towards the stairs. Too late she realised she wasn't alone, and she turned her head sharply, expecting to see Daddy returning with the dustpan. Her mind was racing as she wondered if he'd mention what had just happened, when she realised her companion wasn't either of her parents. At the far end of the gallery where it turned a corner into the newer part of the house where the grown-ups' bedrooms were, there was a movement. A child. No, not a child, just the shape of one. As she'd seen before it was merely a murky outline, a heavy dark-ness moving backwards and forwards in a swaying, fluid motion. As she watched it slowly faded away, just as the child-shadow in the graveyard had. Now she knew she hadn't imagined it, there was no sun beating down on her head to give her hallucinations this time. Keeping her eyes averted from the corner which remained dark, she ran downstairs to the terrace to find the others. She wanted to continue her adventures with Roanie, stay out of her parents' way until their tempers had calmed down and try and blank her mind from what she'd just seen.

It seemed Cordelia and Emily hadn't heard the sound of breaking china because neither of them mentioned it as she flopped down on a sun bed. And Emily wasn't renowned for her ability to keep her mouth shut, even when she'd been told to.

'Pull the lounger out of the direct sun,' Cordelia advised. 'It's supposedly over thirty degrees today and due to get even hotter this week.'

Sarah did as she was told and lay back down. Over the top of her book, she watched Daddy walk from around the corner of the house and alongside the kitchen garden wall and into the woods. She waited for Mummy to appear on the terrace with them, but she didn't and eventually Cordelia announced that she was going to have a large gin and then start dinner. She disappeared back into the house. Despite Cordelia's attempts to keep the atmosphere calm and with a semblance of normality, Sarah could still feel the tension in the air, tightening as though it would snap at any moment and spill forth a torrent of who knew what; something frightening, something terrible.

'I wonder if we will have ice cream for dessert again,' Emily mused as she stripped her dolls of their clothing and laid them on another of the sun beds. 'I wish we didn't have to have salad every night, but the puddings here are ace.' Sarah nodded in agreement. Apparently, Cordelia didn't believe one should eat chips unless you were at the seaside, she'd been quite short with Emily when she'd suggested that an addition of oven chips would enhance some of their dinners. But continuous salad with fish or chicken was neither tasty, nor appetising. Only the desserts kept dinner from being a big disappointment.

Sarah carried on reading her book, the warmth of the afternoon making her eyelids heavy. Beside her Emily's Barbies were involved in an argument, but even her raised voice depicting each doll's opinion didn't stop Sarah from drifting off to sleep.

'Girls, please come and wash your hands.' Cordelia's voice woke her up with a start. 'Sarah, can you go and find your father please and tell him that dinner is almost ready?'

Sarah jumped up and ran towards the wooded area around the tennis court where she'd seen her father disappear. Without a doubt she'd be able to smell the cigarette smoke long before she found him. Sure enough, almost immediately she was able to follow the scent as she ran through the woods calling to him. There was no answer though, the only sound the crunch of brittle leaves and snapping of fallen branches beneath her feet, together with the drumming of a woodpecker high above. A startled pheasant suddenly broke from the undergrowth with a loud, rasping squawk.

As she ran on further, her feet began to slow. The smell of smoke was becoming stronger, but she also knew that she was approaching the nuns' cemetery. After what had happened previously, as well as her experience just hours before, she didn't want to be anywhere near it, and she could feel her heart begin to beat faster. She stopped for a moment and called out.

'Daddy, dinner time!' The woodpecker paused and she waited to listen for a reply but there wasn't one. Walking on slowly, from beneath the leafy boughs shading her she could see in the sunlit clearing Daddy was on his mobile phone, talking to someone and laughing. No wonder he hadn't heard her shouting. She stepped forward cautiously, all the time with her eyes darting around the space looking for the child-shadow, but there was nothing. Just Daddy, sitting on a flat, rectangular gravestone, laughing and chatting on his mobile phone, a cigarette held between two fingers like a paintbrush.

For a moment she forgot the apparition she was trying to avoid, she was so shocked at her father being in a sacred place, as Cordelia called it, and behaving so indifferently as to where he was. He flicked ash onto the stone slab. She was sure that the 'keep out' warnings were for her parents as much as for she and Emily.

'Daddy,' she hissed. It felt wrong to even be shouting here, supposing she woke a spirit up? Perhaps that was what had happened when she'd been here before, although what she'd seen, on both occasions, was only small, a similar size to Emily. And this was a graveyard for the old nuns, and dogs. 'Daddy.' She spoke a little louder and waved her arms above her head until he spotted her. He looked surprised to see her and abruptly ended his call with a series of goodbyes and 'yes, yes, me too' salutations.

'Always issues with the new cohort of students,' he told Sarah as he walked back through the cemetery gate and joined her, 'I seem to be asked to have larger and larger tutor groups every year. And what are you doing here, you know that Cordelia has banned you and Emily from being in this corner of the garden?' He pursed his lips and frowned at her and she bit her lip from pointing out that the rule applied to him as much as it did to her. And she had a legitimate reason, too.

'Cordelia sent me to find you, dinner is almost ready,' she repeated her instruction. As they began to walk towards the house, he caught up her hand in his and squeezed it. Instinctively she knew there was an unspoken agreement that she wouldn't mention where she'd discovered him.

Although Mummy joined them for dinner, the meal was quiet. For once even Emily seemed to notice the strained atmosphere and her usual mindless chatter petered out after a couple of minutes and they ate in silence, the only noises the scraping sound of cutlery on plates – pasta salad, this time with tuna and some corn on the cob – and the soft glug of wine being poured into glasses. Mostly Mummy's, her eyes glittering and becoming sharper the more she drank.

As soon as dinner was finished, and disappointingly with no sign of any dessert whatsoever, Emily asked Sarah if they could go to the rope swing and she immediately agreed. The sooner she could be away from the house, the better. She guessed the atmosphere over dinner had been brought about because Cordelia had found out about the breakage earlier.

Once at the swing she stood and pushed Emily out over the river, her sister shrieking as she went further and further. The water was now even lower than when they'd arrived just weeks earlier and in order to let go and fall in, they both needed to swing out to the middle. Eventually, just as Sarah's arms were beginning to ache, with a final yell Emily let go of the rope and splashed into the water before jumping to her feet and shouting, 'My turn again, my turn again!' as she waded to the bank. Despite her sore arms Sarah acquiesced; she didn't want to provoke a tantrum. She had far too much going on in her head which she needed to sort out into what she could dismiss, and what she needed to worry about.

Unfortunately though, she couldn't find anything that could be dismissed, other than the lack of pudding that evening. Their parents arguing had been a backdrop to the entire holiday and now even that was no longer causing her the consternation it once had. The sight of Daddy in the nun's cemetery had unsettled her a lot, he must know that being in there talking on his phone and smoking was a bad thing to do.

And then there was the other thing, the shadowy figure she'd now seen twice. She was frightened it was something to do with the story that Cordelia had told her, about George the ghost and his rocking horse. If she mentioned it, would Cordelia think she was making it up? She loved being the older, more sensible sister and she didn't want to ruin what she considered to be the illustrious position her godmother had put her in. As if to remind her of her elder status, Emily shouted at her to start pushing again and stepping forwards with her arms outstretched, she began to do so.

40

1571

Despite the darkness I blew my candle out, hoping that in the black I was now plunged into I'd be able to retrace my footsteps. I ran my hand along the rough stone wall until I reached the stairs. Behind me I heard the rasp of the wooden door scraping across the uneven stone floor and then my father-in-law saying, 'Come Blade, find who loiters here and let us drag them out and hang them on the nearest gibbet.' I knew the dog would immediately discover me, and that my status as the duke's stepdaughter and daughter-in-law would not prevent him from murdering me. One more dead stepchild would not make any difference to him.

With him close behind, instead of ascending the stairs in a moment of panic I turned left and ran down the other passage, the one I hadn't yet investigated. Where Blade had growled and frightened Kate and me. I prayed I wouldn't encounter the ghostly monk.

Now rushing even faster, I had my hands on both walls to steady myself, still with no idea of where I was going. This passage was narrower than the others, the floor uneven and slimy beneath my slippers. Suddenly my left hand encountered a gap in the wall and I almost fell as I staggered sideways into a narrow space. I moved further into it until I could only just fit by turning sideways. Carefully I slid along in the darkness holding my breath. It was icy cold and just the sort of place where a portly monk may have once become stuck. Perhaps never lost but trapped.

The sound of Blade sniffing along the damp floor was getting closer and behind him the duke's footfall. I could just see the tiniest glimmer of candlelight approaching. The dog stopped close to where I was wedged into.

'Go away, go away,' I implored silently as I held my breath. Then, just as before, a low snarling growl came from deep within his chest. I realised it wasn't me that had made him halt, it was whatever he thought was inhabiting the space with me.

'What have you found, boy?' The duke had caught him up and the entrance to the gap was illuminated as he held his candle up high. I shrank back against the wall where I huddled just out of reach of the circle of light, the dancing flame illuminated. There was a pause that seemed to go on forever.

'I do believe you are growling at nothing, you stupid dog,' the duke snapped.

The light started to diminish as he turned and walked away, his voice fading as he disappeared into the distance. Still, I remained where I was, unable to move. Every part of my body was now rigid with fear, seized in a stricture, a paralysis. I was sorely afraid Blade had barked at the space I occupied because there was an ancient spirit there with me, and now I was too frightened to move. And I couldn't run away even if I were able, because I didn't know if the duke was still walking the passageways.

Finally, when I'd heard nothing for a long while, I decided I'd have to risk moving, or at least attempt it. There was no telling whether the duke may decide to have the house searched to see if anyone was missing from their beds, or indeed the door I used to enter the passageway may have guards stationed, given that he must know all the entrances and exits to the corridors. If that happened then I would most certainly be found out.

Slowly I moved one foot out to the side then brought the other to meet it as once again I moved like a crab until the space widened enough and I could steal forwards. All was silent, and dark. Very dark. I really began to believe that I was also now lost forever, to walk the desolate corridors for eternity. Turning to my right, although I wasn't convinced I was even going in the correct direction any more, I crept as quickly as I dare, holding the wall with one hand.

Eventually I reached the stairs. I'd dropped my candlestick somewhere in this vicinity and I guessed the duke hadn't seen nor tripped over it, but I wasn't stopping to search now. Instead, I ascended the steps and all but ran along the passage to the door, pushing the latch down and muttering an oath of thanks as it opened to let me out.

Stepping out from behind the tapestry, all was dark. There were no burning torches like the ones the guards carried. I breathed a sigh of relief, if I could now get back to my room undetected, I was safe.

As I hurried along though, I heard raised voices and I saw the bobbing lights of torches being carried. My supposition that the duke would have the house searched seemed to be correct, and almost tripping over my feet, I broke into a run, the men's voices becoming louder as they came upstairs calling to each other. I raced into my chamber where Kate was waiting, her face creased with worry lines.

'Quickly,' I gasped, my heart racing so fast I could barely

speak. 'Help me with the curtains to my bed, then climb into yours with all haste, and lie very still. I will explain later.'

The two of us pulled my drapes closed and I climbed beneath my blankets and coverlet despite my gown hindering my movements. I pulled the covers up to my neck, curling into a little ball. At the last moment I reached up and tugged out my hair adornment, tearing out some of my hair too and making my eyes water. I heard the soft clunk of the door to Kate's sleeping quarters close before just seconds later my bedchamber was full of people. The curtains around my bed were opened and, feigning sleep, I winced at the brightness of a burning torch, holding my hands over my eyes.

'Who are you?' I gasped. 'What are you doing in my chamber? Get out!' I shouted the last two words trying to sound surprised and angry and not smirk as the yeomen in front of me bowed low and apologised.

'We are sent to search the household for intruders on the command of his Lordship,' he explained. 'Every room without exception.'

'Well, I shall be having words with my father-in-law,' I snapped. 'Do you see whatever you are searching for here?'

'No mistress, I do not.' He bowed again and whispering to the other guards he had entered with, they all left.

I lay for a moment ensuring nobody had remained next door in my parlour before climbing out of bed. Kate joined me and wordlessly she started to unlace my gown. I could feel her anger coming in silent waves, burning me. She'd warned me of the danger of my quest and now she knew it hadn't all gone as planned. Although in reality all was well, because I now possessed vital information.

* * *

Two weeks passed and the duke's behaviour displayed how worried he was, however he may try to conceal it. He was no longer eating with the rest of the household, instead having his meals taken to his apartment. And apparently sending it back mostly uneaten, although flasks of wine were frequently refilled. There was a mix of anticipation and fear winding its way stealthily through the house.

I was desperate to inform the Walsinghams of what I knew, and eventually I decided to send a missive to Lady Ursula, hoping Luke would be able to smuggle it out and give it to a messenger boy for me. Kate was furious that I may put him in danger but I couldn't concern myself with her worries, even though I knew how unkind this made me. I would recompense her whenever I was able. She was right, there was a possibility it may be intercepted by people watching the house, which was why I needed to write the letter coded in the only way I knew how. As a poem. Only Sir Francis and Lady Ursula would be able to read between the lines.

I sat all day working out what to write, how I could phrase my words. Never had one been any more important than this one.

> *So many people I greet in London,*
> *A mixing pot of all of Europe, men*
> *Who are Italian or Spanish with their skins as dark,*
> *As burnished gold, brighter than England's sun which*
>   *often greets us rarely for,*
> *Rain has arrived and often falls from the sky,*
> *My heart now sad that I cannot venture out and,*
> *My letters despatched to Norfolk must talk of weather*
>   *dour,*

I would secretly go and visit them, a surprise if they
are blessed with sun, but there
Is no end to the deluge which afflicts them too,
Where our two rivers rise to engulf the land.

Eventually I was happy with it and tearing the sheet of parchment from the book, I wrapped it in a piece of linen with one of my embroidered ruffs. A covering note spoke of sending it as a gift and I hoped anyone who may intercept it would believe the ruff and poem, to simply see it for what they were, a gift from one friend to another.

Once Luke had been despatched, I could do nothing but watch and wait. I knew I would not receive any acknowledgement from Lady Ursula, that was far too dangerous and might potentially incriminate me. Each day crawled past unbearably slowly, the air in the house crackling as though a storm was on the horizon. Being the beginning of September, the weather was still hot, and I wondered if the queen had not yet returned from her progress to be informed of the plot. That may explain why there was no indication yet that my father-in-law was exposed. I could only hope my poem had reached Lady Ursula. Then, three days later, I knew it had.

I was awoken before first light by shouts and horses stamping below my window. I thought for a moment it was the duke preparing to leave London. Knowing what I did, it seemed madness on his part that he was still in situ, a rabbit waiting for the hawk to strike. How typical of his unquestionable confidence.

Opening my shutter gently, I peered down. Beneath me were a large group of men, including several guards wearing the queen's livery, their pewter breastplates glowing in the dawning sunlight. My heart began to beat faster.

Gilbert was at the door trying to prevent them entering, I could hear his voice grow louder as he remonstrated with them, but after a moment there was a scuffle, and he was pushed aside as they marched in. The building vibrated in time with their heavy boots. I could only imagine what was going through the duke's head, I was certain he'd have heard the noise at the door, and I wrapped my arms around myself and squeezed tightly, hardly daring to breathe.

41

2025

Sarah opened her laptop and wondered where to start her research first. Although there were other things in the house she should be doing, she knew she couldn't continue with the task of the logging of Cordelia's possessions until her parents left again. The last thing she needed was them to see her supposedly counting the silver she was about to inherit. Even though she hadn't yet found anything with monetary value, perhaps her father knew of its whereabouts and that was one of the reasons they'd hotfooted it to the hall. So instead, she was hiding in her bedroom to work, confident she wouldn't be disturbed.

She began another search for George and eventually found a more detailed record taken from a sixteenth century news pamphlet of how he'd died at the hall after falling from his rocking horse as the family folklore had told. She gave a shudder knowing she'd now discovered it still in the loft hundreds of years later. The accident had apparently resulted in a head injury and the child's neck broken. It seemed someone ensured the facts were noted down, to never be forgotten. She looked up and stared through the window for a moment, gathering her thoughts. And he was buried with the nuns; at least the family had kept him close.

Getting to her feet she went to find Cordelia, her ears constantly pricked to any indication to the location of her parents so she could avoid them if possible.

Instead of her godmother though, she found Amanda making her way along the gallery with the vacuum cleaner. Running round in front of her so that Amanda could see her, she waited as the vacuum was switched off and became quiet.

'What's the matter?' Amanda was immediately by her side holding her arm. 'Is it Cordelia?'

'No, no, sorry to startle you, everything's fine. I want to speak to her though, is she in the drawing room?'

'She's just having a lie down,' Amanda replied. 'Your parents being here is exhausting for her.'

'I'm not surprised, this must be the last way she'd thought she'd spend the time she has left to her. If I hadn't come, then at least it might have avoided my parents turning up too. It's bad enough for me having to see them again, and here of all places, but I'm feeling stronger than I thought I would, and certainly more than poor Cordelia is. She told me they were once close, good friends as well as related, but there's been a river of water beneath the bridges since then. Two rivers of water.' She paused for a moment, realising that she had just spoken about the ever-present rivers without the thumping of her heart and prickling of sweat across her forehead. Perhaps finally she was starting to feel stronger, accepting of what happened and maybe able to start walking forwards?

'Oh, don't you worry, she's not as frail as she'd have you all believe. I'm quite sure that in any showdown, she'll still hold her own. She must have known they'd turn up, in fact I have a feeling she did it on purpose. To have you all here where your ghosts can finally be laid to rest.'

Even mentioning ghosts made the hairs along Sarah's arms stand up. Amanda was closer to the truth than she realised.

Leaving Amanda to her cleaning, Sarah walked slowly along the wide, long space, the burnished floorboards that had absorbed the steps of so many people for hundreds of years. The nuns, the Dacres, Anne and the Duke of Norfolk. A man, she now realised from her research, who'd had a big part to play in the family history of this house.

And here now at Anne's former home there was something, someone, walking with her as she moved about the house and grounds. If only she knew who it was. Someone who wanted her to untangle the family mystery as much as she did, or someone who already understood it and was trying to show her where to find the answers. Or perhaps someone from the more recent past.

With Cordelia unlikely to be awake for a while, Sarah – still excited by her research – decided to go and find Jed to tell him what she'd discovered. He wasn't in the house and she remembered that morning he'd mentioned clearing the weeds from the edges of the riverbank.

'It's just an excuse to stand in the shallows and cool down,' he had told her. In that case, she wouldn't be going to find him there, not to the river. Not today, not tomorrow, not ever. She'd wait and see him at lunchtime.

However, in the kitchen two hours later, Amanda told her that he'd taken some sandwiches out with him, expecting to be wet and smelly and choosing not to eat in the house with them.

'Okay, I'll see him later anyway,' she answered. 'Has Cordelia mentioned if I'm expected at dinner again tonight? I honestly don't think I can face it. Seeing them now after so many years just makes me feel worse, it brings everything about that summer back to me.'

'Don't worry. When I was helping her to bed last night, she said she'll take all her meals in her room on her own in future. She has a table and chairs in there which she can use.'

'But she shouldn't have to hide in her room,' Sarah said, holding her palms up. 'She needs to send my parents packing. They're doing nothing but causing trouble.'

'I know, but she said she doesn't feel she can ask them to leave. She did say she's happy for you to eat with her though.'

'Good, that's something at least. I'll be in at six for dinner then,' Sarah said.

Going outside she looked over towards the terrace, but her parents were no longer there and she decided to walk through the woods to the graveyard. She'd meant to keep it looking tidy, and then had ended up mostly ignoring it while she spent her time undertaking what Cordelia had asked of her and translating the poems.

Collecting the shears she headed through the woods towards the back corner of the grounds. It was cooler here without the heat of the sun burning down and no rain for weeks had dried everything to a crisp, at danger of wildfires. On the news websites, article after article told of how the countryside was burning, spontaneous fires caused by idiots throwing away cigarette ends, even the sunlight burning through a piece of discarded glass. Nowhere was safe.

Thinking about cigarettes made Sarah realise that, since he'd arrived, she hadn't once smelled the familiar tobacco which had followed her father around during her childhood. At some point he must have finally given up. When, she wondered? There was so much about her parents she no longer knew.

Letting herself into the cemetery through the gate, she began to snip where the grasses had grown up around each gravestone, so ancient they were now sunk deep into the ground, often leaned to the side as they slowly toppled over to be claimed by the earth they stood in. Only George's grave was still upright.

'Mum said you were looking for me.' Her musing was interrupted by Jed's voice behind her.

'You gave me a jump,' she exclaimed putting her hand to her heart as though she could calm it and stop it racing. 'How did you sneak up without me hearing?!'

'Sorry,' he grinned as though he wasn't sorry at all. 'I didn't purposely try and creep up on you. I came through the woods a different way and you were miles away, in fact you were so still for a moment as the sunlight partly obscured you, I thought I'd seen a ghost.' The smile had gone from his face and Sarah could see that now he wasn't joking.

'Have you seen ghosts before then?' she asked.

'No, but there's always the stories, about George, aren't there? And here you are at his grave, crouching down so I couldn't see you properly. I was walking slowly to try and not disturb whatever I thought I was looking at, so it probably was my fault I gave you a fright.'

Sarah considered for a moment whether to tell Jed everything she'd experienced since she'd arrived but decided against it. He was lovely, and she was happy that they were growing closer, but he wasn't family, like Cordelia, and if anyone had felt anything strange in the hall or grounds, it would have been her. These were family ghosts, and they were here waiting for her. She was sure that the old lady knew more than she'd divulged.

'Nope, I've seen nothing. I came down here to tidy up the graveyard like my godmother always did. It seems wrong it's been left to become a wilderness. Especially poor little George.

But, talking of him, come with me – I have something to show you. That's why I was looking for you earlier.'

'I was just at the riverbank, you should have come and found me there,' Jed replied catching her hand and stealing a quick kiss as he fell into step beside her. 'It's much easier to clear when the water's low like it is now. That's one advantage of all this hot weather, even though the grass and flower beds are now just brown frazzled remains of what they once were.'

'They'll soon perk up once it rains again,' Sarah said. She ignored his comment about her going to the river, he must surely know by now why she'd never do that. The memories it would dredge up. 'Come and take a look at my notes, I'm now certain the horse in the attic belonged to George Dacre.'

'That sounds brilliant. I've got to pop into town for some food bits that the online delivery didn't bring, or you won't get any dinner. But how about sharing a bottle of wine back home later and you can tell me?'

'Perfect.' Sarah smiled. She went on to explain how her godmother was now eating privately in her room rather than with her parents. 'I want to keep her company so she isn't eating on her own, although I expect your mum will be there too. I wonder how my parents will feel when they suddenly find themselves dining on their own. Perhaps they won't notice, given how self-centred they are.'

* * *

Cordelia's bedroom, having previously been the dining room, had a heavy oak table – that looked like it had been at the hall since the nuns had been eating off it – pushed up against one wall. The wood was dark and highly polished but pitted with gouges and deep scratches. Amanda had done her best to make it look prettier with a red gingham cloth at one end and a small white jug of sweet peas, their scent filling the room.

'There are few left now with it being so dry,' she said when Sarah admired them.

Dinner was back to being a much calmer affair with just the three of them, although they tried to keep their voices quiet. Sarah explained what she'd discovered earlier in the day and Cordelia was delighted.

'You're definitely getting somewhere,' she exclaimed. 'So, what's next?'

'I need to finish translating the poems, there are only two left. Then I'll go back through the coded parts and see if I can work out the answers to it all with the assumption that it was indeed Anne writing them.'

42

2025

With an idea of who her poetess was, Sarah now felt an even closer connection with the book. It was as though Anne herself was drawing her to it, to understand her story. To send her a message. She still didn't understand the meaning of the coded lines, but by completing the book she hoped to do so.

It was early in the day and only Amanda was up and about. Sarah and Jed had arrived at seven o'clock because, with the weather still baking hot, he was now working first thing in the morning and late in the day, resting in the cool of the hall during the hottest hours. Although Sarah could have driven separately, she was happy to travel with him, a few extra minutes just the two of them. Amanda, however, didn't seem to consider that as being a time to rest and kept giving him small jobs to do inside. After one such instruction over an early lunch, he left the table and with his back turned to his mother he rolled his eyes at Sarah, and she had to use all of her self-control not to start giggling. Clearing her throat, she called out, 'Don't forget your toolbox,' as he disappeared in search of a window which wouldn't open. He waved a hand in acknowledgement, although she wasn't sure how many fingers he was waving, which just made her want to laugh more.

His ability to make her feel light, to take the weight from her shoulders just by his presence had crept up on her, and she was surprised at how right it felt. For so many years she'd kept everyone at arm's length, believing herself unworthy of any sort of relationship, and now her entire being was on a new level. They hadn't yet progressed any further than kissing, but she knew she'd be happy when that moment came. With a wide smile on her face, she went up to the library.

Each time she walked up the steps into the room, she listened for the slightly hollow sound of her feet on the lower two steps. Nobody had noticed it for centuries, other than those who needed to know it was there; somewhere a priest could be hidden. Or a book containing secrets which needed to be concealed.

Opening the book in question she started to transcribe the next poem. She was keen to get it done before her parents rose for the day, although they usually appeared even later than Cordelia. The old lady had an excuse, but theirs was doubtless due to the amount they were drinking every evening, judging by the empty bottles left on the kitchen worktop. As ever it was as though they didn't care about what everyone thought of them.

Within half an hour she was re-reading her notes to double check she understood it correctly, but she was certain she did. It wasn't the coded part this time though that was making her stop and think, it was the last line, 'Where our two rivers rise to engulf the land.' Tears started to fill her eyes and the weight that she thought had lifted descended again, a heavy mantle of despair.

The two rivers rising to engulf the land around Barnham-cross Hall, just as they had twenty-one years ago. From some-where in the house she could hear the scrape of a tool which was doubtless Jed working, but there was someone else she needed to talk to before him. Someone who would truly understand.

As she'd hoped, Cordelia was awake, sitting up in bed with a boiled egg and toast soldiers together with a cup of Earl Grey. If she was surprised to see Sarah burst in through the door, she didn't say anything.

'Sorry, I asked Amanda and she said that you were awake, are you receiving visitors?'

'You, always.' Cordelia smiled and patted the side of the bed and Sarah went and perched beside her feet before handing over the notebook with her next transcription.

'It's the last line,' she said. Cordelia read it all in silence before laying it down on the covers beside her.

'I suppose you think it's a message for you?'

'How can it not be? That last line, what it describes,' Sarah answered.

'I can see how it will have brought everything up again, especially as you've been so brave coming back here for me. But this was written centuries ago and if there is torrential rain then the rivers flood, they always have done. That's why the cemetery is so far from the water and the house. I have no doubt it was worse in the sixteenth century when there was probably no knowledge of clearing the weeds or being conscious of the weir where the rivers converge. It's just a coincidence, my darling.'

Sarah nodded even though she didn't agree.

'And have you worked out if this poem has a secret message like the others?' Cordelia asked.

'Oh, no. I was too busy getting in a state about the final line. Hold on I'll do it now.' Sarah picked out the third word on the relevant lines. '"Italian gold arrived now despatched secretly." It doesn't make any more sense than the previous ones. Who was she telling and why would they care about some Italian gold?'

'What if you think wider,' Cordelia suggested. 'Why might Italian gold be dangerous enough to have to be spoken of only in code? It was obviously top secret.'

'Of course!' Sarah smacked her hand down and almost dislodged Cordelia's tray from the bed.

'Perhaps you'd better move that,' Cordelia laughed and waited while Sarah put it on an ornate, bow-fronted dressing table with a silvered mirror. Like most of the furniture in the house, it was an antique.

'Italian gold,' Sarah said. 'England and Italy, well in partic- ular Rome, weren't on speaking terms. Queen Elizabeth was a protestant and had been excommunicated by the Pope, I remember that from history lessons at school. So, if gold had arrived secretly from Italy, then it must have been for something clandestine. Which would be why Anne had been passing messages in code, although why she was being asked to do so I still haven't yet worked out. And I only have one poem left to transcribe so I'm running out of time.'

'And the family saying, whatever it is that you're looking for, you still haven't worked that out yet,' Cordelia pointed out.

'But I do know now that it originated at the time of George's death or before, because it was engraved on his horse. When Anne was living here. And there's a connection with the Duke of Norfolk because it includes his motto. Argh, I need something that will tie all this together and explain it all, I'm getting frus- trated now.'

'It will happen when you're ready to understand it,' Cordelia said. 'Now could you go and find Amanda and ask if she can help me get up, please? I'd like to be installed in the drawing room before your parents make an appearance.'

Sarah kissed her forehead and, picking up her paperwork, she walked through to the kitchen from where she could hear the food processor working. She crossed her fingers and hoped for more cake.

* * *

Arriving later for lunch, she was surprised to see Cordelia eating with everyone, and she gave her shoulder a quick squeeze as she slipped past to sit down. She felt the bones jutting out beneath the fine linen of her godmother's shirt and it made her swallow hard. The weeks strode relentlessly on.

Amanda came in carrying a plate, on which was a large home-made lasagne. There were several bowls of salad already on the table and, without waiting for anyone else, Sarah placed a small portion of the pasta on both Cordelia's and her own plate, before helping the old lady to some salad and starting to eat. The sooner the meal was finished, the sooner she could return to her work. There was a stony silence from the other side of the table.

'You look like you've had a busy morning,' Cordelia said to Sarah as she leant across and removed a thin trail of cobweb from her hair, letting it drift to the floor.

'I was just in the stables,' she said.

'And what have you found?' Suddenly her father spoke, proving her thought that despite his outward indifference, he was listening to everything she said.

'Sorry?' she looked at him keeping her face blank as though she hadn't even realised he was there.

'Whatever you've found out there, it still belongs to Cordelia, not you,' he said.

'Of course it does.' Sarah spoke slowly, as though not under-standing what he was getting at. 'And she's the proud owner of a rusting garden rotavator and three packing crates containing old dried-up pots of paint.' Turning back to Cordelia, she added, 'I'm probably about halfway through so hopefully I'll be finished in there by the end of today.'

'I hope you find something,' Cordelia said, 'because you're running out of places to look.'

'Look for what?' Getting to her feet, Sarah's mother walked, her gait already unsteady, back to the drinks cabinet where she proceeded to pour herself another gin and tonic. She didn't offer one to anyone else.

'Well, that's a question we cannot answer,' Cordelia replied before Sarah could open her mouth to tell her mother that it was none of her business. 'There has long been a rumour, call it an old family tale if you wish, that something was hidden here that must be found to lay the ghosts of the past. What ghosts, and what object, I have no idea. There's a family motto, *"Search for that which you desire, for here it awaits you, and it shall be yours. Courage alone is invincible."* I've half-heartedly searched over the years but found nothing and so I asked Sarah to try and discover it before I have to leave you all. But unsurprisingly so far, she's turned nothing up. And time is running out.'

'So, something valuable?' her father asked. Suddenly both her parents were sitting more upright, the first time they had properly engaged during the meal.

Cordelia shrugged. 'Unlikely,' she said. 'There's nothing to indicate it's something of value. Honestly it may be nothing, I was told this by my great-uncle and he said no one had ever found it.'

Sarah thought about the poetry book hidden in the library. Although everything seemed to point towards that being what she was searching for, she knew it wasn't the whole story. There was still something missing, and she was certain it had to do with the rocking horse. She kept quiet.

'Perhaps I should come and help you look,' her father said

suddenly. He put his knife and fork together decisively, despite his plate still having a large amount of uneaten food on it. It seemed that he had been distracted from his food by this new piece of information.

'No.' Sarah knew she'd sounded sharp, but she didn't care. For so many years her parents had refused to have anything to do with her and yet suddenly he wanted to spend time together looking for who knew what. She was having trouble just sitting at the same table as them, she certainly wasn't going to spend the rest of the day with him and, with only the two of them there, probably berating her yet again for everything she once did. Or, she considered, perhaps he wanted to get her on her own to persuade her to hand the house straight over to him after Cordelia died? Either way, it wasn't happening. 'I'd rather work on my own, thank you,' she added to try and clarify her comment. 'If I find anything unusual, I'll let you know.'

43

1571

There was a strange hush in the house. When I arrived two hours later in the main hall to look for Kate, who was eating breakfast with Luke, four of the queen's guards stood at the end of the corridor which led to the duke's rooms, their helmets and swords catching the early morning sunlight, whilst two of their brothers-in-arms were sitting at the end of the dining table with plates piled high with food. I could imagine the duke's face if he found out that he was copiously feeding the queen's men too.

Eventually Gilbert appeared and picking up a trencher, he took some food and began to eat, pushing it in and chewing rapidly as though he wished to spend the minimum amount of time amongst the rest of us. This was the chance I needed.

'Gilbert,' I kept my voice low as I moved down the table until I was sitting next to him, 'what is happening? Both Kate and I are sore afraid, and I expect Lady Frances is too.'

'At this moment her ladyship's belongings are being packed and she will leave today for Framlingham Castle.' He spoke in short bursts after swallowing each mouthful as he continued to eat.

'Is it dangerous to stay? Am I in peril too? If so, then I must also leave,' I said. It was the last thing I wanted to do, but now I was becoming worried for my own safety. It hadn't occurred to me before, I was assuming the Walsinghams would speak up for me if my part in exposing the plot was discovered. The image of the Tower rose in my mind, uninvited.

'There has been no word you are to travel,' came the reply. 'At present the duke is to remain here, Sir Henry Neville and Ralph Sadler are with him on orders of Lord Burghley and he is precluded from speaking with any of his staff, myself included. The message came only that Lady Frances must leave.' At that point, his eyes looking shiny as though he may weep at any moment and draining his pewter mug of beer, he left the table. I managed to keep the smile from my face as I also rose from my seat and looked across at Kate, who followed suit.

The following morning the duke's carriage was at the front door, together with a cart piled high with chests and furniture belonging to Lady Frances. She visited me before she left to bid me goodbye and I could see tears hovering at the corner of her pale eyes. Everyone shedding tears for a man who did not warrant them. She was sallow and grey, the lines on her face had noticeably deepened. I wondered if she believed that she would not see her son again.

I searched my heart for any feeling of empathy, of remorse of my part in what may take place, but I found none. Although I felt sorry for the old woman, she'd supported him in everything he'd done. He deserved to pay for all he'd undertaken, and I hoped I'd see that happen.

In the end I had to rely on the servants' gossip to discover what was happening. Gilbert had informed them all that any talk of the duke or the allegations against him would result in instant dismissal, but they simply became more astute about who might hear their whispers. Luke, it seemed, was a confidante to several of the guards, and they in turn were gathering information from those with knowledge in the city. Apparently, the city streets were rife with gossip and pamphlets telling all. I asked Luke if he could acquire one for me, and two days later a crumpled, tatty piece of paper was slipped from his pocket into Kate's as they passed in the corridor, and from her to me.

My heart was beating fast as I sat close to the light, so as to read it better. Kate was avidly waiting for me to tell her everything, leaning forwards to hear my quiet words. We couldn't risk being overheard with the house full of the queen's guards; it would bode very badly for us both if we were found in possession of the newssheet. Whispering, I paraphrased what I was reading.

'It is as Gilbert told me, all is lost for my father-in-law,' I said. 'The gentleman in Shrewsbury tasked with conveying the gold which Barker and Higford delivered ignored his instructions and opened the bags to see what he was carrying, and then ran shouting to the sheriff. There were letters found with the gold, ones that were translated because of the ciphers I found. Both secretaries are now in the Tower being interrogated.' I pulled the corners of my mouth down. I was delighted beyond words that the day was approaching when I would finally see retribution for my dear little brother, but both those men were only following orders and I did not wish them harm. It was probably too late for that. Now the knights on the chessboard were waiting to take the duke, the man who wished to be king, to the castle. Screwing the pamphlet up, I threw it into the fire and watched the flames devour it.

* * *

The air in the house was sharp and still, as though it were dangerous even to breathe it in; to be associated with a man charged with treason, and the possible ramifications which may affect us all. We moved around the house mostly in silence, only Blade's joyful barks when he saw me to break the hush.

The tension, now tight like a skin stretched out to dry, was shattered four days after the guards arrived, when I was awoken in the early hours by shouting and the sound of running. Climbing out from behind the drapes on my bed, I found Kate standing in the doorway to her own sleeping area looking confused.

'Quickly, help me into my night-robe,' I said as I pushed my feet into my velvet house slippers. 'I fear the house is being attacked.'

Once I was decently attired and Kate had thrown a large shawl around her shoulders, we ventured to the door to my apartment. The corridor was empty, but the shouting was becoming louder as more voices joined the cacophony. I heard feet thumping up the stairs towards me; heavy boots, their nailed-on soles making the floor shake. Four of the soldiers who'd been guarding the duke's rooms appeared carrying flaming torches and began running through the apartments on this floor. Within minutes they reached mine and I pushed Kate behind me as the soldier, his dark-skinned face just visible inside his helmet told me to get out of the way so he could search my rooms.

'By all means,' I agreed, stepping aside. 'Can you tell me please what is happening?'

'The duke is missing.' His voice floated back to me as he disappeared into my parlour and from the sounds of it my chamber, as furniture was being flung around as though it were simply kindling for the fire. That was probably all it would be fit for by the time he left.

So, he'd escaped. I wasn't really surprised. The man was wily, a fox in the field had nothing on him, although with the number of guards in the house he must have been very clever this time. He had excelled himself.

As the thoughts tumbled through my head and I listened to my apartment being ransacked, I smacked my hand upon my head. Of course, I knew *exactly* where he would be. I would wager all the gold in my purse on it. The soldier reappeared in the doorway and told us to go back in and not to venture out again. I put up my hand to stay him for a moment.

'I believe I know where the duke will be hiding,' I announced loudly. The house was still in an uproar, and I had to raise my voice so I could be heard. He bent down so his face was level with mine and I could smell ale on his breath as he asked me to repeat myself.

'Wait here,' he told me before running back to the staircase, his torchlight becoming smaller as he disappeared into the distance.

'Are you thinking of where I am thinking?' Kate asked.

'Yes, as far as I am aware other than the two of us, only he knows the whereabouts of the secret passages. It would be simple enough to hide in there until he formulated a plan to get away from the building.'

The soldier, now accompanied by several of the duke's guards and Gilbert, arrived back.

'Tell him,' the soldier nodded towards Gilbert, 'what you just told me.' Gilbert had his hands on his knees and was out of breath from running, but he raised his eyes at me and managed to gasp, 'Mistress?'

I explained about the rumours amongst the servants of secret passages within the house and how they were originally used by the monks.

'No Mistress.' Now standing upright, Gilbert shook his head. 'They are but hearsay, nobody has ever found them.' They all turned to go, an instant dismissal of a deluded young girl.

'Stop,' I raised my voice loud enough to make certain they had all heard me and one by one they all turned back once more. 'I have both seen them, and been in them,' I continued. 'Furthermore, the duke has been in them whilst I was. The servants have not heard ghosts, they have heard my father-in-law.' I turned to Gilbert. 'Do you remember when the gold came with Ridolfi and Blade was sniffing at an arras? It was because he could smell me hiding in the passage behind the door concealed by a hanging. After the duke sent you all away, he followed me in and that is, I am quite certain, where you will find him now. Come, I will show you where I have been entering them.' Any fear I had been feeling left me; I felt a strength more than I'd ever had before course through my body.

If I'd been close enough to Gilbert, I could have probably knocked him over with just a tiny push of my little finger, he looked so astonished. Whether it was because his esteemed employer, the sun in his existence, hadn't divulged the where-abouts of the infamous hidden passages, or the fact that within the space of twelve months I had found them myself, I had no idea. To his horror, I'd just divulged how I'd listened to conversations not meant for my ears. I wondered how long it would be before he realised I was the turncoat who had given his master up. At this point, everyone who was crowded around me stepped aside and accompanied by Kate, I took a torch from one of the guards. Holding it at arm's length to keep the flames away from me, I swept along the corridors until I reached the tapestry covering the door I'd been using. I pulled the hanging to one side and opened the door.

'There is another door at the back of this cupboard,' I said. 'Send Blade in and we will follow him. I can guess where the duke is, but the dog will find him in a few moments.' Even though my father-in-law hadn't found where I had hidden before, I guessed he'd be along that passage.

Blade had been running back and forth and barking loudly at the commotion, so it wasn't difficult to locate him and bring him to the doorway where he ran in despite the darkness.

'The stairs, he'll fall down the stairs,' I gasped and made to run in after him. My arm was immediately gripped by a large hand and I was pulled backwards almost losing my balance.

'No Mistress,' Gilbert said, 'there might be a battle if he is found, he may be armed. You must not accompany the men.' Immediately the passage was filled with soldiers running to where Blade was now waiting at the top of the stairs and barking into the dark. The torches threw grotesque shadows around the narrow interior of the passage, looking like the phantoms of monks who had also used them to escape centuries before. When I turned around, Gilbert had gone and Kate and I were standing in darkness of the hallway, with just the ghosts for company.

44

2025

The following morning, Sarah's parents announced they'd be spending the day with some old friends in Cambridge and within thirty minutes they'd left. With them both gone, the whole household could breathe more easily and Sarah felt her shoulders, permanently hunched around her ears in tension, slowly lower. Her parents had got nowhere trying to persuade Cordelia and she had no idea why they hadn't yet returned to Spain. Despite everything she still needed to do in the house, she decided to take some time off and spend a little time painting. She'd received an email from her agent regarding a new contract for a series of book illustrations and she needed to be thinking about work, or it would be a lean winter.

The day passed peacefully. Dinner was a more cheerful affair, redolent of those the four of them had enjoyed before her parents had arrived. The chatter about the repairs Jed was currently undertaking, how the garden was faring in the relentless heat and Sarah's discovery of the rocking horse and its etched motto filled the spaces between eating. Even the food tasted nicer, probably due to the company and the lack of an uncomfortable atmosphere Sarah thought, the simple roast chicken and new potatoes were light and at much as anyone needed on yet another hot evening. Amanda offered strawberries and cream for dessert, but everyone declined.

'I have one more poem to transcribe,' Sarah explained, 'and I'd like to do that while my parents are out. Less likelihood of being seen and having to explain the book. I wouldn't put it past them to snaffle it into their suitcases if they think it's valuable.'

'Which it most definitely is,' Cordelia stated. 'Primarily to the story of this house and our ancestors of course, but as a historical artifact too. Once you're finished with it, we can organise a proper display case for it in the library for future generations.'

Her comment made Sarah, who was helping Amanda carry the dishes from the table, stop for a moment. In all of their talk about her inheriting the hall, she hadn't given a thought to who it would pass to after her. She had no children, and no likelihood of having any. She didn't even know who her nearest relative was these days, although she had cousins on her father's side, so possibly one of them, or their offspring. Slowly she followed Amanda to the kitchen musing on her realisation. Cordelia must have known this when she changed her will.

Sitting in the library in her usual chair she'd barely started when she heard the front door open, its familiar creak evocative of something from a Hammer House of Horror film, before her parents' raised voices rose through the hall. Its acoustics as a chapel built for voices raised in prayer to ascend to heaven were superb, and even though she was quite away from them, she could hear every word. She quickly slipped everything she'd laid out on the table onto her lap.

'Sarah, your father wishes to speak to you,' her mother called out. Her voice no longer carried as it once did, it had lost the strength it once had. With a sigh, Sarah placed her work on her chair and walked to the top of the big staircase. She didn't want her godmother disturbed. As she ran downstairs holding onto the banister to avoid slipping on the steps, she saw both Amanda and Jed appear from the corridor which led to the kitchen. They'd obviously heard the racket too.

'Do you require some back-up?' Jed asked raising his eyebrows.

Sarah shook her head. 'I'll be fine thanks,' she said. 'Let them say their piece. I can't imagine it's going to be them suddenly accepting Cordelia's decision. Then hopefully they'll just stagger off to bed and we can head back to your house.' Now in the hall, she ushered her parents towards the drawing room, putting her finger to her lips and pointing with the other hand towards the room where Cordelia was now resting. Her mother tutted audibly and her father proceeded, on exaggerated tiptoes, towards the other room. Silently, Sarah went to follow them, although she paused for a moment as Jed scooted across the hall and gave her a quick hug.

Her father immediately went to the drinks cabinet and poured himself a scotch. He held the bottle up and looked across at her mother who was already ensconced in the wing chair as though trying it for size once Cordelia had gone. Surprisingly, her mother shook her head. Without offering one to Sarah, he perched himself on the arm of Cordelia's chair. Sitting on the sofa and leaning forward, her elbows on her knees, she looked at them both.

'Well, what do you want?' she asked. 'Because I need to be getting back to Amanda and Jed's house, and I don't want you waking Cordelia with your shouting.'

'We've come to a decision.' Her father sat up straighter as he began to speak. 'It's not right you inheriting this place when it was always due to come to me. Of all people you shouldn't have it, in fact I can't actually believe you even came back. Being here has upset us both immeasurably, but we felt we had to come and somehow prevent this obscene travesty.' It was nothing different to what they'd already said several times.

'And?' She said looking between the two of them. 'What is this decision? You're returning to Spain?'

'I wish,' her mother muttered.

'As soon as everything here is signed and sealed then yes, we'll be going home,' her father said.

'What's signed and sealed?' Sarah asked, still confused.

'We've decided,' he said, 'that Cordelia can bequeath me Barn-hamcross Hall in her will as it was always meant to be, and then when I die you can inherit it from me. That way it's not changing the true line of succession and you'll still get it eventually, so it's not altering her wishes. We've been to see a solicitor in Cambridge today and they'll be writing to Cordelia. As I told you before, if necessary, we will take you to court, we've got a strong case. Watertight.' His face flushed slightly at the insensitivity of his final word.

'Just what she needs at this point,' Sarah said. 'Do what you like though, if you can get her to consent to your bullying. I've told her I don't want to inherit it, and I didn't want to be here in the first place.'

'So if we get legal papers drawn up, then you'll sign them?' he asked.

'Crack on,' Sarah said getting to her feet. 'I know how you feel about me, and I couldn't feel any worse myself. I have no doubt if Cordelia agrees to your plan then the moment the place is yours, you'll find some subclause to disinherit me, and I don't care.' With her back straight she left the room. She'd said her piece. She already knew what the old lady's reaction would be, her godmother may be desperately ill, but she had an inner strength that would defy them all. Sarah wondered if it was a family trait and whether she could muster some from somewhere, because she imagined she still had a fight on her hands.

She sent a message to Jed telling him she was ready to leave. She knew it was time to tell him about her past.

45

1571

We made our way back to my apartment where Kate lit the candles and we looked at the chaos left in the wake of the soldier ransacking the rooms. The house was now much quieter, although I could still hear the occasional shout from somewhere below. I helped Kate right everything and we sat beside the now re-kindled fire with cups of hippocras, its spiced warmth slowly relaxing us. The fortified wine was supposedly for special occasions but if this wasn't one of those, then I didn't know what was. We were both too shocked to speak; it felt as though there was nothing left to say and we sat together until dawn.

When we crept eventually downstairs to break our fast, all evidence of the soldiers who'd occupied the house had gone. And Luke confirmed in a whisper that he'd been told, as he collected a basket of bread and cold mutton for the gatehouse guards, my father-in-law had been taken to the Tower under the cover of darkness in the early hours. He was gone, and I sighed with relief. Surely now his days were numbered.

* * *

For two weeks we heard very little, other than William Barker and the man called Baillee who'd originally brought the coded letters from France had been released, along with the Bishop of Ross, despite his allegiance to Queen Mary. The other secretary, Robert Higford, had been found guilty of creating the ciphers I stole, and was awaiting execution. I felt guilty about that; it was not my intention to see innocent people sentenced to death, for he was just a pawn in this game, as I was. He had done as he was commanded.

Christmas came and went, a quiet affair with no celebrations or even a special feast. Kate and I secretly exchanged gifts, a pomander for her and, as though she had guessed what I was to give her, some lavender filled bags to go into my own.

Then finally January brought the news I had been waiting for. On the 16 January Luke came to my apartment, his face pink with excitement.

'I cannot stay,' he gasped. He had obviously been hurrying. 'I heard talk on the streets whilst I was running an errand for Gilbert. Who is, incidentally, in a foul mood and has already reduced two young pages to tears, so stay clear of him if you are able.'

'What news, tell me,' I said sitting up a little straighter.

'Early this morning, Sir Peter Carew, a cousin of the queen's pirate, Raleigh, went to the Tower to collect the duke and take him to Westminster Hall. The tides are high and it is too dangerous to travel beneath London Bridge, so instead he was accompanied by seventy-two halberdiers who took him to the Three Cranes inn, in the Vintry. It is said he shall be taken by barge to Westminster later today where the arraignment accusing him of being a traitor is to be read at eight o'clock.'

I pressed my hands to my face unable to stop the smile from

spreading across it. 'George, George,' my lips formed the words against my fingers, 'the time approaches.'

The news from the Tower was printed out every evening on pamphlets to be distributed around London, and every other day I took Kate and a guard into the city to purchase a leaflet. I had a ready excuse if my actions were questioned, after all the trial was of extreme importance to me, it would doubtless decree my husband's future upstanding and financial situation.

Finally I read that the trial, a formality, had been swiftly conducted and the duke would be executed on 31 January.

'Gilbert,' I apprehended him in the duke's gallery. I couldn't stop my eyes wandering to where I'd discovered the ciphers which had brought the plot tumbling down. The steward didn't appear to be doing anything, just picking up items and putting them back down. He looked a broken man and I imagined he would soon be without employment.

'Mistress,' he replied, bowing to me. His manners, whatever he thought of me were, as always, impeccable.

'As the only Howard currently in London, I believe it is my duty to visit my father-in-law before he is executed. To say prayers with him.' I had no intention of praying for his soul, but I needed an excuse to get into the Tower.

'I am sure nobody expects you to attend him,' he protested.

'I do not care about others' expectations, I wish to do this on behalf of his family. I shall send a letter to my good friend Lady Walsingham asking if Sir Francis might arrange it, please ensure it is delivered with due haste. I have heard word the execution is detailed for tomorrow at dawn.'

Gilbert bowed once again. 'You are correct, mistress,' he replied. 'If you wish it, I will send a boy as soon as the ink is dry on the vellum.' Before he could change his mind, I hurried to my parlour to quickly pen my request to Ursula.

* * *

I needed only to pace my rooms for two hours until word came it had all been agreed and that I must present myself at the Tower gatehouse when the clocks struck three after noon. I was allowed to take Kate and one guard, but they would both have to remain at the gates, only I would be allowed in to visit my father-in-law. That suited me perfectly.

I dressed carefully in my most opulent clothing, the dress I'd worn the first time to court. A reminder, although I knew he wouldn't remember, that it had started everything that culminated in his downfall. Like a stone tumbling down a hill and collecting dirt as it went. I was the stone, and he, together with his plot, was the detritus.

As per my instructions, we presented ourselves at the gatehouse at the allotted hour. I had requested Luke to come as my guard so at least Kate would not be unnerved having to wait if she had him with her. After I proved I carried no weapons I followed four guards who marched over to the white tower and from there up a short flight of stairs where a heavy wooden door was unlocked and I was shown into a spacious and comfortable room, not at all as I had imagined a prisoner's accommodation to be. Definitely not as his fellow traitors had been lodged. All while I walked, I kept my head lowered so that the smile that hovered there could not be seen. They believed I hadn't brought a weapon with me, but they were wrong.

Despite the comfort of his surroundings, I was shocked at how old and drawn the duke looked. He was slumped in a chair looking into the flames of the fire which burned brightly, and as he turned to look at me for a moment his countenance lightened.

'You bring me good news, daughter?' He sat up a little

straighter. Did he think I was there to inform him that all was forgiven? He was still so sure of himself, despite all he had done.

'No good news,' I said. 'At least not for you. I come to explain something of great importance.' I sat down in the seat opposite to him. 'I know all that you did, and now I shall tell you of my part in your downfall. So that when you step onto the scaffold you are fully aware of why you are there and not attending your own coronation in Westminster palace.'

He gave a bark of laughter, although it came out hoarsely, and he gestured to a hovering servant to refill his cup of wine. I wasn't offered any. 'I am most interested, and amused,' he said. 'Pray continue.'

Wordlessly I took my weapon from my sleeve. He looked at it, then looked at me.

'It is just your childish volume of poetry, is it not? Please do not say that you have brought it here to recite to me, for I am not as easily entertained as Her Majesty.'

'I have brought it to show you that this, which you are so condescending about, contains more than you considered possible from someone you think of as an innocent child.' Opening it up I began to read out a poem and when I reached the end, I went back and just read out the coded message. His attention, which had been starting to wander, was suddenly brought back to me.

'Read that to me again,' he demanded and, with a straight face, happily I did so. I watched his countenance as the words, and my actions, sank in. 'You betrayed me?' he stuttered disbelievingly.

'I found the ciphers,' I told him. 'I have been passing information to Sir Francis and Lady Ursula through a special code in my poems. Reading them out in front of you at court, and you had no idea. No idea. Your open acquaintance with the Spanish ambassador who, I have been told, is now on a ship back to his home, made you immediately suspicious especially after your previous involvement in a plot. One can only wonder at the sheer foolishness of continuing your desire for the throne having previously escaped death.'

'There is still time for a stay of execution,' he told me, a sneer tugging at the corner of his mouth. 'And then you must pray that I do not reach you before you have gone to ground, like the traitor terrier you are.' It was fine talk of his to direct those words at me.

'Perhaps I shall hide in the secret corridors at Howard House?' I replied.

'That was you?' He smacked the heel of his hand down on the arm of his chair, tiny droplets of spittle falling from his mouth. He drained his goblet of wine and held it out for another refill. 'I thought I was the only person who knew of them. How did you discover their whereabouts?'

I kept my mouth closed. I wouldn't say anything which may incriminate Luke as he'd initially told me of their supposed existence. 'That hardly matters now,' I said. 'And in case you are wondering, not only did I tell the guards where they might find you when you went missing, but I believe you were discovered in the same space in which I myself hid when Blade almost exposed me.'

There was a rap on the door from the outside and a muffled voice through the thick wood called out that I had but a minute left. I got to my feet and prepared to leave.

'Why, Anne?' Remaining seated, the duke looked up at me. 'Why would you do this to me? At least tell me that.'

'As retribution. Why else would I undertake something so dangerous? As you stand on the gallows tomorrow morn, look out over the crowds and maybe you shall see the ghost of a young boy on his rocking horse, riding over the bridges of his childhood home where the two rivers meet. The small boy you had murdered to gain what you desired. Well, now I too have what I desire. You chose your first-born son's wife well, someone as merciless as yourself. And now my blood will run through your grandchildren's veins. With Philip I shall be the head of your family and every one of them will know the truth about you. A child killer, a tyrant, a failure.' I curtsied to him and walked to the door which had just opened and left. I had said all I came to say.

46

1572

When I arrived at Howard House I called for Gilbert and told him that I wished to attend my father-in-law's execution the following day. As I suspected he tried to dissuade me, but I wouldn't be deterred.

'Mistress,' he was shaking his head so violently his hair was whipping across his face, 'if you are seen by the crowds, then you too may be slain. It is far too dangerous.'

I hadn't considered that. 'Then you shall hire me an old horse and I will choose my attire accordingly, so it is not obvious who I am. I still possess my clothes from Barnhamcross and I can easily blend in with a crowd of city folk. And, if I ride with a guard and a groom, neither of them in the duke's livery, I shall be safe. I am also not asking you, I am ordering you. With my husband in Cambridge and the duke and his mother both away from home, I think you will find I now hold responsibility for the house.'

Until the words came out of my mouth, I hadn't even realised that this was true. I felt strong and able to manage the household until we knew what would happen next, I'd grown from the quiet self-conscious girl who arrived a year ago, I moulded myself into my role, and now I would play it.

After glaring at me for several seconds, during which I refused to lower my eyes, he nodded once.

'You may have the men if you feel you must go, although I do not understand your desire to. It will be a sad day that I for one will not want to witness,' he said. 'The head stableman, John, can go with you. He is wily and good with the horses, you shall be safe with him. And I will also instruct the guard to ride a little way behind you, so it does not appear he is accompanying you,' he added.

'Thank you,' I said as I went to go. Then turning back, I added, 'If you knew what treachery my father-in-law wrought within my family you would understand why I wish to, nay need to attend his execution.'

Gilbert looked a little shamefaced then and nodded once. I realised at that moment he must have known what had happened to George. Perhaps now he understood my actions.

* * *

My journey the following day did not go as I had expected as I rode out of the gatehouse just before daybreak wearing a plain gown and my old boots. I was relieved that everything I had undertaken, all the danger, would now show me that it had been worth it. My prize.

As we approached the area around Tower Hill, we began to encounter the crowds making their way to a good vantage point. People grumbled as John pushed his horse through with me following close behind. I assumed the guard could still see me. I didn't feel very safe, and for the first time I wondered if Gilbert had been correct in his warning of my stupidity. It was too late now and kicking my horse, it darted forward.

It was not to be so, though. By the time we'd tied the horses and left them with the guard, I could already hear people moaning and grumbling amongst themselves. Catching hold of the arm of a goodwife walking past, I asked what was happening.

'Tis not going ahead,' she said. 'They are saying that good Queen Bess will not sign the warrant.' A lump rose in my throat preventing me from swallowing. I had been too hasty in gloating, in telling the duke everything I'd done. I explained to John and together we returned to the horses and headed back home.

When I walked in through the door Gilbert was in the hall waiting. He was pretending to do some paperwork at the table but by the way he jumped to his feet I knew he'd been watching for our arrival home. I shook my head.

'The queen will not sign the warrant,' I told him. His shoulders slumped with relief. He'd been working for the duke at Howard House all his life since he'd arrived as a young page and for a moment, I found myself feeling sorry for him. The duke was more than an employer; for Gilbert, my father-in-law was everything, the most important person in his life. I didn't feel guilty for what I'd secretly helped to bring about, but I could understand his distress as his life unravelled.

'Of course,' he replied. 'He is the queen's cousin, she will not want to send him to his death. And if he is executed then she would have no choice but to order the same for Mary Queen of the Scots, and she will never do that.'

Going up to my rooms I quickly told Kate what had happened, guessing that within minutes the news would spread like fire through thatched roofs amongst the servants. I told her to start packing our belongings ready to escape. Now the duke knew everything, and whilst it may have been foolhardy to tell him what I did, I had no regrets. Seeing his face as he'd realised my part in his downfall.

Having changed back into a day gown, I sat at my desk, but was so despondent I could not even pick up my quill to write some of the poetry which usually gladdened my heart. What Gilbert had just said was churning in my head, perhaps he was correct and everything I'd undertaken would come to nought, that the duke was still protected by his close relationship to the queen. I had thought the final result of all my own plotting was to be played out before me, but I was wrong, and I wondered if I'd ever see justice for George.

47

1572

Word came within a week that Robert Higford had been hung, drawn and quartered as befitted a traitor. The newssheets confirmed Ridolfi couldn't be found and was assumed to have been hiding in Europe when the plot was discovered. I had no doubts that was where he'd stay. I spent every waking moment worrying whether to flee or remain where I was. Although his execution had been stayed, the duke was still captive in the Tower.

There were regular reports that the queen had finally signed the warrant for the duke to be executed, but no sooner had word spread, than more rumours would follow saying she'd changed her mind and rescinded it. I couldn't help thinking about his previous stay in the Tower and how he'd later been set free. I was terrified history would repeat itself and all the danger I had put both myself and Kate in, had been for nothing. Increasingly I worried that I had been unwise to go to him gloating.

The rumours and conjecture continued as it was announced that Burghley had suddenly recalled parliament and I hoped he'd done that to try and push for the duke's execution. Usually, they sat every three to four years, and had only been disbanded the previous year, so I could imagine the members' fury at having to return from their estates around the country once again. I avidly read every news pamphlet I could get my hands on, searching for updates.

Finally, and without fanfare, the news I most wished for came on 2 June and by the time I had read about it, it was all over. The warrant had been signed and the duke taken to the scaffold within hours, before it could be withdrawn yet again. I read a full notice, of how he read out a speech admitting he deserved to die, but then declaring himself partly innocent of the crime he'd been found guilty of. He was told to finish his speech quickly because 'the hour has passed' which made me smile, because I'd overheard complaints that the duke was inclined to be overly verbose.

He ended his speech claiming that he was not a Catholic, although I knew this to be an untruth, before saying his good-byes to his friends and forgiving the executioner. The newssheet explained how he'd removed the ruff from his doublet and knelt down with his head on the block, saying one final prayer, before the axe came down and severed his head with one stroke.

He was gone, finally. I expected to feel a huge sense of relief and retribution for George, and yet I did not. I felt empty.

48

2004

The final week of the holiday continued, day by day, towards its wretched finish when they must return home. Sarah had that 'back to school' feeling, the days flashing past faster and faster as she tried to cram in all the fun activities, the rope swing, reading in the hammock and playing with Emily which, only four weeks previously, had seemingly stretched to infinity.

The hot weather showed no sign of ending, although Cordelia told her the weather forecasters had predicted a break and some much-needed rain towards the end of the week. She alternated her time at the rope swing with Emily, where the water was even lower but blissfully cool when they dropped into it, and lazing on the hammock with the last of her new books. It seemed to signal the end of everything she loved about the holiday. When the final page was read, summer would be over.

The tension between her parents had increased steadily, palpably, every day. They'd stopped talking civilly to each other, mealtimes were now conducted in silence. Even Emily, who normally missed any social cues, ate without talking, her eyes flitting between the adults. The quiet which had descended on the house was broken only by frequent bouts of shouting from their parents' bedroom after which Daddy would either jump in the car and drive away, or stalk down the garden to the woods and, Sarah knew, from there to the cemetery. She herself hadn't returned there and now she always ran along the gallery to the stairs looking down at the floor to avoid seeing anything.

On the Friday, Mummy bustled into their bedroom and threw open the curtains letting the early morning sun stream in. Sarah screwed up her eyes and pulled her duvet – now encased in the old Disney cover after Emily had made such a fuss – over her head. From beneath it she could hear a scraping and thumping noise and peeping out she watched as Mummy carried their suitcases into the room and dumped them in the middle.

'It's time to start packing,' she announced. 'We'll need to make an early get away tomorrow morning to try and beat the traffic home. Bank Holiday Saturday is a mad time to be on the roads, but your father always insists we take these whole four weeks. Get washed and dressed and then start please.'

In the other bed Emily began to wail that she didn't want to go home, she liked being at Cordelia's, and Sarah pushed her hands against her ears. She didn't want to go home either, her godmother was safe, she was stable and steady, and if the present atmosphere between her parents was anything to go by, home wasn't going to be a happy place.

Despite her despair Sarah did as she'd been told, before heading down to breakfast. She found Cordelia in the kitchen with the back door open, baking muffins.

'I thought we could have afternoon tea today, as it's your last day, what do you think?' she asked as she got a box of cereal and the milk out and handed them over. 'We could have it on the terrace and pretend we are ladies of yesteryear.'

Sarah nodded as she quickly ate her breakfast, keen to be out of the hot room. She wanted to be down at the river, but as she'd run downstairs, Mummy had whisked past her with their swimming costumes and a warning to not get any clothes wet today because everything needed to be dry to go in the suitcases.

Going back to their room to collect her book from beside her bed for a final lie in the hammock, she paused as she reached the place which led to where she'd seen the strange apparition. Despite having been avoiding looking, now with the clock ticking down to their departure she felt braver. The sun was pouring in through the gallery windows onto the warm floorboards and it all looked perfectly normal. Happy that she'd imagined it all she skipped to her room and collected her book. Emily's case was still empty and her sister was nowhere to be seen.

When she made the return trip along the gallery however, something had changed. Almost as if her thoughts had summoned the spirit. She couldn't see anything different, but the temperature had dropped, although the sunshine was still flooding the gallery as it had been minutes ago.

Then she heard something. A slight, regular creak every couple of seconds, followed by silence and then another one. The rasp of wood on wood. She looked down into the hall below, expecting to see one of the adults dragging a heavy suitcase across the floor, but no one was there. Slowly she swivelled her eyes towards the place where she'd been before. She didn't want to look, but she couldn't help herself, rooted to the floor.

The shadow was there again but this time not moving, just the outline of a person against the window. But not really there, because the sunlight was still visible through whatever she was seeing. The cold seemed to be emanating from it and now Sarah could see her own breath clouding in front of her. The creaking stopped as suddenly as it had started and the shadow clustered on the floor before it faded away. Instantly the cold dissipated. Whatever it was, once again it had left as suddenly as it had arrived. She was certain she'd summoned it. She had no idea why this year she'd seen something and not before, perhaps her ill thought of visit to the cemetery to see where Nero was buried had triggered it.

* * *

The final day raced past. Although she barely noticed her parents arguing now, that day it was constant. Wherever she was in the house or garden she could hear Mummy shouting. She rarely heard her father's raised voice and her sympathy for him increased. At lunchtime neither of their parents appeared and, sitting at the kitchen table, Cordelia placed a plate of ham and some thickly cut bread and butter on the table and left the girls to assemble sandwiches. It seemed even Cordelia had had enough of the atmosphere, it was contaminating everything. Emily squirted ketchup across the table but nothing was said and she swivelled her wide eyes sideways at Sarah in surprise. Sarah gave her a small shake of the head to prevent her from saying anything.

By three o'clock, the allotted time for the promised afternoon tea, dirty white clouds were accumulating on the horizon, the amount of blue sky being squeezed out. As she and Emily made short work of the cakes and cheese scones Cordelia had made that morning, the clouds continued to assemble as though a crowd waiting for the start of a show, buffeting each other, impatient for something to begin. Sarah could feel the tension in the air which made her want to hold her breath and close her eyes tight shut until it went away.

Mummy was on the terrace with them, reading a magazine and steadily making her way down a bottle of wine, pouring glass after glass. Daddy had been in the drawing room but had then disappeared down the garden again. Cordelia wondered out loud whether to go and take him some scones with cream and jam and Sarah prayed that she wouldn't go looking for him because if she found him smoking a cigarette in the graveyard there might be a big argument and they'd never be invited back. Although her parents had behaved so appallingly this time, and when Cordelia eventually discovered the broken ornament they quite possibly wouldn't receive another invitation.

She felt her eyes well up at the thought of no more holidays with her godmother, no more hammock or rope swing or hide and seek. These summers had been idyllic and it felt as if a terrible ending, a crescendo, was waiting in the wings. Was that why the clouds were gathering?

Ignoring Emily's whining about not being allowed to play on the rope swing, Cordelia got out Cluedo and played with them in the dining room until it was time for dinner, a delicious roast chicken. The clouds overhead grew steadily darker and eventually with a blade of lightning splitting the sky in two, heavy drops of rain began to fall, bouncing on the hard ground outside the dining room window and throwing up little puffs of dust.

'Finally, I thought we'd never see rain again,' Cordelia exclaimed as the room was lit up once again and a deluge began to hurtle down in an ever-increasing glistening sheet. 'It's like we're behind a waterfall,' she said as she wandered to the window and looked out, 'I bet the gutters can't cope, the rain will soon be pouring out of them.'

'Just what we need when we have to drive home tomorrow,' Mummy said as she put her knife and fork down, her dinner barely touched.

'You don't have to do the driving though,' Daddy pointed out as he reached over for her plate and scraped her leftovers onto his own. 'I'll be the one crawling through floods where the dry fields can't absorb the water. Do you get floods here?' he asked Cordelia.

'Frequently,' she said. 'But the rivers are low at the moment, they won't burst their banks overnight. Before that they'll start to race from beneath the bridges, the angle at which they were built means the river soon reaches the top of the arches if we have a sudden prolonged downpour; it's like a weir. I should think another couple of hours of this will start to make the crossing a bit precarious. You can leave by turning left at my gates though if the bridges are closed off, there's a well-used diversion when this happens.'

With nothing to do after dinner, Sarah joined Emily in their bedroom where, from the furthest right window they could just see the bridges. As Cordelia had foreseen, it had a white froth of water already churning beneath it.

'I wish we could go and stand on the bridge, just imagine!' Emily said. 'It would be so exciting to see that up close.'

'Don't be daft,' Sarah replied. 'We'd get soaking and you know what Mummy said about not getting ourselves wet.' Once again, she felt a heaviness in her chest as she thought about everything she'd done for the last time this summer. It felt like the end of her childhood. She was about to go up to high school; nothing would ever be the same again.

'Just think what it would be like going on the swing now.' Emily gripped Sarah's arm, her fingers digging in. 'With all the water rushing underneath, it would be amazing, much more fun that when it was just a silly little pool.' Sarah screwed her face up and shook her head. She knew what Emily was like when she got an idea in her head, her stubborn streak wouldn't leave until she'd carried out her plan and there was no way they could escape the house and go out in the rain. She said as much.

'Rubbish,' her sister replied, hands on her hips. It was almost as if by pointing out the flaws in her suggestion, Sarah had already agreed that it would be good fun, which hadn't been her intention. 'Listen,' she held her small hand cupped against her ear, 'Mummy and Daddy are shouting again, I can hear them in their bedroom. And I bet Cordelia is in the drawing room watching *Eastenders*.' It was a strange thing for her academic, sensible godmother to watch, but Emily was right; she rarely missed it.

'That doesn't mean we should go,' Sarah pointed out. 'We'd get in such trouble when the adults found out.'

'*If* they find out,' Emily said, her face so close to Sarah's, she could feel her hot, sweet-smelling breath against her cheeks. 'We can get back and into our pyjamas before anyone notices we've gone. Anyway, nobody has even come up to tuck us in this week, we can just go and find the grown-ups to say goodnight.' She was already on her feet and running from the room and standing up with a heavy heart, Sarah followed her. Outside her parents' room she paused wondering whether to knock and tell them what Emily had planned. No doubt she'd then get in trouble for not dissuading her from the idea, and as she heard Daddy shout some choice swear words, she hurried past the door and downstairs to where she found Emily in the boot room.

'We've only got our plimsolls,' she pointed out. 'They'll get muddy and wet and then the adults will know we've been out.' Emily frowned and nodded and Sarah heaved a sigh of relief. Her sister didn't have an answer for that and the escapade appeared to be abandoned.

'We can find some of the old wellies,' Emily announced. 'I've seen them thrown in the old dairy. Come on, quick.' Before

Sarah could say a word, the back door was open and her sister was racing across the grass, tiny splashes of water rising from each of her feet as they hit the grass. With a sigh, she followed.

Inside the dairy, the rain was so loud as it fell on the corrugated tin roof, Sarah could hardly make out what Emily was saying as she rifled through an old box of wellington boots.

'Cordelia doesn't have big feet, I bet you could fit in her old ones,' she shouted picking up a pair and throwing them towards Sarah before looking around for some for herself. 'Oh yes look, you had these last year when it was raining, remember Daddy buying a pair which didn't fit and Mummy had to take you to get some? These are the ones you didn't wear, they've still got the label on.' She pulled out a pair of pink wellies from the pile and pushed her feet into them. 'A bit big,' she admitted, 'but I can walk in them okay. C'mon, let's go.' She opened the back door to reveal the rain still pouring down and a large puddle stretching from the door towards the kitchen garden.

'Emily, we mustn't.' Sarah grabbed her sister's arm and pulled her back from the doorway. 'We'll get told off. I mean REALLY told off and we might never be allowed to come back and visit.'

'Don't, you're hurting.' Emily pulled her arm free. She jutted her chin out and shouted, 'You big baby, you aren't brave like me.' Before Sarah could grab her again she turned and started running towards the river, her boots now splashing in the puddles already forming on the lawn. Wordlessly Sarah sat on an old armchair in the corner, its stuffing poking through and pulled Cordelia's boots on, surprised that they did indeed almost fit and followed her sister outside.

She took long steps to try and stop water from splashing into the boots. By the time she reached the serried rows of vegetables, now battered down by the rain, the beanpoles and plants laid sideways, the gate to the river was already open and Emily was nowhere to be seen. Sarah felt like using the same swear word she'd heard her father use earlier.

Finally she caught up with her sister at the river which was, as Cordelia had predicted, now a roaring, boiling rush of frothing white water pounding over the rocks, rearing up like a wild animal. Emily's face, now running with water, her dark hair shining and stuck to her cheeks, was lit up with a wide smile.

'Isn't it wonderful?' she shouted above the roar of the water. 'It's like a giant milkshake.' Sarah screwed her face up. The noise was deafening and she was shivering from where she was already soaked through to the skin, but she had to agree with Emily, the noise of the water was exhilarating.

'I've had enough,' she yelled. 'Let's go back before anyone discovers we're missing. Just in case someone comes to tell us it's bedtime.'

'Just one go on the swing.' Emily grabbed the rope and pulled the tyre towards her. 'Imagine flying out over the water now.'

'No!' Sarah tried to take it from her but in her usual defiant way Emily wasn't going to back down. 'You scaredy-cat,' she laughed loudly in Sarah's face, 'I'm going to do it even if you aren't.' Before Sarah could stop her Emily threw her leg over the tyre and with a big kick off the riverbank she swung out over the churning water.

Her wide grin of delight as the water splashed up against her legs was replaced within seconds by a look of shock, her mouth in a perfect 'O' as the wet rope slid from her fingers and she fell backwards into the water.

For a moment Sarah was too shocked to move, and then she ran to the edge of the riverbank, frantically scanning the water for any sign of her sister, but there was nothing. She'd been sucked below the tumultuous, angry water and had disappeared immediately. Turning, Sarah ran back to the house as fast as she could, screaming as loudly as she could the moment she got inside, despite almost having no breath left.

Still wearing the wellingtons and not caring about getting mud on the floor, she ran into the hall.

'Mummy, Daddy, someone come quickly!' Her voice echoed from the ceiling high above her but her parents who were still arguing didn't hear her. Cordelia appeared in the doorway of the drawing room, her face looking as thunderous as the weather outside as she took in Sarah's appearance.

'You were told not to go outside,' she snapped. Sarah had never heard her cross before and she wanted to cry and explain it wasn't her fault, but there was no time.

'Quick, you must come. Emily went on the rope swing, I tried to stop her and she's fallen in the river. She's disappeared.' At this point she did begin to cry. Cordelia ran past her heading for the back door, shouting over her shoulder to go and tell her parents to call an ambulance.

Clumping up the stairs, the wet boots still hindering her, Sarah paused outside her parents' door. Inside her mother was yelling, 'Who is she? Who is she? Are you going to at least tell me that?' She banged as hard as she could.

'Go away!' her mother shouted. Her voice sounded hoarse from the screaming she'd been doing on and off all day. Ignoring her, Sarah wrenched the handle and threw the door open.

Mummy was laid on the bed, her eyes narrowed at the interruption; Daddy was standing at the window which was open a crack so he could flick his cigarette ash outside.

'What did I tell you about getting wet?!' Immediately Mummy shrieked at her. Sarah knew she was in immense trouble, but none of that mattered now.

'It's Emily,' she gasped, 'she's fallen in the river. Cordelia said to ring for an ambulance.'

Her parents' previous inertia turned off like a switch. Daddy ran out onto the landing, calling to ask her where Emily had last been seen and Mummy snatched up her mobile phone and was speaking rapidly, giving out the address.

'Stay here,' she snapped at Sarah, 'and answer the door.' And then she too was gone, her running footsteps receding into the distance.

Walking slowly back downstairs, Sarah sat on the bottom step and removed the wellington boots, padding and slipping in her soaked socks to the kitchen to leave them neatly by the back door. She'd been wearing them for less than fifteen minutes, but it felt like hours.

None of the adults reappeared and within ten minutes the front of the house was lit up by flashing blue lights as an ambulance and two police cars arrived. Sarah showed them where they needed to go, then a nice female police officer made her some hot chocolate and found her a towel for her hair whilst she explained what had happened.

'Will they be able to find her?' she asked. 'Only... she can't swim very well.'

'They will all be trying their hardest,' came the reply. 'We'll wait in here, shall we?'

[illegible faded text from previous page bleeding through]

49

2025

Sarah lay in bed the following morning alternately watching the sunrise and the time on her phone moving on, minute by minute. It was too stifling hot to be able to sleep longer than a few hours and she kept reliving the conversation with her parents the previous evening. When she'd got back to the cottage, she found a note from Jed to say he'd popped to the pub for a cold pint of beer if she wanted to join him. Although part of her had been desperate to be with him, she needed to be alone to get everything in order in her own head first and she'd spent most of the night doing just that.

Eventually by five o'clock she was so desperate for a cup of tea she risked creeping downstairs, but despite her soft footfall, avoiding the step she knew creaked, she wasn't quiet enough to avoid wakening Jed who arrived in the kitchen a few minutes later. With his hair tousled and his face sleepy he looked so attractive that when he wrapped his arms around her and kissed the top of her head, Sarah buried her face in his neck and wished she could forget everything that was going on.

'You're up early,' he said, sitting her down and getting a mug out of the cupboard and placing it next to hers.

'Too hot to sleep,' she said. 'Plus, there was a bit of a confrontation with my parents last night. That's why I just went to bed when I got home, sorry I didn't come and find you.'

Jed waved away her apology. 'It's fine. I was accosted by some of the neighbours and ended up staying far longer than I should have done. Why did your parents kick off? Although I can guess. Drunk again, were they?'

'Of course, nothing changes there.' She went on to explain their threats of involving a solicitor to take Cordelia to court. 'It's not fair that she's got all this hassle in the last few months of her life. Why would they do that to her?'

'Because they're not nice people?' Jed suggested. 'Sorry, I know they're your parents, but they haven't visited for over two decades yet still expected to inherit.'

'Don't apologise, I could be a lot ruder than simply "not nice".'

'Well, I have some news that may cheer you up. Laurie has suggested I have the girls again this weekend, apparently, they haven't stopped banging on about the great time they had here last month. I'm off to collect them this morning, you can come with me if you want?'

Sarah thought for a moment. If she went, it would undoubtedly mean meeting Laurie and it felt too soon for that.

'I won't, thanks,' she replied. 'And with my parents about, I also think it's maybe better you stay here in the village with the girls. I'll take over from your mum, then she can spend some time with you all. Besides I've still got one final poem left to translate and I'm hoping to get that done today. Then maybe tomorrow we could go out with the girls for a few hours, take a picnic somewhere if that's okay?' From the broad grin on his face, she knew it was definitely okay. She didn't know what would happen with him long term, but she was beginning to hope for the first time in her life that there was a future to look forward to. Perhaps with him in it. Although when she eventually explained to him what happened that last summer, what she allowed to happen, he'd probably want nothing to do with her. The thought of it made her heart plummet.

She headed off to the hall when he left to collect the girls, arriving in the kitchen where she found Amanda chopping fruit.

'Cordelia likes a smoothie for breakfast these days,' she explained as she dropped a large spoonful of yogurt into the blender. Sarah turned down the corners of her mouth. It was less than two months since she'd arrived and back then, Cordelia had at least been eating solid food even in small amounts. Sarah's initial horror at having to return to the Hall was now swathed with regret that she hadn't pushed herself to see Cordelia over the years, to have had more time with her godmother. It had been easier to hide everything away and not think about it. Not to open that Pandora's box.

'I assume Jed's told you that he's off to pick up the girls?'

'He has. I was going to make another cake but it's so muggy today I don't think I can face having the oven on. Luckily, I had some ice cream delivered with the weekly shop, I'm sure that will placate them.' Sarah had a flashback to soggy cones, raspberry ripple dripping onto the terrace.

'It certainly is boiling today, even hotter if that were possible. It's overcast though,' Sarah looked out of the window, 'and the clouds have a nasty, dirty blue-grey tinge to them.'

'There's an amber weather warning,' Amanda said as she pressed the button of the blender on and Sarah was saved from having to reply. The last thing she wanted was a storm at the end of a long hot spell. Everything about that summer years ago was rising up, a terrible recurrence. Waving a hand at Amanda she escaped the kitchen and headed for her sanctuary, the library. If the final poem wasn't too difficult, she might be able to do it before Jed returned.

Opening the book, she turned to the final page of writing. Would the code in this one tell her anything that would now help her? She had nowhere else to go if it didn't. This one was longer than the previous ones, the writing erratic and more difficult to read. It took her a few hours to work out what each letter said. She'd become used to being able to recognise most letters, but this was far harder.

She was only halfway through however, when she heard shouts of laughter below her in the hall and smiling, she laid down her pencil and walked out to the landing from where she could look down over the balustrade to where Poppy and Skye were standing, their hair plastered to their faces and their clothes dripping on the floor. Poppy shouted up to her, 'Sarah, it's raining soooo hard! We just got out of the car and ran in the house, and we're soaked! Daddy has gone to get some towels and he told us not to move.' Beside her, Skye appeared not to have paid any attention to Jed's instructions and she was dancing around the floor admiring the pools and drips of water she was creating. She shook one arm and then the other, giggling wildly.

'I'd better come and help him,' Sarah said and leaving her work she nipped to the airing cupboard along the corridor at the top of the next flight of stairs. She'd been concentrating so much, she hadn't even realised the rain had started but looking out of a window she could see a deluge of water falling from the now deep grey sky, rivulets running in lines down the windows. She arrived back in the hall at the same time as Jed, both of them carrying towels in which they wrapped the girls. Before long,

Skye's face was peering out of the top of her towel like a human burrito.

Once the girls were dry and had changed into other clothes from the suitcase Jed had brought from the car, he suggested they stayed at the hall until the rain lessened off. Sarah could hear her mother whingeing about the weather, her voice carrying from the drawing room and she didn't want the two factions of her life, young and old, meeting. Pulling a face at Jed, he immediately picked up on her concerns and led the girls away to the kitchen.

'I think Grandma would love to have you help with some cooking,' Sarah heard him say. 'Then we can get your dolls and books from the car, it's a good thing that you brought some toys with you.'

Returning to the library, Sarah sat and listened to the rain beating against the windows. She couldn't believe she hadn't heard it earlier, but as a brilliant flash outside was followed seconds later by the boom of thunder, she knew she wouldn't be able to concentrate now. The weather had broken in dramatic form, just as it had all those years ago. As if it was tormenting her, playing a game all summer crawling inexorably towards this. With shaking legs, she returned to the table and tried to read back what she'd written earlier.

Lunch came and went, the rain not pausing in its relentless hounding. Sarah had a sandwich with the others, Cordelia apparently deciding to remain in her room. After they'd eaten, Jed relented in the girls' continuous requests to watch the television. Sarah's parents were nowhere to be seen, nor was the decanter of scotch that usually sat on the drinks cabinet. She returned to the library determined to finish what she'd started.

One hour segued into the next; she barely noticed as the words in front of her started to make sense and slowly, finally, the awful truth of what lay before her revealed itself. She put her hands against her mouth as she read it from start to finish.

> *Now my life turns full circle once again,*
> *I can tell my story true,*
> *Of my beloved brother George who*
> *Was slain for his lands and fortune,*
> *By he who promised to protect us*
> *As our dear mother did ask,*
> *I could not protect George,*
> *So revenge I would have,*
> *And send the duke to the scaffold for*
> *He and Ridolfi with the Queen Mary*
> *Did plan to depose our monarch.*
> *Tis done now and my vengeance complete,*
> *My part, my codes, will never be known,*
> *Other than by he who lives no more.*
> *I rest now at my true home where*
> *This volume shall be secreted away forever,*
> *Here that tragedy cloaked us*
> *Where two rivers meet.*
> *Search for that which you desire, for here it awaits*
> *you, and it shall be yours. Sola Virtus Invicta. AH*

Finally this confirmed without a doubt that Anne was the poet. Only she, who'd lived in London, would have known the duke's Latin motto which at some point had also been added to the horse. And with the mention of Ridolfi suddenly everything made sense. In her research she'd read about the plot in which the Duke of Norfolk, Anne's stepfather, attempted to depose Elizabeth Ist and marry Mary Queen of Scots. Which, as Elizabeth's cousin, would have put him on the throne as he'd always wanted. And now with this final poem – no need for code in this one – she realised Anne had been pivotal in his downfall, passing coded messages through her words. As revenge for the death of her brother because she couldn't protect him. Sarah knew exactly how that felt. But it hadn't been Anne's fault because she was just a child herself, she shouldn't have held herself responsible.

As the thoughts tumbled over in her head Sarah gulped with the realisation that they'd both been children; it wasn't for them to ensure the safety of their siblings, and yet they'd both carried the weight of guilt with them. The motto, the one engraved on the rocking horse, the one written here too, didn't mean that she should be searching for a lost item, but rather she should have been searching for her true self, her lost childhood and her confidence. And now, finally, she knew she'd found them, the stasis of her life was ended. If only Anne had been able to do the same.

Jumping to her feet she ran downstairs to find Jed. She could barely hear the television above the noise of the storm still raging above them and casting a darkness outside, even though it wasn't yet five o'clock. The drawing room was empty although one of the French doors had blown open, the torrential rain soaking the carpet. She hurried across and locked and bolted it before continuing down the corridor to the kitchen. A quick check outside the hall window confirmed that Amanda's car was still outside, so Jed hadn't yet taken the girls back to the cottage.

She found him with Amanda, piling up a tray with what looked like party food: small sandwiches, fairy cakes, mini sausages and crisps.

'I've told the girls that, as a special treat, they can have a picnic tea in front of the telly. Do you want to give me a hand?

Could you bring the drinks through please?' He indicated the glasses of squash also on the table.

'No problem. Are they washing their hands? Only I came to find you to tell you I've solved the mystery of the poetry book, I popped my head around the door to the drawing room but it's empty.'

Jed shrugged his shoulders. 'Let's go and look. I hope they aren't playing around in the cloakroom, they got wet enough earlier. If this doesn't let up, Mum said she'd make up some beds so we can stay here. I know it's the last thing you want, with your parents staying, but I suspect the road to the village won't be passable now.' Picking up a tray, he walked through to the drawing room, but it was still empty. Going back to the hall he called to the girls, before reappearing moments later, a frown now creasing his forehead.

'They aren't in the cloakroom,' he said. 'Are you sure you didn't hear them coming upstairs while you were working? Skye has been desperate to play hide and seek here and I wouldn't put it past her to encourage Poppy to disobey my instructions.'

'I didn't,' Sarah said, struck once again by the similarities between the two sisters and her own childhood. 'But I was concentrating, and honestly this weather is so loud, I doubt I would have anyway. And hide and seek is supposed to be a quiet game, so if they did go upstairs they were probably creeping. Especially if you forbade them from playing it.' As if to verify her words another clap of thunder made them both jump.

'Can you come and help me look please? I don't want them disturbing Cordelia, or even worse your parents. It will be quicker with the two of us.'

'Of course. Let's start with the bedrooms in the new part of the hall and make our way along that floor.' Sarah led the way out of the room towards the Georgian side of the house and

together they called for the girls and ran in and out of the rooms
checking in wardrobes and under beds, avoiding her parents'
room which was silent. Amanda soon appeared, she'd gone to
ask the girls if they wanted more sandwiches and had also
realised they weren't where they were supposed to be.

Moving across to the old part of the hall, Sarah knew
someone was going to have to go into the bedroom she'd so far
successfully avoided and taking a deep breath she turned the
handle and stepped inside.

As she'd suspected, it was as though time had stalled. The
beds were stripped, but the books, the collections of bits found
in the garden, their pictures stuck on the wall, it was all there.
The air felt still, as though it was waiting for her, as if she'd
stepped out just a moment before. Not twenty-one years. She
knew instinctively Poppy and Skye weren't in there, all the room
contained was the imprint of two little girls years before. And
also those children centuries before, at the will of a man who
cared nothing for them. Children neither supported nor cared
for by the adults who should have been there for them.

Standing there she could hear the echoes of her parents
continually shouting that last summer. And on that night, the
screams of accusations of her father having an affair. Now, as an
adult, she could see how obvious he'd been, sneaking off to the
graveyard for secret phone calls. Stepping back onto the landing, she shut the door quietly and went to join the others who
were now in the loft, their calls and the thump of feet
above her.

Ten minutes later, the three of them were back in the hall.
Amanda had explained to Cordelia, so she wasn't worried about
the activity.

'Where could they be?' Jed's voice held a falter which
displayed how increasingly worried he was becoming. Sarah

looked across to the drawing room door and then ran back in there. It was still empty.

'When I came in here earlier,' she told them, 'the French door over there was open a little bit. I thought it had blown open with the wind, the carpet was wet. You don't think—' her voice came to a halt. No, please God no, she thought. Jed had obviously come to the same conclusion and together they ran across the room and out into the torrential rain. They were soaked in seconds although neither of them noticed as they ran across the lawn looking around them wildly hoping to spot the bright colour of the girls' matching red T-shirts. Jed was shouting to her, but Sarah couldn't hear his words. He pointed across to the stable and dairy and she felt her stomach lurch remembering huddling in the dairy with Emily. With her sister bossing her about, telling her to put the boots on. And her remonstrating it was too dangerous and that their parents would be very angry. But nothing stopped Emily once she'd made her mind up.

Without a second thought, Sarah turned and ran towards the river. She'd managed to avoid it for the entire summer, but everything led back to here. And it was just as she remembered it. The galloping frothing water spilling over the edge of the bank as it raced past with broken branches bobbing briefly in the water before disappearing beneath it. The roaring of it and the water running down her face making it difficult to see. Another streak of lightning lit up the sky before the crash of thunder made the ground beneath her feet reverberate. As the noise rolled away, she heard a scream and she spotted the red of a T-shirt.

Racing towards it she could see Poppy bent double, but Skye was nowhere to be seen.

'No no no,' Sarah moaned as she ran faster, her breath coming in short gasps, her feet slipping on the wet muddy grass. As she approached, she realised Skye was still there, but Poppy was knelt on the edge of the bank holding her arms as they began to slip. She was moments away from disappearing beneath the roiling waters. Using more speed than she'd ever believed she had, Sarah reached them and with one arm beneath Skye's armpits she scooped her out of the water and onto the grass, where she collapsed down beside her.

Skye was screaming and crying, and Poppy was standing silently, shaking, as though unable to believe what had just occurred.

'Go and find Daddy, he's in the old outbuildings where he keeps the garden tools.' Sarah told her sharply, trying to impress on her the urgency of the situation. She had no more breath left and dragging Skye further away from the edge she sat on the ground, the child curled up in her lap and waited for Jed to arrive. This time she'd done it. This time she'd saved a life, not let it be torn away before she could stop it. Looking out across the river, fleetingly she thought she could see Emily's face as it was swept away, but then she realised she was mistaken. What she was looking at was a small boy on a rocking horse as he turned around to smile at her. Suddenly she felt the warmth of another body and he was gone, as Jed put his arms around her, squashing Skye between them. She felt Poppy's hand laid on her arm and finally she gave in to tears.

50

1572

As my carriage rolled over the three bridges, I looked out at the bubbling rivers as they met and joined before continuing as one. The background to my childhood and so familiar still that I had to wipe tears from my face. I did not want my sisters to see me like this, not when we were all so excited to see each other after our time apart.

Opposite me sat Kate, newly married and no longer in my employ, but she'd asked if she may accompany me to Norfolk as my companion so she could visit her own family. Luke, as part of my guard, was riding alongside us, although it had taken much persuasion of Gilbert to allow him to be away from Howard House for such an extended length of time. Eventually I asked Philip to intervene, and then all was well.

As we turned in through the tall stone gates and continued down the track, my eyes turned instinctively towards the far corner of the grounds where I knew George lay.

We pulled up in front of the hall and immediately the door opened as Elizabeth and Mary, both now taller, came running out to greet me, shouting my name over and over. Luke had to tell them to move away from the door so he could place the steps and assist me down, my heavy gown impeding my progress. I realised from their faces they had not considered how I now must dress in the London fashion, they were still attired in the plain kersey kirtles which I had once worn.

We hugged for several minutes. Over the tops of their heads, I could see my grandmother waiting patiently at the door. She too had aged in the time I'd been away and I was shocked at how the pale, lined skin on her face now sagged. I pushed my sisters from me and reminded them we had many weeks in which to hug each other.

Walking to the door I put my arms around Grandmother and felt her thin, bony body relax against me. The years of little money allocated for the household and the worry of all that had happened in London – I knew that the newssheets from Norwich would have told her everything in lurid detail – had taken its toll on her health.

'I am so pleased to see you home,' she said. I liked the fact that she, like myself, considered Barnhamcross Hall my home.

'I have wanted to return since the moment I left,' I told her. 'And now I do not know where I am to live. All of the duke's titles and estates are gone, including George's. The duke took what was our brother's in the most terrible way, only to lose it anyway.'

'Your husband is not yet of age,' she said. 'He will be appointed a guardian by the crown, and they will tell you where you shall both live. And in the meantime, I very much hope that you may rest here a while. It must have been a terrible shock uncovering the duke's plot.'

I smiled and nodded but said nothing. Upstairs in my trunks which, even now, Kate was probably unpacking despite no longer being my maid, was my poetry book buried beneath the bolts of silks and damask and fine linen ready to be sewn into new clothes for my sisters. I couldn't risk my poems being found in London, I didn't ever want my husband to know the part I'd played in his father's downfall, and I was certain the duke had gone to his death with my secret intact. The shame would have been too much, thwarted by a young girl. He had underestimated me. I decided I would find somewhere to hide the book here, where nobody would find it. And nobody would go looking.

'First, I must visit my brother,' I said.

Grandmother nodded. 'I do not know if anyone has been there for a while. Your sisters do not remember as you and I do, and I am now too frail to walk the uneven path,' she said. I took my leave and after quickly speaking with Kate, who was now joined by my sisters admiring my gowns, I stepped outside.

The warm summer sun had started to bake the ground and all around me I heard the drone of bees and buzzing of flies. A large dragonfly hovered for a moment in front of me before darting back to the rivers behind the house in a flash of colour. I could hear the gentle splash of water as it ran over the stones beside the bank and I finally felt I was properly home. The sound of my childhood, steady and safe.

I had to push tall grasses that reached my waist out of the way as I fought my way down the path to the cemetery. Here, behind the stone wall which had protected the nuns' graves for centuries, lay George. The ground was covered with cornflowers and daisies amongst the grasses shivering in the slight breeze. I walked to where he was, his headstone now becoming weathered with moss and ivy climbing over it, claiming it.

With no thought to my white and soft hands, I began to pull weeds away across the ground in front of his headstone until I had cleared a large space. I hadn't protected him when I should have and although I had now avenged his murder, it did not give me the comfort I had thought it would. I realised nothing would bring him back and now I must let go of the guilt. For my courage had made me invincible.

* * *

The following morning, I arose early, just as the sun was lifting itself from the horizon to light the dancing rivers which I could see from my chamber, glistening like a thousand diamonds.

I had insisted Kate and Luke were given a room in the servants' quarters because it was no longer right that she slept on a pallet outside my room, as she'd done when we lived here previously. Her status as a married woman carried gravitas.

The lack of a maid so early in the morning meant I had to dress myself, pulling an old kirtle over my shift, and slipping my feet into my oldest leather boots. As I crept along the landing, I could hear noises and voices from the kitchen as the day began for the servants. I let myself through the door which led to the loft and where I believed I'd find that which I was searching for.

It lay in a heap, the painted colours and gilt now dimmed with dust and dirt. I knew it had been left here after that terrible day. Nobody had thought of it since, of that I was sure. Kneeling down beside the horse, I took my silver knife brought from London and scratched a message on the horse for those who may come after me. Perhaps if they had need of my words then I could help them so they would not suffer, as I had done. Picking up the rocking horse head, which was heavier than I'd envisaged, I carried it downstairs. After collecting a spade from the stables, I made my way down to the cemetery. Already it was warm, and I could feel my hair, hastily pushed into a coif when I was getting dressed, sticking to my face and neck.

The digging was difficult, the ground hard after weeks of

sunshine. The nuns had known better than to bury their dead close to the rivers, which in bad winters would flood. It took me over an hour to make a hole deep enough and gently I placed the rocking horse head in, so it could lay forever beside my brother. His Hal, his friend, his comrade-in-arms.

I had one last task to do, to complete my story. Entering the abbesses' parlour, I looked around. It was cold in there, and dusty. Grandmother had told me nobody came any more to give the sacrament and thus the conveyance kept for a priest to hide in had been empty for over a year. Once again, I took my knife and with the very tip, I sliced down the binding on the inside back cover. Then, with extreme care, I slid the piece of paper upon which Ursula and I had devised our cipher, inside.

Going to the step, I released the catch and lifted it up, revealing the dusty space beneath, and beyond that, the place I sought. Holding my breath, I leant in and dropped my poetry book, wrapped in a piece of silk embroidered with bees and flowers, watching it thump onto the floor. Nobody would find it there and it could rest in peace, as I hoped my brother now was. Retribution had been exacted and I would move forward with my life, wherever it took me.

Sarah couldn't remember how she got from the riverbank to the kitchen. She was conscious of Jed running with Skye in his arms and Poppy following close behind but other than that, nothing. She'd blanked it all out as the shouting she could hear became confused with that of her parents, years before. The screams of accusation as to why she'd let Emily play on the rope swing, when the river was so high.

But now, as though triggered by what had just happened, she remembered other things about that night. Running inside for her parents, their argument and screaming so loud that they didn't hear her calls for help. Why weren't they there, as Jed had been for Skye? How could it have been her fault, as she'd always been told by them? Would Poppy have been blamed if Skye had not been saved? Sarah had been just a child herself; she wasn't responsible for her sibling. She'd lived with the guilt for so long, but as the motto, Anne's motto, told her, now she needed to let it go and live life in the moment. It hadn't been her fault. Just as it hadn't been Anne's when she couldn't protect George.

* * *

Awaking the following morning, Sarah looked at her phone and realised it was already ten o'clock. They'd all stayed at the Hall rather than going back to the cottage the previous night, and Amanda had put the girls to bed in her and Emily's old room. Sarah had heard Jed reading a story to the girls and she realised it no longer contained any ghosts and, Sarah considered, it was right that it was occupied once more.

Downstairs she found Cordelia already waiting for her in the drawing room.

'You don't need to tell me everything that happened,' she reassured Sarah. 'Amanda came to wake me in the night and then this morning the girls also gave me their versions. Skye is, I think, enjoying the added attention. You must keep an eye on Poppy though.' She looked hard at Sarah for a moment as their eyes met and she knew exactly what her godmother was saying, there were no words needed.

'So now tell me what you discovered about the poetry book before everything kicked off. I gather from Amanda that you have something interesting to tell me?'

'Yes, I think I've solved the mystery.' She went on to explain how the coded poetry had exposed the Duke of Norfolk's involvement in the Ridolfi plot, that ended with him being executed for treason. 'And the final poem explains her motive, that the duke murdered her brother George to gain his lands and money. The family motto I've been chasing, was hers, although it was a message for me, or at least that is how it feels. She felt such guilt that she hadn't been able to protect a younger sibling, but that by finding her courage, she became invincible.'

'Just as you are,' Cordelia said, patting her hand. 'You showed great courage coming back here. I have also carried the guilt, that I didn't prevent it and that you were blamed by your parents. That somehow I couldn't protect you from that. Perhaps Anne has been restlessly waiting for you all these years, so you could both understand.'

'I think you're right,' Sarah agreed, 'I'm not sure how long it will take me to accept that Emily's death wasn't my fault but being here again and – with Anne's help – I hope I can move on with my life. To have everything that I should aspire to; perhaps one day even a husband and family of my own. I read that Anne and her husband Philip went on to have a family and a happy married life. Things I felt I didn't deserve because Emily would never have them. I need to go and speak with my parents; I have something I need to say which I should have said years ago.'

'Whatever they say, this house is yours my dear, and it's right that it should be. I hope you'll live here and fill it with love, and perhaps the laughter of small children.'

Sarah thought about Jed and his daughters. They already filled the hall with everything she now wanted, and who knew? Perhaps in time there might be another child to grow up there, in safety and protection. Her future was an open book for her to write in.

Leaning forwards, she kissed her godmother on the cheek and left the room, finding her parents in the hall, their suitcases beside them. They looked even smaller than when they arrived.

'I'm glad you're leaving, that you've finally realised you're not welcome here,' Sarah's voice echoed around the hall as though it wasn't just her speaking but the ghosts of those who'd had no voice. 'You know what happened here last night. Another child in danger, but this time I saved her. Because I'm an adult now, not a child. You should have been responsible back then, but you were so tied up in yourselves and your own self-centred lives that you left me, an eleven-year-old, to look after my sister. I wasn't to blame – you were. And afterwards I was just a ghost on the periphery of your lives. You wilfully wreaked untold damage on my life, but you know what? It ends here. I can see the past for what it was; a child wrongly burdened with the guilt of a sibling's death. And now those ghosts are set free.'

Her parents seemed to shrink with every word she spoke. Picking up their cases wordlessly, they left, leaving the front door open, fresh air blowing in.

She thought about the small child's laughter she'd been hearing since she arrived, the shadows which drifted across her vision. She didn't know if it was George, or Emily. Or even Anne. Four children, their lives bound together. In fact, now she wondered if it had all been her imagination, the desperation to feel something of her sister still there. But now she very much hoped that, in years to come, the house might become her home and hold the love of her own children. Perhaps they she could find a way to have an apartment in the Georgian half of the house and leave the rest to a national institution. She looked up as she thought she saw a movement on the stairs, but it was nothing, just a trick of the light.

'Ah, here you are.' Jed's voice broke her reverie, as he walked into the hall and she turned to smile at him. Now it was her time, time to find new beginnings, in the place where the two rivers meet.

* * *

MORE FROM CLARE MARCHANT

Another book from Clare Marchant, *The House of the Witch*, is available to order now here:

https://mybook.to/HouseOfTheWitchBackAd

ACKNOWLEDGEMENTS

It is said that it takes a village to raise a child and it has certainly taken more than just me to raise this book, so this is my opportunity to thank everyone who has helped me.

First of all, as ever, a huge thank you to Ella Kahn, my agent, who is so supportive and always at the other end of an email to answer any questions. And also to my amazing editor, Isobel Akenhead, copy editor Debra Newhouse, cover designer Jane Dixon-Smith, proof reader Candida Bradford and the whole team at Boldwood Books, you are all brilliant!

As always, my books require a lot of research and for this book I visited Charterhouse in London, formerly Howard House (if you enjoyed this book, I strongly recommend a visit!). I must thank Barbara Daly for all of her superbly helpful knowledge.

Writing is a solitary profession, and a special bunch of authors are a huge part of my life; I couldn't do this job without their friendship and support. My fellow Fivers, Ian Wilfred, Rosie Hendry, Heidi Swain and Jenni Keer, you are all the very best of folk whom I love dearly. And an extra special mention for Jenni who keeps me company every day, always there for brainstorming and virtual cappuccinos.

A final thank you must go to my husband Des, forever there in the background quietly steering the ship. From the golf course.

ABOUT THE AUTHOR

Clare Marchant is the author of dual timeline historical fiction. Her books have been translated into seven languages, and she is a USA Today bestseller. Clare spends her time writing and exploring local castles, or visiting the nearby coast.

Sign up to Clare Marchant's mailing list for news, competitions and updates on future books.

Follow Clare on social media here:

facebook.com/claremarchantauthor
x.com/claremarchant1
instagram.com/claremarchantauthor
tiktok.com/@claremarchantauthor

ALSO BY CLARE MARCHANT

The House of the Witch

The Shadow on the Bridge

Letters from
the past

Discover page-turning
historical novels from
your favourite authors
and be transported
back in time

Join our book club
Facebook group

https://bit.ly/SixpenceGroup

Sign up to our
newsletter

https://bit.ly/LettersFrom
PastNews

Boldwood

Boldwood Books is an award-winning fiction publishing company seeking out the best stories from around the world.

Find out more at www.boldwoodbooks.com

Join our reader community for brilliant books, competitions and offers!

Follow us
@BoldwoodBooks
@TheBoldBookClub

Sign up to our weekly deals newsletter

https://bit.ly/BoldwoodBNewsletter